The Sacred Shore

(Book III in the Moon Island Series)

Jennifer Fulton

Yellow Rose Books

Nederland, Texas

ISBN 1-932300-35-X

First Printing 2005

9 8 7 6 5 4 3 2 1

Cover design by Donna Pawlowski

Published by:

Yellow Rose Books
PMB 210, 8691 9th Avenue
Port Arthur, Texas 77642-8025

Find us on the World Wide Web at
http://www.regalcrest.biz

Printed in the United States of America

Acknowledgments:

My family, as always, has given me love and encouragement. I am also indebted to Dee, Jan and JD for their intelligent reading, and to Lori L. Lake for her affable editing support.

For FGC, who inspired this one.

MOON ISLAND

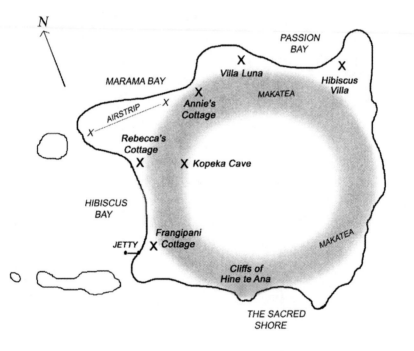

N

PASSION
BAY

MARAMA BAY

X
Villa Luna

X
Hibiscus
Villa

MAKATEA

X
Annie's
Cottage

AIRSTRIP

Rebecca's
Cottage

X Kopeka Cave

X

HIBISCUS
BAY

Frangipani
JETTY X Cottage

MAKATEA

Cliffs of
Hine te Ana

THE SACRED
SHORE

Chapter
One

MERRIS RANDALL CONTEMPLATED the menu. The paper was handmade, the text crisply embossed and silken to the touch. In a few years time no one would remember what real printing felt like, she thought. A subtle watermark caught her eye. Two locked hearts for Valentine's Day. How could she have forgotten? What kind of a Freudian slip was that?

"I don't know what to have," her companion whined, as if it must be restaurant policy to frustrate their patrons with an excess of choice.

Bethany, Merris reminded herself. Or was it Tiffany? She looked like a Tiffany. "The mahi mahi is good here," she suggested.

"I can't eat fish."

Can't. It hung there: the alluring prospect of an evening spent discussing food allergies or, better yet, the burning question of whether fish had souls. Merris allowed the opportunity to slip by.

"I thought you drove a Porsche," Bethany noted after another frown at the menu.

"I used to."

"Oh, no. The ex got it. Bummer." Wide baby-blue eyes plumbed Merris's face for signs of emotion. "But you got the house, right?"

Great. Complete strangers knew the grisly details of her break-up. Merris supposed she had Allegra to thank for that. Her ex mistook everyone she met for her own private talk show audience. Which is how Merris had discovered their relationship was neither happy nor monogamous in the first place.

"The house was mine to begin with," she said in a discouraging tone.

Bethany brightened. "I guess it must be pretty quiet with the kids gone."

Merris knew her lungs were functioning, but her breath

seemed trapped in her chest. She lowered her gaze to the menu. Words waltzed before her, converging into sentences that made no sense at all.

Bethany had the grace to color. "Shit. That was a stupid thing to say."

"It's okay. You're right, anyway. Mealtimes aren't the same without *egg foo yong* being thrown across the table."

Bethany gave a nervous twitter. "I'm never having kids. I'm far too selfish!"

It was socially appropriate to insist otherwise, but why debate the obvious? Merris changed the subject. "Any particular wine preference? Or shall I choose?"

Bethany shrugged. "I'm not fussy. I like the pink ones."

This was a bad idea, Merris decided. Sitting opposite her was an attractive young woman who was willing to dress up for a blind date with a jaded thirty-three-year-old recovering from a messy break-up. For her trouble, she was being judged a shallow dimwit based on a few tactless remarks and an ignorance of wine. *What is your problem?* Merris asked herself. Making an effort, she put the menu down and smiled at her date. "Sam says you volunteer at the animal shelter."

"I help at the thrift store. It's so cool. You get to see all the best stuff first, which is important." By way of explanation, Bethany added, "I'm a Barbie collector."

Merris wanted to say *You have got to be kidding.* Instead she feigned interest. "Really?"

Bethany promptly opened her purse and produced a studio portrait of a blonde Barbie doll posed in front of an Eiffel Tower backdrop. "Nineteen-fifty nine. Mint with her original case. You would not believe what I paid."

"Shock me," Merris invited.

"Twenty dollars!" She was almost squealing. "Some moron has a hissy fit with his wife, so he puts her dolls in a yard sale while she's on vacation. Only she's a collector!"

"You made out on the deal, huh?"

"She's worth like five thousand bucks," Bethany declared, aglow.

Merris gave a low whistle. So much for tech shares. Little girls all over America would make more hanging on to their dolls. Collecting was not a pursuit she fully understood. Some people were in it for the money, but for most it seemed to be a genuine passion. Apparently Barbie really did it for Bethany.

Merris stole a cursory glance around the restaurant. Naturally, it was heaving with couples. Most were holding hands, and none looked gay. In fact, Merris and her date were the only same-sex diners in the place, apart from a group of four women several tables away who were decimating a large pitcher of martini. Merris dwelled for a moment on one of them, a thirty-something in a crimson velvet dress. She was not pretty in any clone-like way you could order from a plastic surgeon. Her mouth was full and uneven, her nose too strong, her dark eyebrows straight and unplucked. She wore her long, silky black hair loosely pulled into a Grecian knot, the effect a cross between formal and bedroom. Her dress echoed the same general theme, cut high enough to avoid the smallest hint of cleavage, yet low enough to showcase a neck and shoulders worthy of one of those yuppie-porn coffee-table books. Merris conjured up a suitable title: *Homage to the Nape*.

She followed the slope of one perfect shoulder down an arm that was smooth and shapely. The left hand was naked of rings, a fact that made Merris's pulse jump irrationally. She checked out the other three women to see if anyone was acting like her partner. They were laughing and touching one another the way gal pals do. The goddess wore a remote smile, as if she were observing her companions from her own tiny island. Merris wondered what she was thinking.

YOU ENTER WITH your dreams intact. You leave them behind, scattered through the rooms you shared, taped to walls that heard too much, swept beneath rugs whose patterns you learned too well during unbearable silences.

How could love fail? Olivia felt like a captain who had scuttled her ship only to discover land was not where it should be. *Passion is not a reliable navigation system. The heart is not a map you can trust.*

Sensible people who were not in love had told her it was doomed from the start. The signs were there for all to see. She was a fool to have convinced herself love would triumph, no matter what. Now, she too could break bread at the table of disillusion. Her friends called this getting real.

"Ah, the *coup de grâce*," Abigail announced as their waiter approached.

"Raspberry bavarois," he intoned, meeting no one's eyes.

Olivia stared at the dessert set before them. It was heart-shaped and shimmering blood red. Oddly, it was served on a platter of wood. Next to it lay a knife that belonged to the shower scene from *Psycho*.

Abigail got to her feet and brandished the murder weapon with a flourish. "Happy Valentine's Day, darlings," she declared and plunged it into the dead center of the heart where it quivered, firmly buried in the board beneath.

"To Olivia!" With over-bright smiles, everyone raised their glasses.

Olivia forced a laugh and sipped her drink. "You wretches. I hate you."

"Do you want to hack it up, sweetie?" Abigail offered. "Or shall I?"

"Be my guest." Olivia looked anywhere but at the mutilated Valentine. The room was a sea of perky couples, drinking champagne and pawing at one another, lovers savoring the bliss of mutual passion. Her eyes flooded suddenly. "Time to powder my nose," she said, lurching to her feet.

"Downstairs through the conservatory, past the Chagall print and to the right," Abigail instructed, the consummate tour guide even on her days off.

Three martinis, Olivia thought, as she made her way unevenly toward the staircase. What she really wanted to do was run as far as she could from the restaurant. In fact, from her life. The banister felt damp beneath her hand, and she stood frozen at the top of the stairs, contemplating whether a fall could be fatal.

Behind her, a woman's voice asked, "Are you okay?"

"I'm sorry." Olivia hastily stepped aside to allow the stranger by, almost losing her balance in the process.

A hand caught her arm. "Allow me."

Olivia glanced sharply sideways, encountering a squarish face, dark ash-blonde hair, and hazel eyes so perceptive they had to be reading *Bitter, broken-hearted woman drowning her sorrows.* Embarrassed, she allowed herself to be guided down the stairs, past the potted palms, to the rest rooms. There the stranger released her arm and held the door open.

With a brief thank you, Olivia found herself mercifully alone in a small marble bathroom that smelled of some pseudo-floral perfume the previous occupant had applied too lavishly. Part of her wanted to open the door and see if the hazel-eyed woman was still there, waiting the way a husband would, a few awkward paces away. Irritated by this train of thought, she ran some cold water and cupped damp hands to her face.

This had seemed like a good idea when Abigail phoned with her screw-Valentine's-Day attitude and dark sense of humor. It was time Olivia returned to the land of the living, she insisted. There were plenty more fish in the sea, if you were still kidding yourself they were worth the price of bait. For a moment Olivia wished she could be an Abigail, a woman for whom love and having sex were unrelated pursuits. Abigail had long ago relinquished the former as nothing but grief, in favor of the latter with its reliable charm. She kept her emotional eggs tucked safely away where they could not be crushed by someone she trusted. As a consequence, she was a happy, confident woman.

Olivia stared at herself in the mirror and tried to remember the face that used to look back at her in the days when she was brimming with joy and hope and awe. In just three years, all trace of that person had been erased. Make-up could conceal the dark rings caused by crying, but not the self-doubt in her eyes. She forced her customary smile and watched the mask she hid behind slide into place. Everyone did this, she supposed. Maybe Abigail did it too. Maybe the entire world was a masked ball and you never really got to see anyone as they were. No wonder love was a fool's paradise. No wonder people became alienated. How could you feel secure if you hid the real you from your partner? On the other hand, if you offered yourself unmasked, rejection was a blow to your very core. Did anyone get over that?

Olivia applied some gothic rose lipstick to her mouth and took a step back from the mirror. Would things have been different if she looked like a *Sports Illustrated* swimsuit model? Was Hunter that superficial?

MERRIS HOVERED NEAR the restroom for a moment, imagining Bethany abducted by aliens and the woman in crimson velvet accepting an invitation to join her for the rest of the evening. They would not discuss Barbie dolls or Merris's divorce, but instead discover a shared passion for walking at night in a strange city. They would laugh that they both knew the date and time and place they had tasted the very best oysters, probably Malpeque or one of those incredible varieties from Brittany. By the end of the evening, they would be snared in an unspoken yes.

She should have asked the goddess her name, she thought. Not that it would make any difference. No self-respecting alien was about to abduct Bethany. And the stranger in the rest room was probably straight and used a database to sort her suitors by charm, wit, sensitivity, skills in the sack, and bank balance. Merris shone in none of those categories. In fact, if Allegra's opinion were any gauge, she stank in all but the bank department.

Bethany was therapy. That much Merris accepted. Her best gay pal, Sam, had fixed them up. She could appreciate his reasoning. A cute, breasty ditz who will have sex on the first date was a reliable bet for anyone with a bruised ego. If Merris had any sense she would take full advantage. What was the worst thing that could happen? She pictured Bethany thinking about Barbie accessories while they were fucking. She needed a cigarette. Shame she'd given up.

By the time she got back to the table, the waiter was lurking nearby with their meals. Bethany had finally ordered the Cornish hen.

"It's the whole bird," she said, aghast.

"You don't have to eat all of it," Merris pointed out. She'd ordered Maine lobster. It was the smaller kind, always the sweetest.

Bethany gave her meal a tentative poke. "It's so awful finding actual bones."

"Would you like me to call the waiter back? They can de-bone it for you in the kitchen."

Bethany seemed charmed by this. "Well, thank you. Sam told me you're a considerate person."

Merris laughed. "Sam was selling me, hmm?"

"He did a good job," Bethany said as the waiter took her hen away. "He said you're considerate, honest, and deserved much better than... well, you know."

That was Sam. No problem taking sides. It was an endearing characteristic in your best friends. Out of the corner of her eye, Merris caught Ms. Neck and Shoulders returning to her table. A moment ago her gal pals had been in a conspiratorial huddle. Now they were animated again and the artsy-looking one who'd been making the toasts seized the goddess's hand, flamboyantly kissing it. Were they together, after all? If so, it must be non-monogamous. Ms. Artsy had been cruising Merris most of the evening.

"Don't mind me," Bethany said.

With a guilty start, Merris returned her attention to her date and realized Bethany was gesturing toward the lobster, thoughtfully suggesting she start her meal.

"It needs to cool off for a bit," Merris said, replenishing their wine for something to do.

Not for the first time recently, she felt profoundly disoriented. Her life had spun out of control. It was as if some cosmic wheels had been set in motion, and nothing she did would make a shred of difference to the outcome. She had no job, no relationship, and no children unless she drove across town to visit them. Everything that had given her life meaning had suddenly been swept away.

"Wow." Bethany greeted the arrival of her Cornish hen à la Gerber. "Extra topping."

All that and she probably ate about three mouthfuls, Merris observed a little later, sucking the last juices from her lobster. Now that she thought about it, she could see Bethany didn't just collect Barbie; she wanted to be Barbie. Eating was clearly out of the question, which explained the disproportionate appearance of the young woman's hands and feet. Average-boned, she could never be truly petite, only thin. Then there were her breasts.

It had always puzzled Merris why any woman would starve herself into a size two, then rush out for implants so she could get back the breasts she'd forced her body to consume. There were people who found big tits hanging off a child's frame a hot look. Merris was not one of them.

Looking past Bethany, she saw the four women leaving. This was her chance. What if she slipped Ms. Artsy her card? It would be worth dating her at least once if it meant getting her gorgeous friend's name and phone number. Merris located a business card and wondered if she were brazen enough to do this. She was out of practice.

"If you'll excuse me." She fed Bethany the same excuse she'd used earlier when she saw the crimson-clad goddess heading for the restrooms. "My beeper just went off again."

"Sure. No problem," Bethany said.

Merris thanked her and went quickly downstairs. In the lobby, she made like she was taking a call on her cell phone. As the four women came down the stairs, she glanced up, all nonchalance. Ms. Artsy gave her a come-hither smile, but before Merris could palm a business card, one of the group began waving at her like she was a long-lost friend.

"Merris! Merris Randall?" She had curly auburn hair and freckles, and Merris had never clapped eyes on her. "You probably don't remember me. Polly Simpson. I was at your commitment ceremony. Allegra's roommate from college." She turned to her friends, gushing, "It was the most romantic day of my life, and it wasn't even me tying the knot. But you know how it is with some couples. You can just tell it's going to be happily ever after. Oh, let me introduce everyone!"

Merris stuck her cell phone back on her belt and shook hands with Polly and a woman called Kate, then with Ms. Artsy, otherwise known as Abigail Zola, a name that could only be made up.

"And this is Olivia Pearce." Polly finally got around to the goddess.

Merris imagined taking that cool outstretched hand and leading its owner out of the building. The evening was ice cold, stars glinting like shattered glass against a midnight sky. They could walk along the darkened streets and pretend to be in Venice. Merris would charm the beautiful Olivia with worldly tales and polished manners, earn her trust by taking no liberties. This was not a woman you grabbed in the dark.

What really happened was that she fumbled the handshake. Worse than that, she blushed, something that had not occurred in living memory. Decently, Olivia pretended not to notice. Maybe from her distant isle she hadn't.

"How do you do?" Her accent was British, her tone low and sweet. She promptly took back her hand.

Merris cleared her throat, searching for something to say. "Well, nice meeting you all," was the best she could muster.

"Tell Allegra hi for me, would you," Polly said. "It's been a while."

"I'll do that if I see her," Merris replied carefully. She didn't want to encourage questions, but she wanted Olivia Pearce to know the much-vaunted happily ever after had not transpired. Olivia appeared indifferent to this information, but Polly's mouth froze in a small O. She started to say something, then looked helplessly at Abigail, whose role was apparently rescuing people who had put their foot in it.

Abigail rose to the occasion with deadpan candor. "Sounds like Merris should have joined us tonight. Valentine's Day is our annual general meeting. The Society for the Romantically Challenged, that is."

Merris grinned. "Dare I ask the eligibility criteria?"

Abigail, a beat ahead, dropped her card into Merris's top pocket. "Call me and we can discuss it. Meantime," she glanced up the stairs, "I believe your date is looking for you."

Halfway down the staircase, Bethany could not hide a pout. Casting a poisonous look at Abigail, she said, "Honey, did you want me to order coffee?"

Oh, great. Merris could almost hear everyone adding two and two. First she makes indirect allusions to her broken relationship. Now a twenty-two-year-old with home-wrecker written all over her is calling her *Honey.* Merris bit back the urge to proclaim, *I am not a cheat.* Not only would it make her sound guilty, but with her supposed 'love' standing right there, a real jerk as well.

Summoning what dignity she could, she said, "Coffee sounds good. I'll be right along." To hell with introducing Bethany like she meant something. Merris knew she already looked like a rat. Did it matter if she shirked the social graces? She bade the women a hasty goodnight.

Only Abigail made eye contact, and Merris had the distinct

impression she knew exactly what was going on and found it highly amusing. As for the goddess, she was already out the door while her companions were still fastening their coats.

Chapter
Two

THE WONDERFUL THING about Cherry Creek was high walls, Merris reflected as she waited for her electronic gates to open. The not-so-wonderful thing was that everybody assumed you were filthy rich if you lived there. The house had been her parents' one big investment. There was no trust fund to support the property taxes and maintenance costs. Instead, Merris had worked like a dog ever since she inherited the place six years earlier.

In hindsight, she could see that Allegra had never really believed she had to earn a living like everyone else. To a girl just one generation from the trailer park, a huge house in Cherry Creek meant you were wealthy, whether or not you wanted to admit it. And Allegra had behaved accordingly, spending Merris's paychecks like so much loose change.

In some regards, this had been a blessing. Merris would never have started her own software company if it hadn't been for all her maxed-out credit cards. It was Allegra's idea. Mortgage the house, get rich in the technology boom, and she'll have a baby. The rest was history.

Rather than join the dot com marketing bubble, Merris's company had developed online security and encryption systems. The business made a lot of money, and Allegra had duly given birth to twin girls. It should have been a happy ending. They had the beautiful house, the beautiful life. How could it have gone so wrong? The twins were sixteen months old when Merris accepted a takeover bid for her company that only an idiot would turn down. That same week she had discovered Allegra was seeing someone else; not just seeing her, but paying her rent and buying her groceries. The affair had been going on for six months. When had Allegra planned to say something?

"I don't see what difference it makes," Allegra said when Merris confronted her. "I'm not going anywhere."

"My partner has been seeing another woman for the past six

months, and it's not supposed to matter to me?"

"I tried to tell you," Allegra muttered.

"You tried! When did you try? Before you rented that love nest with my money?"

"I knew you wouldn't understand. I knew you'd be like this. That's why I couldn't say anything."

"So you cheat on me and lie about it, but it's my fault?"

"I'm sorry, okay? I screwed up. It was meant to be a fling. I was going to stop seeing her, but..."

"But?"

Allegra stared at the floor. "She makes me happy."

Merris drew a deep breath and slowly exhaled, calming herself. "And I don't?"

Allegra ran a hand over her pale curls. It was a weary gesture that communicated her disillusion with no need of verbal embellishment. "People grow apart," she said as if choosing her words very carefully. "You've had other priorities. First it was work, then the girls. There's always something."

Merris stifled a gasp. "I reorganized my entire life for you. I had to work around the clock because you decided to buy twenty thousand dollar pearl necklaces without telling me. Remember?"

"It must be great to rub my face in that every time we fight."

"I'm sorry." Merris reined in her anger. After their last row, she had promised she would stop bringing up that damned necklace. "This just doesn't make any sense," she said, breaking a terse silence. "If you were unhappy with me, why on earth did you get pregnant?"

"We had a deal, remember? You wanted children."

"Are you saying you don't want our daughters?"

"Don't be ridiculous. I'm their mother!" Allegra's mouth trembled. "I didn't plan this, you know."

Merris was silent. Two alternatives presented themselves. She could be a hothead and throw her partner out, or she could find some way to repair their relationship. Having a baby took an emotional toll on any woman. Merris had read the pregnancy books. Every one of them spent pages discussing the difficult transition new mothers had to make. Many felt unattractive and insecure. After a baby, relationships came under stress. People made mistakes. But a committed couple could forgive one another and start again. Sometimes a nightmare like this could strengthen the cloth that bound two people.

Merris studied the fluffy blonde curls Allegra insisted on repressing with mousse and gel. Vibrant and hopelessly spoiled, her partner was accustomed to being the center of attention. Merris could only imagine how devastating it must have felt to be unable to fit her clothes, to find most people no longer related to her as a woman, only as a mother. On top of that, she had to manage not one but two babies when it turns out she didn't want children at all.

By contrast, Merris's life had barely changed after the twins were born. She got up and went to work every day, stayed late if things were hectic, had drinks with friends, traveled on business. She couldn't wait for weekends to spend time with her daughters; it was one of the reasons she had agreed to be bought out of her company. What few personal compromises she'd had to make were well worth it. Her life felt complete and whole and balanced. It had never occurred to her that Allegra did not feel exactly the same way.

Merris took a measured breath. "Look, just answer me this. Do you want our relationship or not?"

"I said I wasn't going anywhere." Allegra's tone was flat. "Nothing in your life needs to change. I'll be here looking after the house and the girls and your clothes and your donations, and making sure the yard guy turns up, and your dinner parties get catered, and your friends get birthday cards. Isn't that what you want?"

"I thought you wanted it, too," Merris said stiffly.

"Whatever. Look, plenty of people have arrangements like this."

Feeling obtuse, Merris asked, "Like what?"

"They stay together for the children and they get their needs met by other people."

"They stay in the material comfort their partner provides and fuck around on the side?" Merris translated.

"You stopped making my sex life any of your business a long time ago."

"That's not true," Merris objected.

"Oh, please. When was the last time you treated me like a lover instead of your fucking housekeeper?" Allegra fell silent as if shaken by her own sudden fury. Her chest rose and fell unevenly. She grabbed a glass of water from the table next to her and took a gulp.

"Are you saying this is all about sex?" Merris was incredulous.

Allegra stared past her to some distant point. "If it makes you feel better, go ahead and make it that simplistic."

"What then? You're in love with this...this Romeo?"

"Her name is Corey, and she makes me feel like a woman. She puts me...us...first."

"And I don't?"

Allegra stared into her glass. "There's no point in this," she said, almost to herself. "You twist everything I say."

Merris could hardly believe what she was hearing. "We have a dry patch so you go get a lover instead of talking to me?"

"You're incredible. I have the twins and our sex life is over. I did talk to you. For months. I was the one asking if we could work on it, remember? I was trying to save our relationship."

"Choosing someone else is a funny way to go about it," Merris retorted.

Allegra released a slow sigh. "It doesn't matter what I say, does it? You're going to make this my fault. I'm the shallow bitch who used you, and you're the wonderful partner who got screwed. It's all about your ego."

Merris controlled the urge to slap her. "No, it's about trust. And loyalty. And honesty. We're in a relationship."

"Is that what you call it!" Allegra hurled her glass at the fireplace.

For a long moment, Merris studied the crystal shards scattered across the hearth. She felt oddly detached, almost dazed. Her gaze shifted to her wristwatch. How could so much change in a single sweep of the second hand? Feeling light-headed, she got to her feet. "Let's stop before we say anything else we'll regret. I'm going to go spend the weekend in Vail. While I'm away I want you to break it off with what's-her-name. When I come back, we'll start again, and I promise things will be different."

Allegra's eyes flooded. "It's too late, Merris. Starve something long enough and it dies."

FOR A WOMAN who claimed she had no head for finances, Allegra had lost no time suing Merris for child support and half her net worth. Merris's lawyers thought a custody suit was the appropriate response, but she could not bring herself to use their daughters as a bargaining chip. Whatever her faults, Allegra was their mother. Eventually they reached a settlement Merris could live with; a trust fund in her daughters' names and a monthly allowance paid to Allegra for their support. In exchange, Merris had full visitation rights, and the girls could not leave Colorado without her consent. As of today, the papers were signed. Officially, they were no longer a family.

Merris stalked through the garage into the house. What she wanted to do was smoke one cigarette after another and get very drunk. Instead she took a shower. It wasn't every day you signed a check for two million bucks to pay off a woman who'd betrayed you. She felt sweaty just thinking about it. For a long time, she stood beneath the water. The hot jets felt so good she didn't want to move. *What now?* she thought.

Chapter
Three

THE BEECH TREES in front of Olivia's house marked the
passage of time. Like love, they came into bud bursting with
promise. Their leaves unfurled, rejoiced in the sun before it
became their enemy, then withered, fell, and were trampled. Ten
months had passed since her break-up with Hunter, and still
each long empty day converged into another just like it. She
knew months had passed and seasons had changed because the
trees told her so. Once more they were barren. This would be her
second winter alone.

A squirrel danced across the red and gold palette of her
lawn, its dainty hands clasping some tidbit. One day soon it
would snow, Olivia thought as she drove out of her garage. The
world would be sugared white. The air would shock her lungs
and paint her cheeks. Thanksgiving would be a very different
holiday this year without the usual influx of Hunter's family.

For an only child, Olivia thought she had handled the
rivalries and informality of Hunter's large family very well.
There were five sisters and four brothers. Most of them had
married young and, like their parents, had more children than
they could afford. But they were a happy crowd and didn't seem
to have a problem with Hunter's sexuality. Life was
straightforward for them. You worked if there was work to be
had, fed your kids, went to church, and belonged to the NRA.
Only rich city folks like Olivia had time for navel gazing.

Olivia had found this uncomplicated approach refreshing. It
was one of the things that had first struck her about Hunter.
Here was a woman who would tell it like it is, she had thought.
No bullshit. No hidden agendas. After a few years in LA, it was
like a glass of fresh mountain water to a parched traveler. Olivia
couldn't get enough. She had never met anyone like Hunter.
They didn't grow them like that where she came from. Women
did not wear Stetsons in London. They did not drink beer, rest
their cowboy boots on the table, or play love songs on a guitar.

Olivia's friends found Hunter anachronistic. Olivia had found her breathtaking from the first hello.

It was a Saturday night almost four years ago, and Benny Berenbaum, Olivia's agent, had said he wanted her to meet someone. She had to wear a low-cut dress and some fancy earrings. It was a cocktail party. They drove to a mock-Tudor mansion in Beverley Hills and were greeted at the door by a butler who, Benny confided, was the real thing from England. He had been headhunted by the guy they were about to eat canapés with, Steve Shaw. Mr. Shaw owned Zane Records. His label had just bought six of Olivia's songs for some discovery they described as 'the new kd lang', as if the old one had already hung up her hat.

"I told him there's plenty more where these came from," Benny said, waving the contract.

"Isn't Zane a country label?" Olivia tried not to sound horrified.

"A great tune is a crossover tune."

"I write blues."

"You write hits," Benny corrected. "Who gives a shit if there's a fiddle involved?"

Steve Shaw saw it that way, too. He loved her work. "Train Rolled By" made him cry the first time he heard it. He took her arm and led her across an expanse of Italian marble to a room where people were congregated around a white Steinway. A bow-tied pianist was playing jazz. Steve interrupted him, waving the room into silence. He thanked some people, made sincere-sounding compliments about someone's new film, said a few words about the Grammys, then announced, "I am proud to introduce the young lady who's going to take the New Country Artist award next year, Hunter Carsen."

The clapping quickly subsided as a latte-flavored voice suffused the air with emotion. "I bruise easily... and you hold me too tight..."

At first Olivia could only see her hat through crowd. But Benny hustled them closer. "I smell platinum," he said, chafing his palms.

Olivia hardly recognized the song as one of hers. Hunter Carsen sang it like she owned it, breathing life and truth into each phrase, infusing the lyrics with meaning Olivia had scarcely realized was there. Her voice was a drug. Steve Shaw was not exaggerating the Grammy potential. This woman was more than a good singer; she was mesmerizing. Whatever that elusive something was that everyone wants a slice of, she had it by the truckload.

Olivia took in her well-worn jeans, cowboy boots, an ornate belt buckle, a plain black shirt, black Stetson, and astonishing lapis blue eyes. Hunter removed the hat when they were introduced. Her hair was short and bleached blonde. She wore no make-up and a smile that was clean and open. Nothing about her was contrived. In a world where people knew they were consumables, she had no need to invent herself. Hunter Carsen was the real thing.

"Songs like yours make me want to sing," she said in low, soft accent Olivia could not place.

"I had no idea my songs were like that until you sang them." Because this was LA, she added, "I'm not just saying that. I mean it."

Hunter smiled full force. "Guess I just sold my first album."

Olivia laughed then blushed. Astonished by the heat in her cheeks, she said, "Where are you staying?"

"At the Hotel California." Hunter's lips twitched. "Only been wantin' to say that my entire life."

Olivia knew her own laughter sounded forced and unnatural. She seemed to have lost control over the muscles in her face. Even Benny noticed her discomposure.

"Glass of water, babe?" he asked.

"Please," Olivia said too quickly. Telling herself to stop acting like a star-struck twelve-year-old over a woman who was not even a star yet, she said lamely, "I've never stayed there." In fact, she had no idea it existed outside the Eagles song.

"Well, actually I was kidding. I'm at the Beverly Hills on Sunset." Hunter's gaze was level and tinted with amusement. "If you're not doing anything later, maybe you could stop by."

"I think Benny has plans for us after this."

"So tell him you're busy," Hunter drawled. Her blue eyes traced a languorous path over Olivia's body. "There's an arrangement I've been working on for one of your songs. I could really use your input."

Olivia felt a flurry in her ears as her pulse quickened. She hesitated, searching Hunter's face.

"You think I'm hitting on you?"

Olivia blinked. "No. I..."

"I wasn't, but I sure would like to."

Olivia knew she should say something sophisticated and neatly sidestep the invitation. This was the music business. You had to make it first, then announce your sexuality, not the other way around. Someone should tell Hunter.

Instead, she said, "Let's get out of here."

That was only four years ago. It seemed like a lifetime.

OLIVIA PRESSED THE play button on her CD as she stopped at another set of lights. The Cherry Creek traffic was already heavy. Everyone went out on Saturday mornings. Finding a place to park near *The Tattered Cover* would be today's karmic test. Either the gods were with her, or against her.

Olivia reminded herself that signs and portents were for grannies gambling their social security checks in Vegas. A well-educated, sensible Englishwoman was not a prisoner of flaky superstition. She would end up in the parking garage anyway, she reasoned. Why circle the block and expose herself to some cosmic lottery? On the other hand, maybe she should be open to the universe, no matter what they'd taught her at the Presbyterian Ladies' College.

Against all the odds, Olivia found a spot on Fillmore. She was still gloating over this triumph ten minutes later as she leafed through a London tourist guide in her favorite bookstore. It was always interesting to see what other people noticed about the place where you were born, she thought. Strangers drew such wonder from the sights you took for granted.

Olivia had grown up in one of the elegant white row buildings that encircle the Kensington Gardens. Her early childhood had revolved around boating on the Serpentine, exploring the local museums, and attending various concerts and political demonstrations in Hyde Park. People traveled from all over the world to experience what she took for granted: the changing of the guard at Buckingham Palace, Big Ben, the Tower of London. Yet these were not the sights she missed most about home. She missed the intense green of England, the clouds of daffodils flanking every country road, the tiny doorframes in pubs that were built hundreds of years ago, when people were not much over five feet tall. Sometimes she even missed the gray skies and the imminent threat of rain almost every day of the year.

Smiling, she turned her attention to the European travel section. Tuscany was always reliable. Prague was fun. Or there was the incomparable Peloponnese, where Paris had stolen Helen of Troy and sparked the Trojan War. As a child, she'd spent many happy summers wandering the Continent with her parents, who considered travel an excellent substitute for formal schooling.

Eventually they had succumbed to social mores and dispatched her to the same boarding school her mother had attended. They still lamented this decision, holding the Presbyterian Ladies' College responsible both for Olivia's meat eating and her penchant for expensive shoes. Like most socialists from upper-class backgrounds, they had chosen a private education for their child only to wallow in perpetual guilt over it.

They would be thrilled to see her, Olivia reflected. It had been a while. If she had to hide somewhere and continue licking her wounds, why not choose the familiar comforts of home? She pictured herself explaining what had happened to her relationship. The sympathetic but unsurprised faces. Going back to England would feel like a defeat when she'd made a whole new life for herself across the pond. She had to find some other way to move on. Almost a year had gone by. Why hadn't the fog lifted?

Olivia had the strangest sense that there was a destination lying in wait for her. Somewhere unknown. The miraculous parking experience this morning was a sign, she decided. She had cast herself upon the mercy of the Fates, and they had answered. Her hands roamed the shelves. A slender volume caught her eye. *Paradise Found*. It was a travel cliché, but she pulled the book anyway. The jacket claimed it was an insiders' guide to Pacific hideaways for travelers who sought privacy. Naturally she did what any self-respecting intellectual would do and went straight to the pictures.

One idyllic beach setting always seemed much the same as another to her. Yet Olivia caught her breath over a long shot that appeared to have been taken from a shady verandah. It depicted a turquoise lagoon encircled by sand that seemed impossibly pearlescent. The caption read *Honeymoon couples can forget about Moon Island. Local custom banishes men from these sacred shores!* Olivia flipped a few pages, only to find that someone had removed the Moon Island section and, just her luck, this was the only copy on the shelf. More annoying still, Moon Island wasn't mentioned in the index of any other book on the region. Perplexed, she headed for the information desk.

"I can't even find the place in an Encyclopedia," she pointed out.

"Your best bet is probably a travel agent," the young woman at the desk said, handing *Paradise Found* back to her. "This is out of print now."

"Of course it is," Olivia rolled her eyes. And if *The Tattered Cover* didn't have any other book that mentioned Moon Island, the place probably didn't exist. Irritated, she bought the defaced book anyway and took it upstairs to the café.

As usual the place was packed, no sign of anyone departing imminently. She'd have to sit with strangers. Normally she didn't mind, but this morning she was not in the mood. At a table nearby someone was enmeshed in a newspaper, their entire face screened. Another anti-social coffee drinker--perfect. Olivia approached the table and politely asked, "Mind if I sit here?"

"No problem." The bent head did not even lift to see who was asking.

Thankful, Olivia set her coffee down and politely angled her chair. Facing away from the stranger, she opened her book and studied the picture anew. Could a place like this actually exist? Olivia allowed herself a daydream: warm sand slipping through her toes, coconut milk on her breath, the reassuring pulse of waves reaching the shore, a romantic sunset, the strum of ukuleles, Hunter kissing her.

MERRIS GLANCED UP sharply at an odd sound from the woman who was sharing her table. Had she choked on something? Peering over her newspaper, she caught her breath in a jolt of recognition. The woman from the restaurant, all those months ago. Olivia Pearce. Today her black hair was in a single heavy braid. On anyone else the style might have looked dowdy. Olivia, however, wore a pair of long ornate gold earrings that drew attention to her perfect ears and of course that long velvet neck. She looked like a Frida Kahlo portrait, Merris thought.

There was a stillness about her that spoke of inner tranquility. Maybe she was Buddhist. Or she meditated or did yoga. She had the poise of a dancer or a model without the brittle self-consciousness. This was a woman disinterested in veneer, Merris decided. How often did you meet someone completely comfortable with herself? She repressed an urge to reach out and touch her as one might a painting, instead striking up conversation with a phony line. "Excuse me. Haven't we met somewhere?"

"I believe you were kind to me in a restaurant once." Polite, but not encouraging.

"Planning a vacation?" Merris indicated the book.

"Tempting myself." A slight smile.

Merris folded her newspaper. "I'm getting another coffee. Want to join me?"

Only the briefest hesitation. "I don't usually take espresso from strangers. But why not?"

Why was she doing this? Merris asked herself as she ordered two double shots. She had flunked the partner test. This was not the time to start looking for anything more than the meaningless encounters that had punctuated the last nine months for her. Since signing that big check, she had done some serious thinking and reached an unavoidable conclusion. She had sabotaged her own relationship. It was a disturbing insight, more so because she had absolutely no idea why.

She set their coffees down and told herself that there was nothing wrong with making a new friend. Just because she found this woman attractive did not mean she was going to do anything about it. For all she knew, Olivia was straight and married.

"I think my friend Abigail was hoping to hear from you," Olivia remarked.

"Oh?" Not the ideal direction for their conversation.

"She mentioned you a few times after that evening in the restaurant."

Was this Olivia's way of letting Merris know her artsy friend was gay, and by inference herself?

"To be honest, I haven't really been seeing anyone," Merris said. "Just the occasional date. You know, so I don't forget how to open the passenger door."

"Ah." No turnabout disclosures. No intrusive questions. Just the slightest nod of empathy, an invitation for Merris to speak or say nothing, as she pleased.

In a bid to get beyond meaningless small talk, Merris said, "I've no idea how long it's supposed to take after a breakup. Maybe I'm slow."

Olivia sipped her coffee, eyes veiled. "Messy?"

"You could say that." Merris surprised herself by adding, "I feel tired. Incredibly tired."

Olivia made eye contact. "You look it."

"Great."

"Amazing, isn't it, the damage we do one another?" A ripple passed beneath the surface tranquility of Olivia's face.

In its wake, Merris glimpsed pain so naked and real it jolted her. "Sounds like you have experience."

"Don't we all?" She wasn't biting.

"You live nearby?" Merris steered the conversation back to safe banality.

"Cherry Creek."

"Me, too. We're probably neighbors."

"If we are, perhaps you could tell your gardener to stop blowing leaves in my yard," Olivia said gravely.

"Fall." Merris groaned. "Don't you hate that leaf pressure?"

"It's like mass paranoia in our street." Humor warmed Olivia's voice. "Last year the guy over the road sent everyone a bill for leaf clearance."

"You're kidding."

"Now he's installed extra security cameras on his gates and — wait for it — they point outward. My yard guy says he's collecting evidence. You know, whose leaves are blowing onto his driveway."

"Schmuck." Merris laughed. "How long have you been in Denver?"

"Two years. I used to live in LA."

"Part of the Californian migration?"

"You could say that. We came for the snow and stayed."

We. On an impulse, Merris said, "Speaking of snow, I'm taking a drive in the mountains tomorrow. I don't suppose you'd care to join me."

There was an unmistakable flicker of interest in the dark eyes, before her face grew shuttered once more. "I can't do that. But thank you for asking."

"Another time." Merris shrugged, guessing that was unlikely.

For some reason this unsettled her. She knew she could not simply say goodbye and walk away. From the moment she first saw Olivia Pearce, the woman had preyed on her mind. It was nothing so simple as a case of lust or the usual post-relationship quest to prove oneself viable. With a shock of awareness, Merris understood that her universe had been disturbed. It was as if a clock, long unwound, had started ticking and she could not escape its persistent hammer. She knew, with a certainty as irrational as it was compelling, that in Olivia she was staring at her destiny.

Queasy all of a sudden, she thrust a hand into her pocket. "If you change your mind, here's my card."

For a split second it seemed Olivia might not accept it. When she did, she did not offer hers in return. She glanced down at the card and immediately looked up again as if pleasantly surprised. "You're just a block from me. I've probably walked past your house a thousand times."

"Well, next time stop in." It took a huge effort to make the invitation sound casual and friendly instead of pleading. *Quit while you're ahead*, Merris told herself. She knew instinctively that Olivia would not respond to being railroaded.

"I may do that some day." Olivia's expression was impossible to read. She tucked the card into her book and slid her chair back. Merris made a mental note of the title, *Paradise Found*. Something about the Pacific Islands. "It's been nice talking with you." Olivia gathered up her coat and purse. "Enjoy the mountains."

"I always do." Merris found a casual smile. "Take care of

yourself, Olivia."

Willing her to look back, but not expecting her to, she watched Olivia walk away. Her shoes seemed too frivolous for her dark pencil skirt and cream blouse, and Merris felt her jaw drop a fraction as she noticed something else. Stockings. With seams up the back. Merris knew she was wearing a stupefied expression when Olivia glanced back. Casting the merest ghost of a smile at Merris, she lifted a hand in farewell.

With every fiber of her being, Merris wanted to run after her and insist on taking her home or at least carrying her parcel to the car. Telling herself to get real, she waved back, picked up the newspaper and opened it at random. The first headline she saw proclaimed, "*Lovestruck Drivers A Menace Says Report*".

Chapter
Four

"CODY?" ANNABEL WORTH gathered up her leather flying jacket and aviator sunglasses and headed for the door.

Her lover reclined on a hammock on the verandah, dark head drooping, a gruesome-looking mystery novel splayed across her stomach. Her small breasts rose and fell in the tempo of slumber. It was that kind of day, hot and tranquil, palm trees inert against a cloudless sky, the pulse of the ocean sluggish, insects too lethargic to fly.

Even after five years on Moon Island, Annabel still found the concept of endless summer astonishing. It was an East Coast thing, she figured. Thirty years in Boston, and you came to expect foul weather right around the corner. She contemplated awakening Cody, but instead stooped to drop a soft kiss on her forehead.

Before Annabel could retreat, her arm was seized. "Not so fast," Cody wrestled her into the hammock. "You're not sneaking off without a proper kiss!"

"This thing will collapse," Annabel protested.

Cody's dusky gray eyes regarded her with a mixture of mischief and invitation. "Not if we stay very, very still." She kissed Annabel with slow deliberation, and began easing her shirt from her pants.

Annabel swatted her hands away. "Don't even think about it, Cody Stanton. We have guests waiting to be taken to Raro." Dodging further kisses, Annabel struggled to her feet and pointedly dusted herself off.

Cody groaned. "Sometimes I wish this place wasn't so popular."

"So that you could spend your entire life reading detective novels?"

"So we could make love any time we felt like it," Cody said huffily. "I get sick of sharing you. Who's coming this week? Another closet case having a fling behind her girlfriend's back?"

"Honey, it's no business of ours what our guests get up to. We run a resort, not a correctional institution."

"I don't like home-wreckers."

"Well I don't think we have any arriving in the near future." Annabel consulted her introduction sheet. "Tomorrow there's a Chris Thompson coming off a cruise boat."

"Rich and lonely mid-fifties who lucked out at the Dinah Shore," Cody interpreted.

"Then there's those anthropologists from UCLA coming for the Hine te Ana rituals."

"Oh, great." Cody pulled a face. "I forgot about them. It'll be Birkenstocks on every doorstep. Naturally Dr. Whatever is a vegan."

"Dr. Glenn Howick," Annabel supplied. "We're going to make them very welcome. The University has offered a scholarship to a young Cook Island woman."

"In exchange, Dr. Howick gets to treat this place like a human zoo?"

"I've spoken to her and she seems very sincere. Look, it says right here in the file she's a world authority on ancient tribal religion and practices in the South Pacific. She has written seven highly regarded texts on the subject."

Cody grunted.

"You are going to be charming to her," Annabel reiterated.

"She's wasting her time anyway," Cody muttered. "It's not as if she can watch the ceremony unless the island women invite her, and that's not happening."

"She says she wants to explore the sacred sites and interview some of the women who participate. It sounds harmless enough."

Annabel had informed Dr. Howick that the rituals the local women conducted on Moon Island were secret. Men were forbidden, and non-Islanders could only attend if invited by the *ruahine*. Like most pre-Christian traditions, the Moon Island rituals had been stamped out by missionaries in the previous century, and for many years women who persisted in making the dangerous canoe journey to the island were punished when they returned. Eventually no one came, and Moon Island lay abandoned.

Finally, in the 1960s, Annabel's aunt Annie had moved to the island with her lover and child. Local women interpreted this as a sign from the old gods that they too should return, and before long a *ruahine*, or priestess, was appointed. Nowadays, once each year, the local women held a special ceremony in honor of Hine te Ana, one of three goddesses believed to dwell on Moon Island.

According to legend, Hine te Ana was a princess washed ashore after trying to save the life of her small daughter who was claimed by the sea god Tangaroa. Stricken, she had climbed the dangerous cliffs above the beach and retreated into a cave to mourn her child. There her tears formed a great pool and when Marama, the moon goddess, looked down into the cave and saw Hine's weeping reflection in the silver waters, she took pity on her. For one night she granted the princess's greatest wish: to see her daughter again.

To this day, the islanders believed that any woman invited by the goddess to look into the magical waters inside the cave was granted a wish. However, any trespasser looking down into the sacred pool without her blessing was cursed. The cave's exact location was a mystery, but during the rituals it was said the goddess sometimes singled out a woman and led her there.

No one made the journey to Moon Island by canoe any more. Annabel picked up the *ruahine* and other participants on Rarotonga and flew them in. Cody then delivered them by boat to the Sacred Shore, as Hine's beach was known. They were picked up two days later. What happened in the intervening period was strictly *tapu*, or sacred, and discussing it was forbidden.

"Where are we putting the doctor?" Cody asked. "Over the other side of the island, I trust."

"They'll be in Marama Bay where we can keep an eye on them."

"I can hardly wait," Cody mumbled.

"You are completely incorrigible."

"Let's go make out on the beach, while we've still got the place to ourselves."

There was an edge to Cody's voice Annabel seldom heard. She tilted her head in unspoken question.

"I want you," Cody said. "Is that so hard to believe?"

"When it's in that tone. Yes." Annabel touched her arm. "You seem cranky. Want to talk about it?"

Cody swung her feet to the wooden boards. "I feel like we never get any time together. And it's not just that. Ever since that fight about the baby, you've been distant from me. I hate it."

Annabel shook her head, bemused. "I have no idea what you're talking about. We're together all the time. And this is the busy season."

"Let's go away somewhere. Just us." An urgency entered Cody's tone. "We could shut the place up for a month or two."

"Darling, we're booked solid. We won't have any time clear until the middle of next year."

Cody sighed. "Can't we say something has come up? There are plenty of other islands 'round here."

"None that are women only. Our guests choose us because that's important to them."

"Okay, so let's plan a time and take no reservations."

"Good idea," Annabel took Cody's hands and lifted them to her mouth, tenderly kissing the palms. "I love you," she said, very serious. "I'm sorry if you feel I've been shutting you out."

"I don't blame you, after what I said."

Annabel shrugged. "Well, you were right. I'm not the motherly type."

Cody colored. "It was a stupid and cruel thing to say and I'm sorry. Anyway, I didn't rule out the whole idea," she added defensively. "I said I had to think about it."

"That was six weeks ago."

"There's a time limit?"

Annabel felt a quick surge of frustration. She had promised herself they wouldn't have this discussion again. Her lover wasn't ready for a baby. It was that simple. Cody was five years younger than she. Annabel's biological clock was ticking, and Cody's was not.

Like a fool, Annabel had convinced herself that Cody would be completely thrilled with the idea of starting a family. She had broached the subject one night after they had made love, anticipating that they would fall asleep in one another's arms united in their decision to begin a wonderful new chapter of their lives. Instead, Cody had behaved as if Annabel must be kidding. Then, when she realized Annabel was serious, she had made her opinions very clear. Cody had no interest in raising a child and, even more discouraging, she seemed to think Annabel would make a lousy mother.

Annabel had spent the rest of the night crying in the spare bedroom, and for the next few days they had barely spoken. Finally, Cody accused Annabel of using emotional blackmail to get her way, and they had a fight even worse than the first. They made up eventually, but the damage was done. If she were honest with herself, Annabel knew Cody was right. She had been distant ever since, not trusting herself to have another discussion. The issue was too emotional.

Forcing an even tone, Annabel said, "Let's not go there. Okay? Can you understand that because it was important to me, I wanted it to be important to you, too. I'm just coming to terms with the fact that it's different for each of us. If I seem to be pushing you away, I'm truly sorry."

Cody's mouth trembled. "I know you want a baby. I know

it's important. I was trying to give it time, that's all. You know, trying to picture how it would be. It's been just the two of us for five years, and it feels perfect. I can't imagine us any other way." She broke off and wiped tears from her eyes with the back of her arm. "I'm sorry I was such an idiot. Please, can we talk about his again when I've gotten used to the idea?"

Touched, Annabel kissed her lover's wet cheek. With a flash of insight, she understood Cody had her own process to go through, and she was just doing her best. Annabel had been thinking about a baby for at least a year. In her excitement at having made her own decision, she had expected Cody to come to terms with the idea in less than five minutes. "I haven't been fair about this. We can talk whenever you're ready," she said. "I'm sorry, honey."

Cody held her tight. "Maybe I'm pre-menstrual."

"Well, we can do something about that later," Annabel said. "But first..."

"I know." Cody made a face. "Someone has to unload the pineapples."

FOUR THOUSAND MILES away, Riley Mason checked her watch and jiggled her car keys impatiently.

"That comes to twenty-six dollars fifty," the librarian at the returns desk informed her tonelessly. "One of these was on reserve."

"I'm sorry." Riley foraged in her satchel. Her wallet was trapped beneath a heavy binder. She could hear the next guy in line swearing beneath his breath. "Here..." She located a couple of crumpled twenties.

Without lifting her head, the librarian indicated a sign that said. WE DO NOT GIVE CHANGE. PLEASE PAY FINES IN CORRECT DENOMINATIONS.

Riley stuffed her hands into her jeans pockets and produced a handful of quarters. "Look, all I need is five bucks. Can you..."

"There are people waiting." The librarian glanced pointedly at the growing line. "You can make change at the help desk."

"And wait in line again? Please, Sarah." Riley humiliated herself by begging, "I've got a class, and I need to get this re-issued. It's for Dr. Howick."

Sarah was unmoved. "Then she will need to come down personally. I'll put the book aside."

The moral–never date a librarian. Riley had only gone out with Sarah for three weeks. There was no chemistry. Their lovemaking had been mutually unrewarding, and they had little to say to one another when they weren't in bed. But Sarah still referred to "our relationship" long after their fling was over and had told everyone that Riley Mason had internalized homophobia and a hang-up about oral sex. Since then, the offers had flooded in. Not!

"Okay, you win." Riley pocketed the unwanted cash and snatched the books out of the indignant Sarah's hands. They were already late. How much worse could it get? She would go get the goddamned change and stand in line again. She was taking that book to the Cook Islands tomorrow. Period.

"By the way," Sarah called after her. "Those Nikes you left at my place. I gave them to the Salvation Army."

Why? Riley asked herself two hours later in the local Starbucks. What did she do that brought out the very worst in women? She glanced at a group of students sitting at a window table. They were deep in important-sounding conversation, laughing and touching and making the occasional sweep of the room to ensure they were being noticed, preferably by someone cute.

Riley caught herself returning a flirtatious stare and hurriedly swung her attention back to her laptop. Didn't she have enough problems? She had an essay to complete before she could leave town. Her subject was the impact of deforestation on female spirit mediums in Pattani province, Thailand. Naturally, she would get a C. Faculty don't enjoy being dumped any more than librarians, especially when they've risked their career to date a student. This campus wasn't big enough for her and twenty crazed ex-girlfriends. She was getting out in the nick of time.

She had been stunned when Dr. Howick invited her to join the Moon Island research team. The woman was her idol. Intense. Scholarly. Self-assured. Deeply hot. They would be sharing a cottage on a tropical island. Riley could barely draw breath at the thought. They would be working into the night, perhaps taking moonlit walks on the beach to clear their heads. The stars would be low and bright, the sea an expanse of shimmering ripples. They would discuss the socio-economics of gender oppression in the Asia Pacific region. Glenn Howick's throaty voice was such a distraction that her words would be lost even as Riley fantasized about silencing them with kisses.

"In your dreams," she mumbled to herself. It wasn't going to happen. For a start, who knew if Dr. Howick was even a lesbian? There were rumors, but no one had ever heard of her with a partner of either gender. The *Time* magazine article Riley had pinned on her bedroom wall described her as "intensely private," a well-known press euphemism for closet queer. But Riley wasn't so sure. She was an expert at spotting lesbians in deep cover, and so far the mysterious professor had stayed under the gaydar. Dr. Howick revealed nothing of herself to anyone, it seemed. She kept her students at a distance and made people respect her boundaries. No one had an ounce of dirt on the woman. Was she human?

Riley pictured herself at Glenn Howick's side, taking notes that would eventually be forged into a seminal work on female tribal customs. People already said Howick was the next Margaret Mead. This book would make her a world authority. She would need a faithful assistant on her lecture tours. By the time they had finished their study on Moon Island, Riley planned to be the prime contender.

Chapter Five

CHRIS THOMPSON STARED down at the boat-shaped papaya dessert on her plate. Tucked beneath it was a decorative slice of rubbery coconut cut in the shape of a flower. Hibiscus adorned the table, orange and red hues as vivid as the sunset she had enjoyed from the deck that evening. In the background, a band in white dinner jackets played uninspiring jazz.

The bald man seated next to her invited her to dance, explaining, "My wife's seasick."

Chris declined the offer. "I'm lucky. I haven't been sick once since we left Hawaii."

"You traveling alone?"

She had been asked the same question at least a hundred times during the past week. "That's right."

He responded with a sly wink. "Give it time."

Did she look like she was on the make? Chris took stock of herself as others might see her; a sturdy woman in a plain cream shirt and olive pants, silver-threaded sandy brown hair brushed back from her forehead, her face free of make-up. She glanced across the table at the other unaccompanied female present at the evening meal. They had spoken briefly at the swimming pool that morning. The woman, clutching a cocktail extravaganza with a slab of a pineapple clinging to the side, had introduced herself as Linda. She had no intention of swimming, she'd said, offering to reserve a deckchair while Chris swam a few lengths. She'd had her legs waxed that morning and looked like a plucked chicken.

Linda *was* on the make. She had spent the evening sizing up the men at their table and asking those she found interesting to pass her various condiments. She had danced with a couple of the married ones, perhaps so she wouldn't seem too obvious. Catching Chris's eye, she smiled conspiratorially, as though they were fellow strategists in the same man-hunt.

Chris returned a smile that was politely discouraging. She

was not sure if this cruise had been such a good idea. Certainly she had relaxed, exercised, tanned, and eaten well. She had met some pleasant people — versions of her parents, mid-west folk on the vacation of a lifetime. She had considered going on a women-only cruise, but did not feel ready for the cut and thrust of the meat market. It was eighteen years since she had been 'out there.' Besides, she still felt married to Elaine.

She'd spotted a few lesbians on board the cruise boat, mostly closeted couples who seemed anxious to remain so. They had not encouraged her overtures of friendship. Perhaps she looked too lesbian. Her unfeminine appearance was guaranteed to draw speculative attention to any woman she was with. Or perhaps the couples she encountered were simply in love and snatching precious time together. Three was a crowd. Her hand moved to the heavy locket suspended between her breasts. She could remember that feeling.

"Going ashore tomorrow?" her bald neighbor inquired, adding, when she turned blank eyes toward him, "Rarotonga?"

"Yes. Actually, I'm leaving the cruise. I'm spending the rest of my vacation on one of the islands."

"You don't say." Chuckling, he lowered his voice. "Now you watch out. They eat white folks 'round these parts."

Chris swallowed her final mouthful of papaya, doubting the guy had any idea how offensive he'd been. "Well, I'll look forward to that," she said solemnly. "It's been a while."

"IT'S JUST WRITER'S block," Polly said. "You'll get past it."

"It's sexual frustration," Abigail corrected.

Olivia rolled her eyes. "I can't write because I'm not getting any?"

"How many entire albums did you write when you and Hunter got together?" Abigail demanded. "And how many songs over the past year? You do the math."

"I think it's slightly more complicated than that," Olivia said.

Abigail was unimpressed. "Whatever. But a change of scene is exactly what you need. Trust me. You won't believe this place."

"It sounds fantastic," Polly enthused, reading from the brochure, "The undiscovered jewel of the Cook Island group. A paradise decreed by ancient tribal tradition to be for women only."

"I've reserved the two-week Celebrity Seclusion package," Abigail continued. "They even offer discreet bodyguard surveillance as an option."

Polly giggled. "Imagine it. Some hunky butch hanging around holding your towel."

"Oh, please." Olivia groaned. "And I don't need a celebrity package, for God's sake."

"Just thought you might be missing the excitement...stretch limos, TV cameras, sycophantic hangers-on..." Abigail said, all innocence.

"Uh huh." Olivia had detested the relentless public scrutiny life with Hunter entailed, and her friends knew it.

"So you'll do the luxury getaway instead?" Abigail typed into her laptop, which, thanks to wireless technology, was no longer relegated to its case when they dined out. "Your own secluded cottage...private beach...snorkeling...scenic flights..."

"It could be worse," Kate chipped in. "I mean if you can't write songs on a desert island, where can you write them?"

Olivia removed the olive from her martini and chewed it thoughtfully. She had begun to wonder if she would ever write again. It happens. No one can come up with hits indefinitely. Maybe songwriters only had so many great ideas and once these were all on paper, you were condemned to recycling. It didn't help that every time Olivia thought of a line, she heard it in Hunter's voice.

"It's not like I need to write another song in my entire life," she said candidly. "All it takes is one hit, and thanks to Hunter, I have six."

"But it's not just the money, is it?" Kate said. "You wrote songs for years without making a dime."

"They were not very good songs," Olivia pointed out.

"Oh, I don't know. I always liked that one about the wilting rose. How does it go?" Polly forged a few words together with some off-key humming.

Olivia winced. Here was a solution to her creative angst. If it were Polly's voice instead of Hunter's she heard as she composed, she wouldn't miss her work at all.

"Guess what. We scored a cancellation, so you leave at midday tomorrow," Abigail announced. "I'll house-sit."

"Tomorrow?" Olivia was aghast. "I can't leave tomorrow."

"Why not. You've started packing, haven't you?"

"It's not that. It's just—"

Abigail tapped her squared off nails on the table. "Give me one good reason why you should wait."

TWO HOURS LATER, with piles of folded clothing all over her bed, Olivia still couldn't come up with a single excuse to cancel. Somehow, she had known she would journey to Moon Island from the moment she had picked up that book in *The Tattered Cover*. When she'd raised the topic with her friends, Abigail had immediately insisted it was the perfect destination. She knew about the place from colleagues in the travel industry. It was one of those best-kept secrets. And being women only, families and straight honeymooners were ruled out. What could be more ideal?

Olivia studied the brochure again. The photographs depicted expanses of white beach, palm trees, crimson sunsets on a shimmering sea. The place was operated by two women. A picture showed them standing in front of a gorgeous tropical villa, obviously a couple. Everyone who stayed there was probably a couple, too, Olivia thought. How depressing.

The phone rang, and for a moment she vacillated. She didn't recognize the caller ID. Probably a sales call. She picked up impatiently. "Hello?"

Silence. Then, "Olivia?"

Had she responded? Olivia didn't know. Her mouth was frozen.

"I'm in town," Hunter's voice poured into her ear. "Can I see you?"

Olivia held the phone away from her face and took several short sharp breaths. She felt winded. Hunter was here? What did she want?

"That's not possible," she finally managed.

"Please." That low husky beg she'd never been able to resist. "It's important."

Olivia closed her eyes. The phone was slippery with sweat. She knew she should say no, but she couldn't.

Ten minutes later, Hunter stood slouched against the sitting room fireplace, thumb in her belt, a booted toe awkwardly tracing a pattern on the tile. "You look great," she said.

"You look awful." Olivia handed her a shot of Sazerac, reminding herself to throw the bottle out later. There was no reason to keep rye whisky in the house any more.

"We're recording." Hunter said as if to explain her pallor and reddened eyes. She drank the shot and handed the glass back for another. "It's all my own stuff."

Since when was Hunter any kind of songwriter? "Your fans will be thrilled," Olivia commented dryly. These days Hunter only had to breathe into a mike and you could hear the money being printed.

"It sounds like shit. Nothing's working."

"Too much coke, not enough sleep?" Olivia suggested, pouring a second shot.

Hunter looked defensive. "It's the songs. Steve is pissed. He says my writing sucks."

Olivia shrugged. This was news? "Well I'm sorry to hear that," she said insincerely. "It doesn't explain what you're doing here."

"Not exactly the welcome I was hoping for." There it was. That crooked flash of a smile. Those wayward eyes making promises they both knew she could keep.

Olivia could feel color swamping her cheeks. It seemed at any moment her heart would force her ribcage open like a clam. She willed her legs to carry her back across the room to the liquor cabinet. With shaking hands she poured some vodka on ice and made a show of sipping it. Hunter was flirting with her. She flirted with every woman, Olivia reminded herself.

"Baby, I'm sorry," Hunter burst out. "I'm sorry I hurt you. You were the best thing that ever happened to me, and I blew it." She sidled across the room to stand just a touch away from Olivia. "I've been practicing this for months, and I always figure you'll slap my face about now. So knock yourself out." She inclined her head and tapped her cheek lightly.

Despite herself, Olivia smiled. Her heart had lost all sense of rhythm. Hunter had come to apologize. It had taken the best part of a year, but she was here, and the look in her eyes told Olivia she really meant it.

"I want to make it up to you," she continued huskily. "I can't handle this not-talking shit any more. Nothing works when you're not there."

Olivia was struck by her thinness. The torn 501s were hanging from her. She must have lost fifteen pounds since they broke up. Of course, without Olivia around to rain on everyone's parade, Hunter was surrounded by people who only said yes. There were no limits. No drug she couldn't buy. No one she couldn't bed.

"Are you using again?" Olivia wrapped her suspicions in a neutral tone.

"Shit. You sound like my mother." It was Hunter's standard response to anything she didn't want to hear.

"God forbid the people who love you actually give a damn," Olivia remarked.

Hunter grinned. Her eyes were softly challenging. "That sounds like you're saying you care."

Olivia was overwhelmed with the urge to say yes, to seize

whatever it was Hunter was offering. Yet something jarred. This was not the Hunter who had colonized her mind every waking moment since the day they met. The singer seemed to have aged ten years in ten months. There was a brittleness about her, a tautness in her face Olivia had never seen.

Hunter had always maintained that she could control her drug use, insisting that getting high occasionally did not mean she had a problem. When occasionally became every day, she went into denial. From the look of her, Olivia was certain she was at the every day stage. "I can help you," she said. "I'll make some calls right now and check you into rehab. No one needs to know."

As if she hadn't heard a word, Hunter slid her arms around Olivia and drew her close. "You feel amazing," she murmured. "I've missed this. I miss us."

Me, too, Olivia thought. For a few seconds, she managed to hold her body stiff. Then her flesh began melting against Hunter's. People messed up, she reasoned with herself, especially in this business. There was so much temptation, so few boundaries. One minute Hunter was a complete unknown; the next, women were throwing their panties at her. Was it any surprise she had trouble staying grounded? If they were back together, Olivia could help her get clean and stay clean. This time everything would be different.

Hunter's mouth was on her neck, the kisses slow and hot, and suddenly Olivia was where she had longed to be every painful day since they parted.

"Remember Aspen," Hunter murmured. "Those songs you wrote."

In bed. Between lovemaking. Days in a row. Olivia caught Hunter's shirt in her hand, twisting her closer. How often had she played this scene in her mind? Hunter coming back to her, full of remorse, knowing she'd made a mistake, knowing they belonged together, and promising nothing and no-one would ever come between them again.

"I miss that," Hunter whispered in her ear. "I miss your words. What have you been writing lately?"

"Nothing much," Olivia admitted. "My work's shit, too."

They laughed softly against one another. "I'm guessing that could change," Hunter said.

Her blouse was on the floor, Olivia noticed. And Hunter's hands were unfastening her bra. Now was a good time to stop, she thought. Instead she reached for Hunter's belt.

Hunter caught her wrists and pulled her to the sofa. "Will you do something for me?" she asked, softly biting Olivia's throat.

"Opportunist." Olivia released a sharp sigh as Hunter's teeth moved to a nipple.

"Write." Hunter placed her hands over Olivia's hips. "Now. Like we used to. Write something wonderful." She slid her knee between Olivia's thighs.

Olivia did not even pretend to resist. A tiny voice in the back of her mind shouted warnings, but listening would mean sending Hunter away, and that was something she couldn't do. The fog that had enveloped her for almost a year had suddenly parted to reveal a bright, blazing world. All Olivia wanted to do was run toward it. Hope and elation evicted all doubt from her mind. The Fates were sending her a signal. Hunter would not be here; Olivia would not feel so right in her arms, unless they were meant to be together once more.

Mock reluctant, she said, "I don't have pen and paper." She'd once written a song in felt marker on Hunter's back during lovemaking.

Hunter promptly got off the sofa and made a show of looking around the room.

"Tease," Olivia pointed to the notebook and pens on her desk. They had played this game before. Hunter would make it worth her while.

"Take those off first," Hunter said, indicating Olivia's garter belt and stockings.

Arms folded, she watched Olivia unsnap her garters and roll down her stockings, and held out a hand to take them. "Now go get that paper."

Obediently Olivia crossed the room and collected what she needed. When she returned, Hunter was sitting on the sofa, still fully dressed, legs carelessly extended, hands linked behind her head. She might have been watching a football game. Her hot stare said otherwise.

Olivia knelt beside her, rested the paper on Hunter's denim-clad knees and pondered a first line. Anticipating how she would be rewarded focused her mind like nothing else. She scribbled, "Restless heart. You play me too well," and offered it up to Hunter.

A fingertip trawled the length of her spine. "Touché. It even sounds like a country song." Hunter moved a caressing hand over her ass.

That irritating little voice in the back of her mind borrowed a megaphone, informing Olivia, *Yes ma'am, heartbreak and betrayal make for great material.*

"It's blues," Olivia said. This was a standing joke. She wrote blues and Hunter labeled it country.

"We'll see." Hunter set the paper in front of her once more.

Olivia had no problem with a second line, then a third, and the chorus; notes and lyric in effortless tandem. She was writing. Just like that. All the proof she would ever need that without Hunter she was incomplete as an artist and as a woman.

As lines filled the page, their lovemaking shifted from exquisite teasing to that familiar fierce cadence Olivia had missed so desperately. By the time the song was complete, she was astride Hunter's lap, sweating, shaking, consumed by her creature self. There was nothing but sensation, converging in the sweet hot core where her thighs met. Blood coursed through her body, sweeping aside the numbness she had known for months. She was present in her skin so intensely it was as if the pores were imploding.

Her release, when it came, was more than mere letting go. It was at once surrender and empowerment, the truest expression of her secret self. Eyes closed, her breath coming in small gasps, she felt that heady rush she had thought was lost to her forever. Once more she was perfect and whole, part of the universal organic harmony that connected every living soul.

Hunter ran the tip of her tongue across Olivia's bottom lip. "Let's do this again very soon."

Olivia stretched her arms languidly above her head. "How does later tonight sound?"

Hunter groaned. "I wish. But I need to go, baby."

"Go? Where?"

Hunter looked abashed. "I have to drop someone off. She's waiting in the car. I wasn't expecting...this. I thought you'd throw me out after five minutes."

It was a bucket of ice water. Olivia's stomach knotted. "Who is she?"

"No one. There was a party last night. Her ride went without her or something."

Olivia had heard it all before. Mechanically, she swung her legs to the floor and gathered her clothing.

"C'mon baby. Don't give me a hard time."

"Did I say a word?"

Olivia pulled on her blouse, suddenly chilled. Her teeth began chattering. She seemed to have become two people. One set about buttoning the garment over her naked breasts, the other walked from the room and floated out the front door into the chill solace of night sky. "It's none of my business what you do," the earthbound Olivia said as her moon-clad twin drifted far, far away. "We broke up. Remember?"

"Don't be like that. Didn't I just make it up to you?" Hunter finished buttoning her jeans. Her body language was indolent, almost cocky. She pulled on her boots, polishing the tops against the back of her jeans, one foot at a time as she always did. With slow deliberation, she buckled her belt, the performer seducing her audience. The bold sensuality that had once been so unselfconscious was now calculated and premeditated. Hunter had said the power was addictive. At first she'd felt uncomfortable with it, then it excited her, now she could not function without it.

Was that what tonight was about? Had Hunter set out to prove she could win back her toughest critic and most disillusioned fan? Olivia used to laugh at the absurdity of magazine features that promised the real Hunter Carsen, as if her interviews and candid shots were anything but scripted and stage-managed image building. All media was advertising, Benny Berenbaum always said. Olivia had understood a long time ago that Hunter was never off-stage. Not even in their personal life.

"Why did you come here?" she asked flatly.

Hunter folded the two sheets of lyrics Olivia had just written. "I told you. I miss us. I want you back in my life." She slid the song into her pocket. A small white corner protruded, trapping Olivia's stare.

Hunter was still talking her talk. But Olivia heard nothing she said. Between one breath and the next, she understood what she had never understood. Hunter did not love *her*, Olivia, the person. She loved what Olivia could do for her. She had not come back to Olivia, she had come back to her music. There had been no epiphany for Hunter. She did not wake up one day and realize she truly loved Olivia; she woke up and realized her next album would stink. She had just made love to Olivia because that's what it took to get a song she could use.

There was a time when Olivia would have convinced herself that this judgment was unfair and cynical, colored by her own insecurities. Not any more. She knew with absolute certainty it was the truth, a truth she had concealed from herself. Hunter was a user. She used people the same way she used smack, and with as little regard to the consequences.

"I can't wait to have you back in the studio, baby," Hunter said. "I'll call you tomorrow. Okay?"

"I won't be here."

Hunter gave her a knowing look. "Oh, I think you will." She collected Olivia's panties on the toe of her boot and flicked them into her hand — another of her stage tricks. "Mind if I keep these?" she said, tucking them into her belt with a candid grin.

Olivia was vaguely aware of Hunter dropping a hard confident kiss on her mouth, of her boots echoing in the hall, the front door closing with hollow finality. Then she sank slowly down to the floor and curled up on her side. In the corridors of her mind, doors slammed, windows shuttered, walls closed in. Unable to move or think, Olivia listened to her grandfather clock tick the night away. Just before dawn, she got stiffly to her feet and gazed out the window. It had snowed. Her world was white and cold and silent.

Chapter
Six

WHEN A B-17 Flying Fortress is your guest transport, you get used to twitchy passengers. *Lonesome Lady* was a genuine warbird rebuilt after World War II and now converted into a comfortable passenger plane. She was as safe and reliable as any commercial craft. At least that's what Annabel told skittish arrivals who seemed reluctant to hand over their luggage and climb aboard.

The sandy-haired woman standing on the tarmac today had no such problems. "I don't believe this," she exclaimed. "Is she for real?"

"Eight missions over Berlin." Annabel indicated some flak marks. "Very few of these ever came back. There's less than fifty in the world."

Chris whistled. "My dad was a Spitfire pilot. I can't wait to tell him about this." She pulled a camera from her cabin bag and asked, "Would you mind?"

Obligingly, Annabel snapped their new guest in a classic pose in front of the plane one arm resting on the twin .50 caliber machine gun protruding from the nose. She did not seem the kind of woman who would be taking a vacation alone. Guests of Chris Thompson's age and common-sense demeanor typically came to Moon Island with a partner. Singles out shopping after a broken relationship went where they could find a crowd.

"You ought to give this a plug in your brochure," Chris remarked. "It's a real marketing plus."

Annabel refrained from pointing out that the thought of flying to the island in a sixty-year-old bomber did not float many skirts in her experience. Their guests had enough problems coping with an antiquated telephone system and electricity that seemed to function at random. Moon Island was a far cry from the Cancun Club Med. Annabel handed Chris's luggage over to Smithy with the usual pang of guilt.

Now almost eighty years old, Smithy, the wiry little British engineer, still insisted on loading the plane. "Got another passenger for yer," he said, waving toward the hangar. "Turned up 'ere yesterday. Told 'er she'd be waiting a while."

Puzzled, Annabel consulted her guest roster. "Are you sure she's for us?" Sometimes the Information desk at Rarotonga International sent people over on the off chance of a charter. Bevan, who co-owned the *Lady*, ran joy-rides around the islands on his fly days and would take strays if he had enough room. Annabel generally restricted her flying to the shuttle between Moon Island and Rarotonga. It was her concession to Cody, who had wanted her to quit flying altogether after she crashed their last plane on Solarim Atoll.

With a friendly smile at Chris, she said, "If you'd like to step aboard and choose a seat, we'll push off shortly. I'll go see what's happening with this other passenger."

Chris looked delighted. "Mind if I explore?"

"Feel free. If you have any questions, Smithy will be able to help. He serviced these during the war."

Chris grinned at the Englishman. "I'll bet you have some stories."

"Chris's dad was a fighter pilot," Annabel commented. As far as Smithy was concerned there were civilians and there were heroes. He had very little to say to the former, and a wealth of conversation for the latter and their kin. He'd have Chris in the top turret taking aim at imaginary bandits at twelve o'clock high before she could blink.

Annabel strolled across to the hangar, her cotton slouch hat pulled down low to cut the painful glare from the tarmac. A woman sat in Smithy's favorite armchair in front of the cooling fan. Her head drooped to one side. In her arms lay a young baby. They were both sound asleep in the muggy afternoon heat.

Annabel removed her hat and sunglasses, and crouched down for a better look at the woman's face. "Melanie?" She gave the woman a gentle shake. "Is that you?"

A pair of sweet doe eyes blinked back at her and her cousin's delicate features lifted in a smile.

"My God," Annabel exclaimed. "What are you doing here?"

Melanie pulled herself up slightly in her chair, careful not to wake the baby. "Don't tell me I've arrived on the wrong day." She extended an arm and gave Annabel a hug. "I'm so happy to see you."

"The wrong day? Mel, I hate to sound like an idiot, but I don't seem to have a reservation for you."

"You don't?" Melanie looked stunned. "Are you saying I can't come?"

"No, no! I just wasn't expecting you. I mean I'm thrilled

you're here, but it's a surprise. That's all."

"Oh dear," Melanie's voice grew thin. "This is probably really inconvenient for you. I was worried when your mom suggested we write. I suppose the letter hasn't even arrived yet. Look, I'll make other arrangements."

"Don't be silly!" Annabel laughed. "I love that you've come. And you brought the baby." She drew the light cotton shawl aside gently and lowered her voice. "Oh, she's gorgeous. Briar, isn't it?"

Melanie nodded. "She's just getting her first tooth, so she's exhausted, poor darling."

Damp black curls clung to the baby's tiny head like silk rosettes. In her sleep, her mouth puckered every now and then in a sucking motion. Annabel was overwhelmed with tenderness. "Let me take her," she said, "And we'll get you on board."

To Annabel's astonishment, Melanie burst into tears. "I'm sorry, you'll have to help me. I'm so tired. I just can't do it." Wiping her face, she reached for something behind her chair.

Shocked, Annabel noticed a folded wheelchair propped against the workbench. What on earth had happened that Mel needed this? She lifted Briar gently against her shoulder and pulled the wheelchair out.

"It's not that I can't walk," Melanie said. "But when I'm tired, I..." She broke off and eased herself into the chair. "It's all in the letter."

Annabel returned Briar to her and knelt beside the wheelchair, her mind spinning. "Did you have an accident? No one told me..."

"No, nothing like that. I haven't been well for a while and having Briar was hard. You know, the pregnancy."

She was terribly pale and her skin felt clammy. Melanie had never been heavy, but she was as slight as a reed now. "What on earth is wrong?"

Melanie hesitated. Obviously it was a difficult subject. "I have ALS. It seems to be progressing very fast." Reading Annabel's puzzlement, she explained, "The medical term is amyotrophic lateral sclerosis."

Annabel must have looked as mystified as she felt. "Is that like multiple sclerosis?"

With a weary sigh, Melanie took her hand. "Can we talk about this later?"

CHRIS WADED ALONG Passion Bay at water's edge. The ocean was warm and shimmering, more clear and blue than any ocean she could have imagined. Beneath her feet, fine white sand sucked and swirled. The sun was sinking slowly against the vast curve of the Pacific horizon, a blood-orange curtain descending with it. The Cook Islands were the only land for thousand of miles. No wonder the mutiny on the Bounty had happened in these waters, she reflected. Imagine months at sea without sight of land and suddenly the heady vision of a blue lagoon and islands so beautiful they must have seemed the stuff of myth.

Elaine would have been enchanted. She had always wanted to travel further than Hawaii and Key West, where they vacationed most years. They had often discussed their dream holiday in the South Pacific, starting with a tour of Australia and New Zealand, continuing with a cruise around the islands, and finally stopping somewhere hopelessly romantic where they would have a second honeymoon.

"I'm so sorry," Chris said aloud, closing her fist over the locket she always wore.

They had put the trip off year after year. There was always some reason they could not take a month out of their careers and spend a lot of money. Finally their time had run out. Chris had kissed Elaine goodbye one morning, like any other morning, only it was their last. Elaine was killed twenty minutes from their home. Chris had passed the wreckage herself and recognized the car. Nothing in life prepares you to watch your partner carried from a mangled pile of metal, her body so torn and broken they urge you not to look.

Chris opened the heavy gold keepsake and stared down at the face imprisoned there. Elaine had liked to say she was plain and nothing would change that fact. But Chris saw only beauty in the warmth of her eyes and the way her face crinkled when she smiled, which was often. She loved the silken softness of her fine straight hair. Its style had never changed from the time Elaine was in elementary school. She wore it bobbed, parted on one side and pinned back on the other with a tortoiseshell slide.

As the gathering darkness swallowed that familiar face, Chris wondered if there would ever be a time when she could think of her lover without this terrible grief. There was so much she wished she had said while she still could. Of the two of them, Elaine was the more expressive. It was Elaine who lit candles and made romantic dinners, Elaine who cried over films that made Chris cringe. She had always seemed to understand that it was not in Chris's nature to be demonstrative.

Now Chris wondered if she'd made Elaine as happy as she deserved. There had been times when she'd caught a wistful expression on her lover's face when she saw a couple holding hands or one of those grandiose movie kisses. Had Elaine just settled for what they had in default of anything better? Had she had regrets?

What exactly would it have cost her to be a more romantic lover? Chris berated herself. Instead, she had allowed months to become years and had made no effort to change her comfortable habits. She hated to think of the opportunities she had squandered to enrich their life together. Since the accident, she had become acutely conscious of her failings as a partner. The worst of these, it seemed to her, was that she had allowed Elaine to walk out the door alone that morning.

It didn't have to happen that way. Most of the time they drove into work together. Elaine had waited for her that day, but Chris had taken a call when she should have been in the shower. Eventually Elaine had left without her, irritated and running late. Knowing Elaine, she would have driven a little faster than usual, passed a few more cars, taken extra risks. She loathed being late for a meeting.

If only Chris had made different choices that morning. If only the phone hadn't rung. If only she had told the caller she would phone him back later. They would have left in the same car. Chris would have been driving. Maybe the accident would never have happened. Or maybe it would have and Chris would have been killed instead of Elaine. Or perhaps they would both have died. Anything would have been better than what transpired that day.

Chris retreated up the beach and sat in the warm sand to watch the sun vanish into the sea. In theory, she knew it was not her fault Elaine was dead. But she was haunted by the *what ifs*. She pictured Elaine beside her right now, leaning against her the way she did. "I love you," she said. "I wish you were here."

"WHAT ARE YOU doing?" Cody rolled over, squinting at Annabel's bedside lamp.

Annabel was dragging something bulky into their bedroom. It looked like a chair. "Everything's fine," she insisted. "Go back to sleep. We'll talk later."

Rubbing her eyes, Cody sat up in bed. "It's three in the morning."

Annabel arranged the chair in the corner of the room near her side of the bed. "I'll be back in a minute," she said, heading out the door.

Cody got out of bed and shambled into the bathroom. First she comes home with some long-lost cousin and her baby, then the two of them disappear together for the rest of the evening. Now she was moving furniture in the middle of the night. What would be next?

As Cody dried her hands, she became aware of some peculiar sounds. Sticking her head around the door, she asked, "Is that you making those weird noises?"

"Not exactly," Annabel replied. She was sitting in the chair, a strangely contented expression on her face. In her arms, Melanie's baby was making all kinds of grunting, crooning, and sucking sounds as it drank its bottle.

Cody was dumbstruck. Not only had Annabel moved an armchair into their room, there was a bassinet right next to the bed.

"If it's okay with you, I think Briar should sleep in here tonight," Annabel said as if it were no big deal. "Mel needs to get some sleep. The travel was rough on her."

"Sure," Cody said. Like she had a choice. She sat on the end of the bed, struck by the sight of Annabel tenderly looking down at Melanie's baby, her pale hair spilling across the blue silk of her kimono. Somehow Cody had never been able to imagine Annabel with a baby, yet she seemed completely at ease, like she knew exactly what she was doing. And she looked as beautiful as Cody had ever seen.

Annabel caught her eye. "Isn't she adorable?"

"Amazing." Cody hoped she didn't sound as unenthusiastic as she felt. "I didn't realize you knew this stuff. Baby stuff, I mean."

"I don't," Annabel replied. "But it can't be that hard. They're just little people who need us." She lifted the baby against her shoulder and slowly rubbed her back.

"So how long is your cousin going to be staying?"

Annabel wiped the baby's mouth where she had spat up, and cradled her close. "It's hard to say." Her face grew serious. "There's something I need to tell you."

Cody felt a small prickle of alarm. Annabel looked upset, as if it was a struggle to speak. Cody braced herself for alarming information. Did Annabel want to go back to Boston to help her sick cousin for a while? It seemed like the woman meant a lot to her, and clearly the baby was a draw card.

"It's Melanie. She's sick. Really sick. That's why she's here. Both her parents are dead and her older brother is the family nut job. So she was staying with Mother last month and they cooked this up between them." Annabel shifted position, set the bottle aside and slowly rocked the baby. "She and Briar will have to stay in the Villa with us. She can't manage alone."

"Sure, no worries," Cody agreed, thankful that Annabel wasn't about to go anywhere. It wasn't going to be easy having two extras in the house during a busy period, but it wouldn't be for long, she figured. "Maybe the climate will help her. Is that what she's thinking?"

Annabel got up and put the baby in the bassinette. "Honey, she has something called ALS. It's a motor neuron disease. She has about six months left to live. Maybe less." Tears rolled down her face.

Cody was at a loss for words, consumed with guilt for resenting the woman's unexpected arrival. "That's awful. She's so young."

Annabel leaned heavily against her shoulder. "It's funny, we barely saw one another when I was little. But we were at Radcliffe together and we had a blast. It was great. Just like having a sister all of a sudden."

Cody stroked her hair. "I remember you telling me about her." She found a tissue and wiped Annabel's tears.

"Mel is a fantastic person. I can't imagine how terrible this is for her."

"Did she know?" Cody asked. "I mean before she got pregnant?"

Annabel shook her head. "She had some early symptoms but she thought it was nothing. She didn't even go to a doctor. After Briar was born, she got very sick and that's when they found out."

Cody stared down at the sleeping baby. "God, the poor little thing. She won't know her mother."

"Or her father," Annabel said. "It was donor insemination."

"Great. She can't even say her first word and she'll be an orphan." Cody lay down with Annabel and pulled the sheet up over them.

Annabel curled against her. "No child should have to suffer that."

Her voice was thick with sorrow. Cody could tell the subject pushed buttons. In a sense Annabel had been orphaned too, brought up without knowing that the woman she thought was an aunt was, in fact, her birth mother. Annabel's parents had adopted her as a baby and had kept the truth from her. It was only when her "aunt" had died that Annabel learned of her true identity.

"We'll do everything we can for her," Cody said, gently caressing her back until she could feel Annabel starting to drift back to sleep.

"I knew you'd say that," Annabel murmured against her

shoulder. "I love you."

Cody bent and kissed her partner's warm, damp cheek. "I love you, too."

Chapter Seven

MERRIS SHIFTED DOWN and drove past Olivia's house at a crawl. It was only the hundredth time she'd done this since that coffee encounter at The Tattered Cover Bookstore a few weeks ago. *You're behaving like a stalker*, a warning voice insisted. *Either ring the bell, or go home and get on with your life.* Bad enough she had scoured the telephone directory for Olivia's address, let alone she'd all but staked out the place. She knew what days Olivia went shopping, when she took her long walks, how often her housekeeper came. Destiny or not, it wasn't healthy.

Merris stopped the car at Olivia's wrought iron gates and got out. It was biting cold, and the late afternoon light was fast fading. An ominous sky had long ago swallowed the mountains. Heavy snows were forecast for the next few days. She planned on spending these blimped in front of her widescreen TV watching Julianne Moore movies and ordering in pizza, activities unlikely to appeal to a woman like Olivia. That was okay. Merris had a Plan B. If Olivia seemed receptive, she would suggest an elegant dinner. They would have a romantic evening, then say goodnight. She would phone the next day and invite her on another date.

Clutching her peacoat together and wishing she'd had the wit to wear a woolly hat, Merris pressed the buzzer. A disembodied voice answered. Merris gave her name and said, "I have something to drop off for Ms. Pearce."

The gates opened, and she drove toward a sprawling white mansion that made her place look like a crab shack. She wondered how Olivia came to own real estate like this at her age, which Merris guessed was barely thirty. She had moved here from LA, Merris recalled, wondering what kind of business she was in. Something that paid silly amounts of money. Movies, maybe.

It was beginning to flurry more intensely, a haze of snowflakes congealing across the windshield. Merris halted at the front entrance behind a black BMW she supposed must be another of Olivia's cars. When Olivia wasn't driving the practical fully-optioned Subaru it seemed everyone in Colorado had to own, she was in one of several highly idiosyncratic vehicles. There was a decrepit green Jaguar with seats that had been re-covered in astonishing peach suede, and a perfectly restored cherry red '67 Mustang convertible. She probably had others, Merris guessed with a glance at the vast garaging.

Grabbing a small package from the passenger seat, she headed for the front door, rehearsing what she was going to say. Before she could get her first sentence together, the door opened, and she found herself facing Olivia's artsy friend, who looked somewhat taken aback to see her.

"Well, well," she greeted Merris. "Fancy meeting you here. Abigail Zola, in case you've forgotten." She stuck out a hand.

Collecting herself, Merris produced an urbane smile and the requisite handshake. "I'm sure people don't easily forget you, Abigail," she remarked, meaning it.

Olivia's pal had one of those bad angel faces with a wide wicked smile and innocent blue-green eyes. This she framed with some very expensive hair tinting that converted dull mouse to multi-hued honey. If you couldn't remember her face, she made sure you would remember her appearance. Numerous silver and glass bead bangles were stacked up each arm. Her neck was festooned with more of the same, and her nails were individually painted with a flowery design on a background of pale iridescent blue. She wore a tight top of matching blue lace that called attention to the tiniest breasts Merris had ever seen on a grown woman. In keeping with this summer-in-December theme were strappy high-heeled sandals and a rose pink chiffon skirt of many layers. Olivia must keep the house pretty warm, Merris surmised.

Her breath fogging in wreaths, she said, "I have something for Olivia."

"I'm sure you do." Abigail gave her an old fashioned look. "She's not home right now, but that's no reason to leave you out there freezing to death. Come in, for Chrissakes." She beckoned for Merris to follow her. "Your timing's perfect. I was about to mix a martini."

"Sounds good," Merris said, distracted by the swish and cling of the pink skirt as Abigail walked ahead. "So, will Olivia be long?" She hoped not. She knew Abigail would flirt with her, and it didn't seem diplomatic to piss off Olivia's buddy by not playing along. On the other hand, she didn't want to give anyone the wrong impression, especially Olivia.

The room they entered would have been named the den in an average home, but in Olivia's mansion it was obviously the library. Breathing a silent *wow*, Merris removed her coat and glanced around. At least fifty feet long and lined with hundreds, if not thousands, of books, the room was warm and restful. At the far end, a black baby grand piano stood surrounded by huge potted palms in Chinese porcelain planters. In the center of the room, club leather chairs and a sofa were arranged before a crackling log fire. Dark wood paneling set off a modest but carefully chosen collection of art works.

One of these, a huge painting hanging above the fireplace, made Merris catch her breath. It was a nude: a woman sitting in a window, her body modestly turned to the landscape beyond. But she looked back across her shoulder, directly at her viewer. Her expression was not the inviting tease so typical of vanity portraits and pseudo-art. It was more of a challenge, as if she had caught someone watching her without permission. There was no doubt it was Olivia.

Abigail was listening to the kind of droning new age music Merris loathed. She turned it down and took Merris's coat, inviting, "Make yourself at home." It seemed she had no plans to answer Merris's earlier question about Olivia's return.

Merris chose a big leather armchair near the fire and stretched out her hands to be thawed. "This is a great place," she remarked.

"I know. Aren't I lucky getting to house-sit?" Abigail draped Merris's coat over the back of a nearby sofa and began hauling bottles out of a liquor cabinet.

Merris's heart sank. If Abigail was house-sitting, that meant Olivia hadn't just stepped out for a few minutes. Cursing her timing, she asked, "Olivia's away?"

Abigail sloshed some Vodka into a shaker. "You just missed her. She left this morning." Merris guessed her face must have told a gloomy story, because her companion added archly, "Cheer up. *I* don't have plans for this evening."

Merris forced a smile. On a small table near the fire was a chess set with a game in progress. Indicating it, she asked, "Do you play?"

"Good Lord, no. It's way too slow for me. Olivia's the grand master 'round here."

Merris eyed the board. If she was not mistaken, white was mounting a Nimzovich defense. Unorthodox, but frequently effective.

"I suppose you play," Abigail remarked. "Was that one olive or two?'

"Two, thanks. And make mine a little dirty."

"I knew that." A wicked glance. "So, what did you get her?"

"A book." Merris removed it from the bag. "*The Happy Isles of Oceania* by Paul Theroux."

"Sounds like the sequel to *Prozac Nation*," Abigail quipped. Waving a bony hand around the library, she added, "Well, you brought it to the right place."

"She was reading something about the Pacific Islands last time I saw her," Merris explained. "So I thought she might like this."

"Very resourceful," Abigail handed over a great looking martini. "I hate to tell you, but you're wasting your time."

"What do you mean?"

"Do you know anything about Olivia? I mean, have you two been seeing each other or anything?"

"No. Nothing like that." Merris felt uncomfortable.

"I didn't think so. Olivia said she thought you were interested. But I got the impression she wasn't going to do anything about it."

Merris felt herself flush. This was not a conversation she wanted to be having with a pal of Olivia's. She took an unsociable slug of her drink and glanced at her watch. "I should go before the snow gets heavier."

Abigail shrugged. "Suit yourself. But don't you want to know why Olivia won't date you?" She had Merris's attention and she knew it. Toying with her bracelets, she said, "Hey. I'm her best friend. I don't usually talk behind her back either. Okay?"

"Okay." Merris set her cocktail down on the coffee table. "By the way, this is a great martini."

"I know. But thanks anyway...for the endorsement."

Merris found herself warming to Abigail Zola. People probably misjudged her all the time. She was so much sharper than her flaky appearance suggested. "So, what makes you think Olivia won't date me?"

"You mean other than her telling me she was never going to have another relationship as long as she lived?" Not the answer Merris had hoped for. "I know," Abigail commiserated. "Kind of discouraging, wouldn't you say?"

Merris was not sure what to feel. The good news was she had made enough of an impression that Olivia had discussed her with a close friend. The bad news was that Olivia seemed to be contemplating entering a nunnery some time soon. "Do I look like her type?" she enquired, guessing that Olivia's preferences probably did not include average-looking, moderately conservative linear thinkers like herself.

Abigail kicked off her sandals and tucked her feet up underneath her. "In a word, no. You're completely different from most of her exes. But trust me, that's a huge plus. Her last girlfriend...what a piece of work!"

It was always helpful to win over the best friend, Merris told herself. Abigail apparently cared a great deal for Olivia and wanted her to be happy. "You're saying she has lousy taste in women?"

Abigail responded with an exaggerated shrug. "You didn't hear it from me, sugar."

"How long ago did she break up with the er...piece of work?" Merris asked, keeping things rolling in the right direction.

"Almost a year ago. But you would not believe the cheek of this bitch. She turns up here last night and screws around with Olivia's head some more. I arrive this morning to take her to the airport, and she's a complete mess. Not dressed. Not packed. Not waxed. Nothing. I could kill that woman."

Perfect, Merris thought gloomily. Olivia was stuck on her ex. "How long were they together?"

"About three years. You've probably heard of her. Hunter Carsen. She's a country singer."

Merris took her time processing that fact. Hunter Carsen was a household name, at least in lesbian households anyway. And if the media were any indication, she was huge in the straight country market, too. Allegra had all her CDs and had dragged Merris to one of her concerts a couple of years ago. The woman had an astounding voice, Merris conceded. And she was hot. If that was Olivia's type, Merris didn't have a prayer. "So, what happened?" she asked.

"Olivia threw her out. Hunter was fucking around. I think there was more to it than that, but who knows what goes on in someone's relationship?" Abigail fell silent for a moment, seemingly weighing her next remark. "You broke up about the same time, didn't you?"

"Yep. There was someone else involved. My ex is living with her now."

Abigail pulled a wry face. "And people wonder why I won't have a relationship."

"There *are* good ones out there," Merris said.

"I take it you're the marrying type?"

"I guess I am." Not that it had stopped her messing up. No matter how much she wanted to blame Allegra for everything that had gone wrong between them, the depressing truth was that she had allowed their relationship to disintegrate. The signs had been there, loud and clear. But for some reason, she had imagined she could ignore them and everything would stay the same. Now her daughters would be stuck with the consequences.

"Pity," Abigail said with dry candor. "I guess I can't interest you in a cheap encounter, then?"

Merris laughed. "Actually, you probably could. But I get the impression that wouldn't play well with Olivia."

Abigail held her eyes in a frank stare for a long moment, then heaved a playful sigh. "Okay, so we got that out of the way. Don't keep me in suspense. What's your plan? How are you going to woo her?"

"Woo her!" Who used that expression any more?

"You can't seriously imagine Olivia is just going to fall into the sack with you," Abigail said bluntly. "She's no pushover. You need a plan."

"Well, I thought I'd ask her out to dinner and...take it from there."

"Dinner with you is going to rock her world?"

Merris reminded herself she was a mature, intelligent, reasonably attractive woman of thirty-three. "I'm good company."

"So is a dog." Abigail ate an olive.

"Do you have a better idea?"

"Actually, I do," she said without guile.

"I'm all ears."

Abigail's smooth forehead crinkled as though she'd just been struck by some puzzling thought. "Just by the bye. You seem like an intelligent woman. How could you not notice your partner was shacked up with someone else?" Catching Merris's dismay, she said, "C'mon. This is a small town and your ex is a blabbermouth. Polly—you remember her?—well she told me everything."

Merris groaned inwardly. "And you told Olivia?"

"I left out the stuff about your sexual performance," Abigail said, like butter wouldn't melt. "So, do you see much of your kids—what were their names?"

"Anaïs and Chloe," Merris supplied.

Abigail's sharp eyes widened with amused alarm. "Tell me your ex didn't name her children after perfumes."

"What can I say?" She really did know everything, Merris thought, appalled. "I have them twice a month for the weekend." The girls had found it upsetting to be shuttled back and forth each week, so after a few hellish weeks she and Allegra had agreed on bi-monthly visits.

Abigail pondered on this for a moment. "Painless parenting. You get the fun, she gets the chores. Sounds ideal!"

"I guess it would be. For someone who didn't like kids."

Abigail waved a *tsk tsk* finger at the inference. "Another martini?"

"I should get going."

"Oh come on. I'm teasing. I promise I'm going to tell you how to win the fair Olivia." Abigail gave the fire a tentative poke, sending a fountain of bright orange sparks spraying in all directions. "Oops." She grabbed a sandal and slapped a couple of embers off the Persian rug near their chairs.

"May I?" Merris took the poker from her and rearranged the logs, adding some fresh wood.

"Just what I don't need," Abigail muttered almost inaudibly. "To burn down Olivia's house while she's basking on a beach in the Cook Islands."

"The Cook Islands?" Merris echoed.

"I know." Abigail glanced at the book Merris brought over. "Very serendipitous. And now, since you've been so patient and I've decided you might be exactly what Olivia needs, I'm going to tell you what I think you should do. But first, let's get really trashed." Grabbing Merris's glass, she headed back to the bar.

It could be worse, Merris thought. It was a lousy night and she was sitting in front of a great fire with Olivia's best friend, who was kind of fun and actually seemed to like her. With any luck, she would leave with a plan that would help her win the woman who had occupied her thoughts almost constantly since they'd met. Tonight was not what she had expected, but maybe it was all part of some bigger and better picture.

She raised her fresh martini in a toast. "To Plan B."

Abigail tapped glasses, adding with suitable drama, "Conquer or die."

Chapter
Eight

A SIGN OUTSIDE the Rarotonga International Airport terminal said *Moon Island*. Sitting on the bench beneath it was a woman with glossy black hair combed severely into a braided knot. She was reading a book, dark glasses screening her eyes. Muted lipstick set off the most perfect skin Riley had ever seen. The color of gardenia petals, it looked impossibly cool and soft in the tropical heat.

She would have been gorgeous wearing a sack, but this woman was in a tangerine sundress with a tight bodice and a big skirt. She looked like one of those 1950s pinups. Betty Paige, Riley decided, only more French or something. Babe-struck, Riley dumped her luggage on the pavement close by. "I guess we wait here," she remarked for something to say.

"It would seem so." The accent and dry wit were not French, but unmistakably British.

"You're from England?"

The woman closed her book with a small firm movement that hinted at irritation. "Originally. But I live in Denver these days."

"So did you come in on the LA flight?" Riley asked, amazed she could have missed this hottie at the departure gates. "I didn't see you."

"I stayed in the lounge 'til the last minute."

Riley contemplated making a weather remark, but that would be pathetic. Instead she said, "I'm Riley Mason. I'm here with a UCLA research team for a couple of weeks."

"Olivia Pearce," the pinup returned politely. "What are you researching?"

"You might have heard of Dr. Glenn Howick, the cultural anthropologist. She's leading a study into some secret rituals Rarotongan women conduct on Moon Island."

"Ah, so they won't be secret anymore," Olivia remarked in a tone that was vaguely schoolmarmish.

Her cool reserve reminded Riley of Glenn, only Glenn would never be seen dead in peep-toe turquoise high heels with little orange bows on the top. "Dr. Howick is very culturally sensitive," she said a little defensively.

"I'm happy for her." Olivia's attention crept down to her book. Clearly, she was not in the mood for chitchat.

Riley repeated her name silently. It sounded strangely familiar. "If you don't mind me asking, are you an actress?"

There was a long pause. She was probably someone famous trying to get away from the public gaze, Riley deduced with a pang. And here she was, pestering her with snoopy questions. No wonder the reception was frosty.

"Forget I said that," she hastened. "It's none of my business. Your name just seemed familiar, that's all."

The woman removed her dark glasses and regarded Riley with a calm direct stare. Her eyes were somber gray, almost granite-colored, and heavily lashed. Something in their depths unnerved Riley. It was as if Olivia saw straight through her and, within a split second, had compiled a mental laundry list of Riley's yearnings, secrets and pretensions. "I'm not an actress," she said in her clipped English way. "I'm a songwriter. Perhaps you've seen my name on a CD label and tucked it away in your subconscious."

"That must be it." Riley was aware that her usual charm had abandoned her. The woman made her feel like a gauche eighth-grader. "Well I won't interrupt you any more," she apologized, with a glance at the novel.

"It's okay. I'm feeling anti-social today. Don't take it personally."

"Well, you've come to the right place." Riley relaxed as the temperature between them rose a few degrees from icy to lukewarm. "I hear this island is incredibly private."

"I'm counting on it," Olivia said with dry humor. She indicated the bench next to her. "Do sit down."

"I'm fine." Riley glanced around. "I think we're supposed to be met any minute."

A woman pushed a laden baggage cart toward them, but she didn't look like their pilot. Riley was slack-jawed at the sight of platinum hair in bunches secured with big plastic daisies, cotton candy pedal pushers, and a thin white nipple-enhancing shirt knotted below unnaturally round breasts. Naturally she was chewing gum, which she removed and folded around one finger to greet them.

God, Riley thought, *a porn star.*

"Hey, there. I'm Trudy." The new arrival beamed a white,

perfect smile and gazed around, her frosted pink mouth parted in moist surprise. "Way cool. This is like...*Survivor*."

Or maybe *Clueless*. Riley exchanged a brief look with Olivia, who seemed completely unfazed. "I'm Riley and this is Olivia. I don't know where our ride is."

"They better show up soon." Trudy pulled off her little round sunglasses and cleaned them with the tail of her shirt. "Is your mascara, like, melting?" she asked no one in particular.

"Totally chocolate syrup," Olivia replied without missing a beat.

Trudy collapsed on the bench, fanning herself with her hand. "So I guess it's true then," she said with a pointed look at Riley. "The man ban, I mean."

"Moon Island is women only," Riley responded, bracing herself for the homophobic remarks.

Trudy was fishing around in her purse. "I thought Daddy was kidding me!" She produced a mirror and set about fixing her lipstick. "So are you two gay and everything?" Catching Riley's frown, she added, "Hey, I'm cool with that. I like girls, too. You know, whatever."

"You're bi?" Olivia enquired.

"I'm not into labels." Trudy shared her philosophy. "I'm like...a feel-good person. You know what I mean. Whatever feels good."

Olivia gave a thoughtful nod. "How about you, Riley?" she enquired, chatty all of a sudden.

Riley had the distinct impression Olivia was toying with them. This was paranoid, of course. She simply had good manners. She was trying to put this intellectual pygmy at ease by conversing on her level.

"Sure. I'm into feeling good," Riley said, playing along. "So long as it involves a woman."

"Lesbian and polyamorous?" Olivia interpreted.

"Polyamorous..." Trudy repeated the big word.

"Multiple sexual partners," Olivia supplied.

They both waited expectantly for Riley's response.

Feeling about as sophisticated as string cheese, she said, "Single and playing pretty well sums it up."

"So you'd be monogamous if you were in a relationship?" Olivia continued the twenty-one questions.

"Hopefully," Riley said, ignoring her history. If she were in a relationship with someone like Glenn Howick she would never play around. She was quite sure of that. "Your turn," she told Olivia. "Sexuality. Relationship status. Monogamy."

Olivia tilted her head slightly and gazed past her with a

bland smile. "Alas, I think we'll have to put this riveting conversation on hold."

Riley turned her head as a strikingly fair woman in fawn fatigues gave a casual wave. She was dragging a huge, empty baggage trolley with a black leather bomber jacket slung over the handle.

"Welcome to the Cook Islands," she said. "I'm Annabel Worth, your pilot, and that's our plane, the *Lonesome Lady*." She gestured toward an aircraft parked in front of a hangar a few hundred yards away.

It was like something out of a war movie. Painted light khaki green, a pin-up decorating the fuselage, it still had machine guns sticking out from its nose and turrets. Riley was shocked that any self-respecting feminist would consider using a retired war plane to take guests to an island that must be one of the only places on earth free of male energy.

Annabel started loading their bags onto the cart. Hastily, Riley lent a hand. Hard as she tried to overcome her cultural conditioning, she was uneasy that their pilot was a woman. Not just a woman, but a woman with long straight blonde hair who looked like she'd be more at home in a shampoo commercial than flying a plane.

Annabel handed out earplugs, casually explaining, "You'll be needing these. She gets kind of noisy. Now if you'd follow me..."

She didn't protest when Riley insisted on dragging the baggage cart, instead asking them socially appropriate questions about their flights and the cold weather they'd left behind.

Trudy seemed ecstatic at the prospect of taking a ride in the museum piece. "Do the guns actually work?" she breathed as their luggage was getting stowed.

"They would if we loaded them," Annabel replied. "You know that expression, the whole nine yards? That's how much linked ammunition was fed through one of these Browning machine guns at a time."

"Wow." Trudy twiddled with her hair. "That was like...what...a hundred years ago?"

"Sixty," Annabel said. "She's a World War Two bomber."

"Oh right," Trudy said gravely. "Hitler and stuff."

"I didn't know that...about the whole nine yards." Olivia commented. "These were high-altitude bombers, weren't they?"

"They could reach thirty-five thousand feet, but they usually flew at around eighteen thousand," Annabel replied. "No heating. No pressurization. Don't worry. We won't be doing that today. There are coats and blankets on board, and if any of you want socks, you'll find them in the mesh baskets by your seats."

"How cold those boys must have been before they died." Olivia's voice was suddenly thick with emotion.

She was almost in tears, Riley noted with astonishment. Evidently her detachment was reserved for people in the here and now. "Shit, Olivia," she said. "What kind of songs did you say you wrote?"

For a moment it seemed as if the glamorous British woman might have taken offence, then her mouth twitched and the permafreeze cracked just enough for Riley to glimpse a whole different person. "That would be blues."

"Uh, no kidding."

Olivia laughed. Her eyes were still sparkling twenty minutes later, as Rarotonga receded in the distance and they leveled out above the vast blue of the Pacific Ocean.

CHRIS ROLLED ONTO her stomach and turned her face toward the palm trees at the far end of Passion Bay. She could just make out the gabled rooftop of Villa Luna, the beautiful home where the island's owners lived. What a lifestyle, she thought with brief envy. No morning commute, no office politics, no lamebrain clients destroying their own carefully constructed case in the courtroom.

Sleepily she closed her eyes. She had only been sunbathing for an hour beneath a huge shade umbrella, and already she felt soporific. A lazy tide lapped at the white sand, its sluggish pulse inviting even the most determined reader to fall asleep in the middle of a thriller. Her hosts had warned her about over-doing it. This was the tropics. It was easy to become dehydrated or burnt to a crisp.

At first, Chris felt sure Annabel had been exaggerating. Understandably, she was neurotic about the sun because of her pale skin. Chris couldn't imagine how difficult it was for an albino to live in the South Pacific. The sun was one thing. But with her strange lavender-colored eyes and dead straight white-blonde hair, Annabel Worth must attract all kinds of attention among the tanned tourists and local Polynesian population.

Returning her concentration to her book, she managed another few pages before she found herself drifting toward sleep again. This was another one of those times when she felt terribly alone. If Elaine were here, Chris would have asked her to keep an eye on the time and wake her up after an hour or so. Instead, she would either have to get up right now and go for a swim, or take refuge indoors. It was simply too risky to fall asleep alone on a beach in this heat. Slipping the marker in her book, she got to her feet and strolled down to the water's edge.

The lagoon was incredibly warm and bright turquoise blue, a color she hadn't thought existed except in travel magazines. Chris splashed her face and waded out to her knees, stopping every now and then to pick up unusual shells. Passion Bay was not a vast beach, but with its crescent of white sand, tranquil waters and swaying palms, it was storybook perfect.

She hadn't had a chance to explore the other beaches around the island yet, but she planned to take a hike the next day. The guest information in her cottage said something about caves in the *makatea*, a fossilized coral reef that was now covered in jungle. One of these was home to a rare swallow that used sonar to navigate in the darkness beneath the earth. Chris was keen to see it, if only because that's what Elaine would have wanted.

Adjusting her cotton hat, she glanced over her shoulder. There was no one around, yet she had the oddest sense that she was being watched. Neck prickling, she gazed west, then east. The beach was deserted. A little unnerved, she crossed the sand toward a belt of coconut palms and stood in the shade, careful to avoid the drop zone directly beneath the heavy clusters of fruit.

It was not the first time since Elaine had gone that she'd felt another presence when no one was around. At first Chris had ruthlessly ignored the sensation, ascribing it to her heightened emotional state. But lately she had started to wonder if Elaine's ghost was trying to communicate its presence somehow. Was it really such a farfetched idea?

Guided by the faint thud of music coming from the hilltop above, Chris began climbing the slope toward Villa Luna. Now seemed as good a time as any to ask for directions to the caves she wanted to visit tomorrow. The music grew louder as she cut her way up through mango trees, frangipani, and banana palms, their musky sweetness flooding her nostrils. Recognizing an old Fleetwood Mac hit, she hummed along, trying to put all thought of the supernatural out of her mind.

As Cody and Annabel's gracious looking plantation villa loomed through the trees, Chris halted, gazing up at a towering mango seductive with ripe golden fruit. All over the island, mangoes plopped periodically to the ground, creating one of the distinctive nighttime sounds her hosts had mentioned. Stepping over fallen fruit, Chris smiled to herself. Could anything be more tropical than a front yard littered with mangoes? It was not Minnesota; that was for sure.

Someone turned down the music as she drew closer to the house, and a dark-haired woman on a cane chaise lounge waved from the vast front verandah. "Hello. Come on up."

"Hey there." Chris waved back. "I didn't see you. I'm Chris Thompson." She climbed the wooden steps and shook hands with a woman who looked exactly like Audrey Hepburn, only thinner, if that were possible.

"Melanie Worth. I've been watching you. Want some iced tea?" She gestured at a pitcher on a nearby table.

"Don't mind if I do." Chris poured a tall glass. She felt a mixture of relief and disappointment that it was this woman's regard she had sensed, not some spiritual presence. Raising the pitcher, she asked, "Would you care for some more?"

"Thanks. It's a wonder I haven't floated away. I've done nothing but guzzle fluids since I got here."

"Are you staying close?" There were other cottages dotted around the island, but Chris didn't know how many were occupied.

"Actually, I'm here in the villa. Annabel is a cousin of mine." Melanie smiled as Chris shot her a quizzical second glance. "I know. Incredible family likeness." She reached for her glass but her hand was so shaky she withdrew it, plainly embarrassed.

For a split second Chris wondered if she were drunk, then she started adding two and two. A wheelchair was propped against the wall, and several bottles of medication stood next to Melanie's glass. Then there was the dull pallor of her skin. Without fuss, Chris lifted the drink for her, releasing it only when she had a firm grasp.

Melanie thanked her sweetly, adding, "This is getting old."

"Not one of those people who love getting sick so they can be a patient?"

"It's not all it's cracked up to be."

Chris repressed the urge to ask what was wrong. Not everyone wanted to discuss their health problems with complete strangers.

"Cody won't be long," Melanie said. "She had to go get some of the cottages ready for new guests."

Chris claimed an armchair and drank her iced tea. The deep verandah was a welcome respite from the heat, and it provided a breathtaking view of Passion Bay. "I'll hang out 'til she gets back if that's okay," she said. "I need some directions for a hike I'm doing tomorrow."

Melanie perked up. "I love hiking. This would be a great place to explore. It's so beautiful."

"If you're feeling better tomorrow, maybe you could come. It's kind of strange doing everything alone." Chris fell silent for a moment, her throat tight. Surprising herself, she did not change the subject, but instead said, "I lost my partner recently. A car accident."

"Oh, no." Sympathy flooded Melanie's voice. "I'm so sorry."

"We were together eighteen years."

"I don't know what to say. It's such a shock, isn't it? When something happens and your life is changed forever. You're so powerless."

Exactly, Chris thought. She had taken for granted her complete control over her life. She was healthy, she had a successful career, a nice home, a lifestyle that was comfortable in every material way. Yet she had lost the person who meant the most to her in the world, and nothing she did could change that. "I guess it's part of the grieving process. Anger. Helplessness. Self-blame."

"I think they should call it the *twenty*-five stages of grief," Melanie pronounced.

"Yeah. Then they could include impatience, rudeness, and bad driving." Chris knew she sounded harsher than she intended, but Melanie seemed unfazed.

"No kidding." The sweet-faced young woman grew animated. "Don't people say such stupid things!"

"My personal favorite is *You'll find someone else*. As if Elaine was...hell, I don't know...a piece of furniture or something."

"I know just what you're saying. The trouble is there's no etiquette for tragedy. People feel guilty that it's you and not them, and you end up feeling responsible for making them uncomfortable. So you avoid talking about it, and everyone starts pretending nothing is happening." Melanie broke off, her expression rueful. "I'm sorry. You got me started."

"Hey, it's fine by me. You sound like an expert."

"What can I say? I have a terminal illness." Her light, laughing tone almost convinced Chris she was joking. But her eyes told another story. With a small shrug, she added, "I have ALS. Most people don't know what it is. Not that it really matters. It's incurable. I'm dying. There's no nice way to say it." She met Chris's eyes and they remained silent for a long moment, as if each knew exactly what the other was feeling.

On an impulse, Chris reached over and took Melanie's hand. It felt frail, the skin tautly stretched. Even without her illness, she would have been a slightly built person, but she was wasting away. Chris had no idea how ALS was treated. All she knew was that people lost their muscle function.

In silence, they sat looking out to sea, two strangers sharing a moment of empathy. For the first time since Elaine's death, Chris felt truly comforted by another person. The slight pressure of Melanie's fingers communicated more plainly than words. Chris squeezed back, tears welling, and Melanie tugged her hand gently, saying, "Come sit with me."

A little awkwardly, Chris perched on the edge of the chaise lounge. They were still holding hands, but she could feel Melanie's grip fading and wished she could transfer some of her own strength to the young woman.

"I truly believe we see the people we love again," Melanie said with conviction. "I'll see my daughter, one day. And you'll see your partner."

"You have a daughter?" Chris was surprised, then dismayed.

"Briar. She's nine months old." Melanie glanced toward the house. "She's sleeping. Would you like to see her?"

"I'd love to." It felt only natural to lean over and lift Melanie like a child. "Put your arms around my neck."

Melanie uttered a giggling protest as Chris swung her off the chaise.

Grinning, Chris said, "Oh please. This is what I pay gym fees for," and headed down the hallway to a door Melanie indicated.

The room they entered was airy and plain. Wide-slatted plantation blinds screened out the intense afternoon light and a huge ceiling fan languidly moved the warm air. Chris set Melanie down next to a bassinette shrouded in filmy white mosquito nets. It was an ancient-looking wood and wicker affair decorated with brightly colored beads. The name *Lucy Annabel Adams* was carved into a small, heart-shaped plaque at the head. Melanie's baby lay within, sound asleep on her tummy, head turned to one side, hands balled into little fists.

"She's so tiny," Chris whispered, parting the nets for a better look. *Briar.* The name suited her. She was an unusually beautiful baby, Chris decided, calling to mind the few she had seen. Most were bald and scrunched. Melanie's baby was like a miniature of her mother, the same delicate features evident already.

"She's the best thing I ever did." Melanie wobbled slightly and Chris slid a supporting arm around her waist. She had so many questions. Where was Briar's father? What was going to happen to her afterwards? She was filled with pain for Melanie. How terrible to know she would have to leave her child, would never see her grow up.

Melanie seemed to sense her train of thought. "I didn't know I was sick when I was planning her. And even if I did...it's hard to say. She makes everything worth it."

"Her father's back home?" Chris asked.

Melanie was silent for a moment. "She doesn't really have a father. I never met anyone I wanted children with, so in the end I used a donor program."

"Shit," Chris muttered before she could bite back the reaction.

Melanie met her eyes. "I know."

SALT AIR STUNG Olivia's cheeks. Holding her skirt down with one hand and tightly clutching a metal grip on the side of the boat, she gazed at the brilliant colors swirling beneath the water. She'd had no idea coral came in so many hues: loud pink, bruised violet and soft gold.

Normally, the extraordinary beauty of this sight would have enchanted and inspired her. Yet she felt oddly detached from her own responses. Intellectually she knew she was seeing something wonderful. Emotionally, she drew a blank. She had Hunter to thank for that, Olivia reflected. Like a physical blow, anger shook her body. White-hot and gut-wrenching, it shocked the breath from her.

Eyes stinging, Olivia tightened her grip on the rail to steady herself. Yesterday's degrading encounter had played over and over in her mind throughout the journey here. How could she have allowed herself to be treated that way? Did she have no pride? Olivia pulled herself together. She had to stop thinking about it. She had to find some way to let it go. Only, she had no idea how.

"Hibiscus Bay," Cody shouted above the noise of the motor. Pointing up at a jungle covered slope, she added, "There's your cottage."

Olivia compelled her clenched fists to relax. She could vaguely discern a thatched roof amidst a mass of green. Her accommodations were every bit as secluded as the brochure had promised.

Cody wheeled the outboard in a semi-circle and slowed to a puttering crawl. As they approached a jetty jutting from the rocky point at the southern end of the bay, she said, "We used to row people in." She indicated a small dinghy on the beach. "That's yours if you want to row around to the Villa any time. But I can pick you up if you'd rather not take your chances."

"Actually, I rowed for Cambridge University," Olivia said, slightly peeved by the inference. In all fairness, Cody wasn't to know she'd once prided herself on her skills.

"Get outta here!" her host exclaimed. She secured the boat and tossed Olivia's luggage onto the wooden planks. "We should race one day."

"I'm not exactly in shape." Olivia sized up the woman in

front of her. Lean, tanned and athletic, Cody Stanton looked as if she was never out of peak condition.

To make matters worse, her would-be opponent said, "I'll even give you a head start."

Olivia laughed. "Those are fighting words."

Something about Cody reminded her of Hunter as she used to be: fun-loving, self-assured, seductively ingenuous, very charming.

Cody pushed a cabin bag at her and calmly picked up the other eighty pounds of luggage. With a dubious look at Olivia's footwear, she said, "It's a bit of a walk up to the cottage."

They set off up a winding path through dense fleshy tropical plants. Trailing behind, Olivia felt as if she'd been dismissed as a hopeless wuss, a one-time athlete gone to seed. She contemplated pulling off her sandals so she could keep up, but instead decided to keep her feet clean and avenge herself on the water.

"You're on," she said, as they emerged from a thicket of frangipani. "For the race, I mean."

"That's the spirit." With a grin, Cody deposited the luggage in the front yard of the cottage. "Tell you what. I'll give you a week to train. Just be careful where you row. It gets rough heading south and that side of the island is off-limits to guests anyway."

"I can take care of myself," Olivia said, picking flowers out of her hair. Before her, Frangipani Cottage stood picture-perfect in a setting Hollywood could not have invented. Huge pink, cream and apricot flowers spilled from wall trellises. Glossy creepers tangled with bougainvillea along the verandah. The warm air was thick with the green crush of jungle foliage and a sweet mix of vanilla and jasmine that made her senses reel.

It was for such a glimpse of paradise Gauguin had left Paris, Olivia thought. "It's perfect," she said.

"There's another cottage that way," Cody pointed at a jungle path that led north. "There'll be a new guest in there tomorrow. Mary. No..." She frowned slightly and cocked her head. "Merris. That's her name."

Olivia gave a small start. The name was quite a co-incidence. She had thought about Merris Randall on and off ever since they'd first met. If things had been different, she would have accepted her invitation to drive in the mountains that day. She still had the card Merris had given her at the bookstore. Several times she had come close to calling, but she always changed her mind at the last minute.

Lately she had seen her a few times at a distance. Once she

was in the parking lot at the supermarket loading groceries and Merris drove past her. Their eyes had met briefly, then she was gone. Olivia had felt a little piqued that she did not bother to stop and say hello. But then, why should she? The last time they'd spoken, Merris had left the ball in her court. And Olivia hadn't phoned.

It was not that she found Merris unattractive—quite the opposite. Perhaps that was the problem. Sometimes she felt as if any woman she was ever attracted to treated her badly. Even Abigail had commented on her lousy taste in girlfriends. How did a person break out of a pattern like that? After Hunter, Olivia doubted she would ever trust her own judgment again.

"We don't lock doors," Cody said as she ferried Olivia's luggage into the cottage. "The only way anyone can get here is by air or sea, so you don't have to worry about security. And there are no wild animals. At least, not the man-eating kind."

The room they entered was airy and unpretentious. Woven mats decorated a painted wooden floor, and the whitewashed walls were hung with colorful *tivaevae* quilts like those she'd seen on display at Rarotonga airport. Olivia gazed out the deep bay window that overlooked the ocean. She could be comfortable here. She would get some space. Maybe she would even write. And maybe she would find some way to move on.

Chapter
Nine

RILEY AWOKE TO the sound of tapping on her door. Disoriented and half asleep, she stumbled out of bed and tweaked the wooden plantation blind so she could see behind it. No one was there. Yawning, she wandered out onto the balcony and looked around.

It was barely daybreak. High above, the moon was a watery gold, almost green. To the south, above the dark hills in the center of the island, the first tentative blush of dawn slithered across the sky. Beyond her cottage, the jungle was still but for the first birdcalls of the day. To Riley, the silence was velvet and unreal. Never in her life had she awoken to such tranquility. She heard the tapping again and turned sharply to see a plump pigeon sitting on the railing with an expectant look on its face. Instead of flying away when she swooshed her hand, it hopped calmly along the balcony toward her.

"Oh, I get it," Riley said. "You're here for breakfast."

She went back indoors, contemplating her options. There didn't seem any point returning to bed. She had already slept for hours. Flying thousands of miles did that, she supposed. The time zone changed, you were exhausted and dehydrated, and there was something anti-climactic about arriving at an exotic destination like this and having no one to share the moment with. Glenn Howick was not due until tomorrow. Riley intended to be fully prepared, proving herself worthy of Glenn's confidence. She would need to rig up platforms for camera gear, cordon off locations, and make preliminary notes.

She had already requested a boat for this morning so she could scout the search areas Glenn had flagged. Cody said she would take her to Passion Bay, where the boat was anchored. Hopefully she would show up soon.

Riley inspected the contents of her refrigerator with interest. There was a bowl of what looked like purple custard and a platter of chopped fruit and assorted muffins. The previous evening she'd sampled some exquisite juice from a pitcher labeled fruit cocktail. A couple of other delicious-sounding combinations were lined up beside it. She opted for pineapple and papaya smoothie, spooned some of the custard and fruit into a small bowl, and chose a muffin.

This gratified her visitor, who perched on the opposite side of the small outdoor table to solicit crumbs. In just another day, it would be Glenn sitting there, eating slices of mango and drinking tea that Riley had freshly brewed. She had packed a box of Twinings Lady Grey, Glenn's preference, as well as a pot of the imported ginger marmalade she liked to have on toast. By the time they left the island, Glenn was going to find her indispensable.

Riley often wondered where Glenn was from. She was American, but her accent was devoid of the characteristic vowels that signified either North or South. She spoke quickly, which made Riley suspect New York, but her consonants were very soft. All anyone seemed to know was that she'd earned her Ph.D. from Cornell and she had taught at Minnesota State before joining the UCLA faculty. In her late thirties, she was already a keynote speaker published in every important academic journal in her field.

Riley had no idea why, of all her post-grad students, Glenn had singled her out for a place in her handpicked tutorial class and now this coveted assignment. Her grades were mediocre at best, and she had never had much success ingratiating herself with her teachers. Glenn said she found Riley's essays fresh and well considered. Everyone else thought she was overly opinionated and took short cuts in her research. Riley was both thrilled and bewildered that Glenn was taking such a special interest in her. Could it be personal?

She took another mouthful of the purple custard, which was actually a coconut-flavored rice pudding unlike anything she had ever tasted. The rice was kind of nutty and chewy, bursting sweet coconut across her tongue. It was to die for with the chunks of mango and banana she had piled on top. After a breakfast like this, how did anyone go back to pancakes at IHOP?

Riley spread out a map of the island and leafed through Glenn's notes again to make sure she hadn't missed anything. Glenn had written pages on the myth of Hine te Ana's cave. One of her aims was to investigate the cave's existence. She had identified an area northeast of the cliffs of Hine te Ana as a probable location. If they could prove the cave actually existed, it would suggest the legend of the goddess could have a basis in real events. For a passionate scholar of pre-Christian wisdom and traditions like Glenn, this was a big deal. Determined to contribute in any way she could to her idol's professional kudos, Riley rushed through the rest of her breakfast, tossed the leftovers to the pigeon, and set about preparing equipment for the day.

LESS THAN AN hour later, Cody led Kahlo along the narrow pathway through the jungle toward Annie's Cottage. The coal-black mare knew the way by heart, like most of the tracks around the island. She always noticed the slightest change in their surroundings, lifting her head and whickering with interest if they passed a different coconut palm or encountered an article of clothing some guest had slung over a branch. This morning she was acutely interested in the camera equipment piled in front of the cottage doorway. From the look of it all, Cody could only assume Riley Mason was planning an entry for Sundance.

Tethering the mare to a banana palm at the rear of the cottage, Cody unloaded fruit and sodas from the saddlebags. A chef prepared most of the meals on the island, leaving platters of food in a refrigerated room at Villa Luna. Guests had the option of dining at the Villa each night or having their meals delivered. During the day, Cody dropped fresh snacks and drinks into each cottage and provided any advice and information women needed.

Annie's Cottage was their most recently constructed guest accommodation, featuring two bedrooms and a big sitting room all with balconies that overlooked Marama Bay. Cody had built most of it herself. Carpentry was an essential skill when you lived in a hurricane zone and your partner could not hammer a nail.

In the five years they'd lived on Moon Island, they had experienced only one major hurricane, but it had virtually flattened the place, destroying the small cottages in the west and laying waste to many of the mature mango and guava trees that covered the island. Since then, they had systematically replanted and rebuilt, adding additional cottages to cope with expanding demand for accommodations. They could easily treble the rooms they had and still fall short, but neither she nor Annabel wanted to increase guest numbers. Moon Island was their home. It was one thing to have a few guests share it, quite another to operate a tourist mecca.

"You're right on time." Their new guest emerged wearing hiking gear and a big grin. Appreciative dark eyes traveled over

Cody's face and down her body. "Need a hand?"

Annabel always said a little flirtation was harmless, but Cody saw it as an affront to her relationship. It never failed to irritate her when one of their guests acted like the host was served up with the rest of their holiday package. Cody had lost count of the times she had ended up in some woman's cottage on one or another phony pretext. She gave Riley a stony little smile and shoved a couple of pineapples at her chest.

It was time she took a break from the public, Cody decided. This young woman hadn't done a thing and already she was fantasizing about pushing her out of the boat. Feeling guilty, she made an effort to sound enthusiastic. "So, where are we going this morning?"

"I'll show you." Riley dumped the pineapples on the kitchen counter and squatted down by her pack. "This is the area Dr. Howick is interested in," she said, pulling out a map and pointing to a big red circle.

Loading the refrigerator, Cody glanced over her shoulder. "That is only the most inaccessible place on the whole island."

"I figured we could land on this beach, then climb up here." Riley traced a finger from the Sacred Shore to the cliffs of Hine te Ana.

"We could if we had a death wish. It's the wrong time of day to approach the cliffs from the sea. The currents would sweep us against the cliffs if we tried to row ashore. And you can't swim it. There's a rip current that drags you out and dumps you over a ledge."

Riley looked startled. "Then how does anyone get to it? Don't they swim in for the rituals?"

"Not unless they're completely nuts. That's why the legend of the goddess is a big deal. It's impossible to swim in there, but supposedly she did it."

"They used to row canoes over from Rarotonga, didn't they?"

"Once upon a time. These days I boat them in, and when the currents are right we take a Zodiac ashore. After the ceremonies, I pick them up, or some of them walk out as far as Hibiscus Bay. There's a pathway up one of the cliffs from the Sacred Shore."

"Can you show me?"

"I'm not sure exactly where it is, but I can take you to the trailhead for the cliffs." Cody pictured Riley Mason wandering in circles, trying to find the right pathway. The jungle southeast of Hibiscus Bay was the thickest and the *makatea* the steepest on the island. "You'll need a compass."

Riley adjusted a ball cap over her short, spiky brown hair

and flashed a flirtatious smile. "I'd prefer a guide."

"I wish I could help," Cody said in a solemn voice. "But if I don't get all my chores done Annabel beats me."

It took Riley a couple of blinks to realize she was kidding. "You shouldn't joke about domestic violence."

"I know." Cody adopted a hangdog air. "Shame on me."

IT HAD RAINED in the night and, inland, the jungle smelled intensely green and fecund. Chris was sweating profusely, her shorts and tank top soaked. She stopped for a moment to catch her breath, inhaling air thick with evaporating moisture. The route Cody had explained took her deep inland across the *makatea*, a fossilized coral reef that had originally been underwater. Evidently, this geographic phenomenon was found on a number of islands in the Cook group. Some of the ancient coral formations were hundreds of feet high. Cody had shown her photographs of the precipitous cliffs at the southernmost tip of Moon Island, explaining that these were also part of the *makatea*.

Carefully Chris picked her way down a steep slope. The *makatea* was razor-sharp and pockmarked with holes, most of which were invisible beneath a fleshy tangle of creepers and plants. To avoid ankle sprains, she had converted a broken branch into a makeshift hiking pole, testing the ground as she went. The track to the *kopeka* cave was helpfully signposted with coconut shells spray painted glow-in-the-dark yellow. There would always be someone dumb enough to try and find their way out of the jungle after nightfall, Chris supposed, reaching for her water flask.

She was keenly aware of trespassing in a world that did not belong to human beings but to the countless unseen creatures that made the undergrowth stir and creak. Strange, shrill cries pierced the jungle around her, as if every living thing within ten miles was warning of an intruder in their midst. An audience of tiny apricot-and-brown birds maintained a constant twittering commentary on her progress, darting along the route ahead of her and hopping from branch to branch to scrutinize her every move.

Chris wondered if they were *kakarori*, an endangered species Cody had said she might see. Conservationists had recently established several populations of rare birds on Moon Island, which was one of the few Pacific islands free of rats. She halted and stood very still, extending an arm. To her delight, one of the birds swooped down and landed on her wrist. It was similar to a sparrow but much prettier, with its pale apricot breast feathers and brown speckled wings and tail. Like the starlings and fruit doves that assembled each morning outside her villa, it seemed remarkably unafraid of human beings.

She could almost feel Elaine standing next to her, thrilled by this encounter with a rare species. Elaine had always brought along binoculars and bird-watching guides when they went hiking, and she lived for the chance of a sighting she could report. Maybe she was watching now, Chris thought. Despite her own innate skepticism, she kept coming back to the idea that ghosts might actually exist. Sometimes she felt a prickling certainty that Elaine was present and trying to speak to her. Was it such a crazy idea? After all, if things had been the other way around, and had she died instead of Elaine, wouldn't she try to communicate?

On the off chance, Chris said, "I wish I could hear you." She stood very still, willing her mind to clear. Talk to me now, she thought and waited. The jungle clicked and vibrated with life, but there was no white light, no disembodied voice. Telling herself she had watched *Ghost* too many times, Chris turned her attention back to the track.

Abruptly, the descent grew steeper and she realized she was entering the huge mouth of a cave. Setting her pack down, she located her flashlight and camera. Once you were deep inside, the *kopeka* birds could supposedly be seen hanging like bats from the roof. If you got really lucky, they would descend and buzz you.

Some people found this pretty creepy, Cody had warned. The occasional guest panicked and broke an ankle trying to get out of the cave in a big hurry. Chris could see why. The entrance rapidly contracted to a dim passageway, the cave itself yawning darkly ahead. Already she was being strafed by tiny creatures that felt like bats. That would be enough to send most nervous types back where they came from. But Chris wasn't prone to claustrophobia or vampire fantasies.

Blinking rapidly to adjust to the darkness, she eased herself over a rocky lip and dropped down into a huge limestone chamber. Enormous stalactites dripped from above illuminated by an eerie light that seemed almost phosphorescent. This was filtered through a series of narrow chimneys that also supplied the cave with air. The place smelled musty but not foul.

The first chamber she encountered was like a ballroom, oval in shape with a high vaulted ceiling and shawls of pinkish limestone draping the walls. Shining her flashlight around, she made out the remains of several campfires. Some adventurous guest had spent a night or two down here, she surmised.

Immediately beyond the campsite, several immense limestone columns marked the entrance to a smaller cavern where it seemed most of the *kopeka* birds were gathered. As Chris entered, she was met with a swirling mass of wings. Laughing and covering her face, she backed up a few steps only to lose her footing on the slippery rocks at the base of the farthest column. Struggling to regain her balance, she found herself on a steep pathway that had not been visible from the campsite. Pitch black, and lined with what felt like bunches of hard slithery grapes, it narrowed sharply, forcing Chris onto her butt. As the ceiling closed in and the passageway became little more than a hole, she shimmied down the wet rock for five or six feet, wishing her flashlight were more powerful. She could see maybe twenty feet ahead and it seemed like the hole might lead to another cave. But if it didn't, getting back up the slippery neck was going to be a problem.

Deciding discretion was the better part of valor, Chris stuffed her camera inside her shirt, dug her feet in, and turned back. A few years ago she would have made it up the narrow hole with a modest effort. She had basic caving skills. The ascent was awkward but well within her fitness level. Instead, she lost traction, dropped her flashlight, and slithered down the hole, unable to control the speed of her descent. This is it, she thought without emotion. At the same moment, the passage leveled out and she managed to brake herself with her feet before she hit bottom.

Heart pounding, she groped around. As far as she could tell, she was not in any immediate danger. This was not some narrow ledge that spilled into a chasm. The walls around her were solid, and there didn't seem to be anywhere else she could fall. Searching systematically, she located the flashlight. Like her, it was still intact, and it revealed a sight that would warm the heart of any caver. Directly ahead, a wide fissure parted the rock. Beyond this, Chris could make out a cavern. With any luck there would be a way out of it. Sucking in her stomach, she squeezed through the gap.

The sight that greeted her made her blood freeze. Someone else had also fallen down the hole, only they hadn't made it back. Reclining in a hollow fringed with tiny stalactites, a human skeleton leered at her.

Chris's yelp of horror bounced off the cave walls like echo on a bad long-distance call. Breathing hard, she swung her flashlight around to ensure no one else was there. It was silly, of course. The skeleton could do her no harm and any companions the unfortunate caver had were obviously long gone. The truth was, she was in no danger from anything but her own poor judgment. If only she'd been content to see the nice birdies, then climb back out, none of this would be happening. As it was, she would probably be stuck here until help arrived. It could be days. Her batteries would run out. She would be in pitch darkness. And starving.

Willing herself to chill out and stop with the disaster scenarios, Chris trained her flashlight on the skeleton. It was in a sitting position, one leg bent, the other extended. The skull was tilted to the side, cradled against a rock protrusion. Hanging from the yellowed frame were the remnants of a long-sleeved shirt and a pair of pants with what looked like a sash tied around the middle. Men's clothing, Chris decided, squatting down for a closer look. Tracing the legs, she saw the one extended was broken not far above the ankle, eloquently revealing the fate of its owner. He had died sitting here, probably waiting for rescuers who never came. Somewhere in an old newspaper there would no doubt be mention of a fisherman lost at sea.

Chris wondered if he was carrying any identification. Delicately she inspected his pants. There were no pockets and she was surprised by their stiff texture. They were suede leather, old and rigid, not at all what you would expect to find a Polynesian fisherman wearing. Chris checked the walls nearby for a satchel or pack and was intrigued to find a pair of boots. They were unlike anything she had ever seen; tall, with wide tops that folded down and laced up at the back. One boot was much heavier than the other and Chris slid her hand cautiously inside, hoping she was not invading the living quarters of one of those huge, hairy spiders that lived in places like this. She withdrew several objects and laid them on a dry rock in front of her.

The deceased had not died this century, she deduced, fascinated. His pistol belonged in a museum; a flintlock made of wood with ornate silver fittings, it looked about two hundred years old. Several large gold coins appeared to hail from the same era. They featured a coat of arms on one side and a man's head on the other. There was a Latin inscription around the rim, and below the coat of arms, Chris could just make out the year 1791.

Her fingers trembled as she set the coins down and picked up the most intriguing discovery of all, a vellum roll heavily sealed with wax. Written along the sealed edge were the words *Kaua e whàki, waiho kia muna ana.* Chris was almost afraid to break the seal. She glanced at the hollow-eyed skull with a pang.

Whoever this man was, he must have written the letter she was about to open. It was important enough that he had sealed it to prevent it being read by just anyone.

Chris pictured a woman waiting tirelessly for word of her sailor husband. She had died without ever knowing his fate or his final words to her. Respectfully, she unfurled the stiff vellum. At first she was puzzled, then her heart accelerated and she felt sweat bead on her forehead. She was not looking at some long-lost sailor's love letter, but a map. Her eyes flew straight to a point in the center that was marked with a large X. All she could think was, *Buried treasure.*

Chapter
Ten

BEHIND A GAUZY film of cloud, the moon seemed screen-printed against the night sky. Like candlelight, its muted glow spread across Hibiscus Bay, transforming the ocean surface to buttery quicksilver.

It was almost enough, Merris thought. If nothing else happened to make this trip memorable, it was worth it just to see this. She had slept for a few hours after unpacking, and it was dark when she awoke. So much for her plan to watch the sun set on her first night. Intending to have a nightcap on her verandah and contemplate the universe, she pulled on a t-shirt and shorts. But the moon soon lured her down the short pathway, through the stand of palms below her cottage to the long white beach beyond.

A hesitant breeze cooled the heat that had built up during the day and swept the voluptuous scents of different flowers as far as the waterline. Sitting there, with the languid tide lapping at her feet, Merris tilted her head back and inhaled deeply. Maybe she would sleep here, beneath the stars, in the warm safe cocoon of the tropical night, she mused. This train of thought was so completely out of character, no one at Randall Software would have believed their one-time boss capable of it.

With a sigh of satisfaction, she lay back on the sand and closed her eyes. She was here, and she was just a few minutes walk from Olivia's cottage. Getting a reservation had not been easy. At first, the island's owners were oddly reluctant to take her proposal to the couple who were supposed to be spending the next three weeks in Merris's cottage. But, as Merris had pointed out, twenty grand plus a first class all-expenses-paid vacation in a luxury villa in Tuscany was the kind of offer people had a right to hear about.

"Oh!" said a startled voice. "I almost fell over you." A woman in a sarong materialized at Merris's feet. Dark hair cascaded over shoulders as creamy and lustrous as a South Sea pearl. Her face was cast into shadow, but it was unmistakably Olivia. "You must be my neighbor. I'm so sorry to disturb you."

Hastily, Merris sat up. "Don't be." She grappled for the perfect thing to say. The best she could manage was, "Beautiful night, isn't it?"

Olivia moved a little closer, her head cocked to one side. "Merris? Merris from Cherry Creek?"

"Olivia?" Merris hoped she sounded every bit as astonished as her companion.

"Good grief. It is you."

"How bizarre," Merris said.

"I know. What an incredible coincidence." She didn't sound suspicious. In fact, Merris thought she detected a note of pleasure.

"How long have you been here?" Merris asked.

"Only a day. I can't believe this. What a surprise. I mean, it's a good surprise."

"You don't sound so sure about that."

Olivia laughed softly. "No, I am. Really. I guess I just never expected to run in to anyone I know."

"Me either," Merris said with plausible conviction.

Olivia sat down on the sand an arm's length away. "What made you come here of all places?"

"Well, for a start, I'd never heard of it. So I figured no one else would have either."

"Exactly my thought," Olivia chimed in.

"I needed a vacation, and I figured, if you're going to get away from it all, why not go the whole hog?"

"How ironic. We both came thousands of miles so we wouldn't see anyone we knew and..."

"Here we are." Merris finished her sentence.

Caught off-guard, Olivia seemed open, girlish somehow. Being somewhere new and far away made it easier to step outside of normal behavior patterns, Merris guessed.

"Well, it could be worse," Olivia mused aloud. "At least we get along. Imagine coming all the way here and finding yourself next door to...I don't know..."

"The ex," Merris suggested.

Olivia hesitated for a fraction of a second. "Appalling. The ultimate negative fantasy."

"Weird isn't it? When you fall out of love." Merris made the observation almost without thinking.

Olivia met her eyes and looked quickly away. Her voice tightened a little. "My friend Abigail has a theory about that. She says being in love lasts two years because that buys enough time for the real thing to take root and grow. Assuming it's going to."

"So when the rose-tinted specs come off you've either got something or you don't," Merris said. "Hence those folks who only ever have one two-year relationship after the next."

"Addicted to the in-love high," Olivia concluded with a small sigh. "I blame our culture. We're sold the idea that's what the real thing is supposed to feel like. If we don't have the whole many-splendored deal, by definition we don't have love."

Merris detected a shift in her mood. The playfulness had gone and there was a pensive sobriety in its place. Opting for a lighter note, she said, "Well, speaking for the huddled masses who have no idea what the *in-love* feeling is actually like, I am happy to report that I don't miss it at all."

There was silence for a moment, then Olivia released a peal of laughter. "How did this conversation happen?" she said in mock protest.

"I can answer that," Merris adopted a professorial tone. "We are two people at crossroads in our lives. We traveled far, hoping for perspective, and stumbled upon one another at the very same intersection of place and time. Which means the dice are rolling and all bets are off."

"Very philosophical. And of course, travel is always a license to do all manner of things we would never permit ourselves back home...to write our own rules."

"You bet," Merris agreed, determined to exploit this unexpected rapport. "For example, we could have a rule that you and I will meet here every night and talk about absolutely anything we want."

"Unmasked."

Olivia spoke so softly, Merris was not sure she caught the word.

"Why not? What's to lose?"

"All manner of things. The comfort of shallow small talk...our respective mystiques..."

"You flatter me," Merris said with irony. "I have about as much mystique as a barbecue grill. What you see is what you get. Now, you, on the other hand..."

"Pray continue," Olivia invited.

"No, you tell me," Merris countered.

After the briefest pause, Olivia said softly, "What you see is what you want to see."

"And you think *I'm* philosophical."

Olivia was silent, resting her forehead on her knees. Slowly she turned her head on its side to face Merris. "I should have called you."

Merris heart jumped into her throat. "It's not too late."

A faint smile. "That's relative."

"No, that's opportunism."

Olivia laughed. "You're funny."

"So, it's a deal then?" Merris went for the close. "Tomorrow. Same time, same beach. We talk about anything we like, no strings."

"You're not in car sales, are you?"

Merris grinned and got to her feet, dusting the sand from her limbs. "I'll be here waiting for you."

"Okay, it's a deal."

There was a gratifying hint of disappointment in Olivia's voice, as if she wasn't quite ready to end their conversation. Yet Merris steadfastly pulled on her sandals and said goodnight.

She could feel Olivia's eyes on her as she strolled up the beach. It took real willpower, but she did exactly what Abigail had told her to do; she exercised restraint. Not a wave, no looking back, no finding an excuse to linger. According to Abigail, Olivia was like a cat. If you were too easy, she would lose interest.

DISGRUNTLED, RILEY SLOUCHED her way along Marama Bay, wondering what she was going to say to Glenn tomorrow. No thanks to Cody, she had finally stumbled onto the cliff tops above the Sacred Shore. There was a sheer drop of a couple of hundred feet down to the small beach where the rituals would take place. Nowhere did any reasonable vantage point for observation or filming present itself. As for a pathway down, Riley had almost gotten herself killed exploring one dead end after the next. If Hine te Ana's cave was anywhere in the vicinity, she had no idea how anyone would ever get to it from the beach. The more she explored, the more convinced she was that the cave was one hundred percent myth.

She had done the best she could to prepare the site, flagging a couple of spots near the cliff edge where they could mount a camera, and marking out the areas she had already searched. It wasn't what she had hoped for, but tomorrow was another day. She plunked herself down on the beach and popped the cap off a beer. Once Glenn was here, everything would fall into place. She had a way of making that happen.

Riley took an experimental swig of the local ale. It was surprisingly good; smooth and ice cold. As she lowered the bottle, her heart sank. She had company, but not the kind a dyke alone on a romantic moonlit beach hoped for.

Trudy the porn star tossed a towel down next to her, coyly demanding, "Got another one of those?"

Why she bothered to wear that shred of string pretending to be a bikini, Riley could not imagine. It wasn't like her breasts needed support; they appeared to be helium filled. She produced another beer from her shoulder bag and handed it over. Trudy stared at the cap like it was radioactive. Taking the hint, Riley plucked the bottle from her hand and removed the offending top. This earned a breathless thank you.

"This beach is so cool." Trudy observed after a moment lost in thought. "Imagine a five star resort right over there." She waved a hand in the general direction of Annie's cottage, adding, "Of course, the man ban would have to go."

"It's a local tradition," Riley said. "The Cook Islanders think any man who sleeps on this island, or sets foot on it without permission, will be cursed."

"Oh, like anyone believes that stuff. My Daddy says it's amazing how fast a story changes when there's money to be made."

"Sounds like your daddy has friends in low places."

Trudy blinked. "You shouldn't say mean things about someone you don't even know." Her father's proud mouthpiece, she declared, "Daddy isn't a crook. He's legitimate."

Riley took that to mean the guy had laundered enough money that he was now part of the establishment — yet another fine American tradition. She recalled an essay by Gore Vidal which referred to the United States of Amnesia. The old guy had a point. "What line of work is your father in?" she enquired, expecting to hear 'garbage disposal'.

"He's in post-life."

"Which is a euphemism for...?"

"You know," Trudy trotted out some more double-speak, "Pre-need services, memorial real estate."

"The funeral business?"

"Uh huh." She rearranged her towel and fidgeted with a conch anklet.

Death was a socially awkward topic, all the more so for those who made their living from it, Riley concluded. She changed the subject. "So, what made you pick this place for a vacation? It doesn't seem your style."

Trudy took a moment. In a slightly breathless tone, she said, "If I tell you, you have to promise not to say a word to anyone."

"Wait, let me guess. You're a CIA operative."

"Just promise."

"I promise, okay? Now what's the big secret?"

"Well, Daddy thinks this could be like...ground zero for his new concept." She paused for dramatic effect, then intoned, "Deluxe Transition Retreats. The bereaved accompany their loved one to an exotic destination to commence his or her final slumber. All compassionate services take place in a customized luxury environment; the viewing, the funeral, catered mourning functions, and of course five star accommodations with therapeutic activities available...like, say, golf."

Clearly, she had memorized the entire promotional pamphlet. Riley wanted to laugh, but it wasn't that funny. "You're saying your father wants to set up cemeteries in far off places and run a kind of funeral getaway. Kill two birds with one stone, as it were."

"Cool, huh?"

It was not the word Riley would have used. "So, you're here to scope the place out?" She wondered if Cody and Annabel knew.

"Virgin real estate doesn't grow on trees, and when you find it, there's usually a catch. That's what I'm here for. To see what it will take to make the problems go away."

"So, is there a catch with Moon Island?" As if she couldn't guess.

"The way I see it, the problem is those two women, Cody and Annabel. They really don't get the bigger picture. Like, this could be a Sandals St. Lucia for the bereaved. Daddy would do a sweetheart deal. But you can lead a horse to water... "

Amused, Riley finished her beer. "Money isn't everything for some people. If you assume it is, you'll never get to square one."

Trudy appeared to weigh this novel idea carefully. "If it's not money, it's sex...usually it's both." Giggling, she said, "That could be fun."

"Are you saying you'd have sex with someone so they'll do business with your father?" Riley was appalled. What sort of man pimped his daughter to build a cemetery?

"No, silly!" Trudy gave her a soft kick. "With guys, I just pay them some attention. Make them feel... you know, big." She let the word linger. "Then Daddy closes the deal."

"Somehow I don't see that approach working with Cody and Annabel."

Trudy sighed. "I know. It's so weird. Like, guys think I'm hot. And lesbians are supposed to be into girls. But I tested the waters, and they are so not going there. I mean what's up with that?"

"Cody and Annabel are a couple," Riley stated the obvious.

"Anyway, just because men find you sexy doesn't mean a lesbian will."

"You've got that way wrong." Trudy's voice got a little squeaky. "I've fooled around with untold girls. They were into it."

"Wild guess. They were straight or bisexual."

"I don't see what that has to do with it."

"That's because you're not a dyke."

Trudy rolled her eyes. "You people are obsessed with labels. C'mon, be honest. Do you think I'm sexy?"

"Being honest, you're not my type," Riley said, sparing her feelings.

Trudy set down her beer bottle, crawled across their towels and linked her arms seductively around Riley's neck. "Really?" She teased Riley's ear lobe with the tip of her tongue. "Prove it."

Riley gave the idea room to breathe. She had just endured two celibate months after the Sarah disaster and she was feeling pretty horny. Why not have a little fun? She tried to picture herself between Trudy's legs. It wasn't happening. "Look I need to get some sleep," she said, disengaging herself as politely as she could. "I'm working tomorrow."

Trudy's bewildered pout was evident even in the moonlit shadows. "Okay. Whatever." She watched Riley pick up her gear. "Come to think of it, you're not my type either."

Happy to leave it at that, Riley gathered up the empties and said goodnight. It would be the decent thing to walk Trudy back home, but who needed the excitement? "See you 'round," she said like a real cad. "Have fun."

"I plan to," Trudy replied, sweet as ant poison.

Chapter
Eleven

OLIVIA ROLLED ONTO her back and tuned into the vibrant cacophony of the new day. She had gone to bed with her windows wide open so she could fall asleep to the distant pulse of the ocean. This morning the wind was up, making the palms sigh and groan, and chasing scented gusts of frangipani into her room. The jungle spilled over with birdsong and the toil of tiny creatures getting about the bustle of life.

Dangling her feet over the side of the bed, she wiggled her toes in the cool green air. She felt strangely contented to be here. It was as if her real life had been frozen in time and she had stumbled, instead, into another dimension. She would have to go back in the end, but for now she was happy to be lying in this simple room, inhaling tropical aromas and contemplating a day that could be anything she wanted it to be.

Her mind raced ahead to the evening and her rendezvous with Merris Randall. There had to be some reason the Fates had thrown them together. It could not be random coincidence. Her imagination instantly generated a snapshot of Merris here in her bed, trapping her hands and kissing her. Disconcerted, she sat up and pushed her hair back from her face.

In the entire time she was with Hunter, she had never once thought about making love with any other woman. Even now, almost a year after their break-up, the very idea made her feel queasy and disloyal. Yet Merris preyed on her mind. And why not? Olivia reasoned. She was attractive and interesting. Tonight they would spend some time getting to know one another. Why limit the options to friendship only?

Olivia tried to imagine herself having a casual encounter. It was hardly her style. But since when had her style paid off? She had spent the past ten years not falling into bed with just anybody. She had dated eight women. Of these, only four had become steady girlfriends. None of her relationships had come to a good end. Sometimes she wondered if she had limited her own romantic experience far too much. Maybe she kept picking lemons because that was all she knew. Here, far from home and familiar habits, it seemed the Fates were offering her a chance to do something different. Why not be open to it? Didn't she owe herself that much?

Feeling edgy, Olivia knotted a sarong over her breasts and headed for the bathroom. Her cheeks were hot and her pulse was uneven. She splashed cold water on her face and told herself firmly that she was a normal woman with normal needs. There was no need to panic because she'd had a sexual thought about a woman she barely knew. In fact, it was healthy. They were two adults on vacation in a place made for romance. Other people would hook up and have some fun. Why not her? Assuming Merris was interested, which seemed obvious.

Olivia scrubbed her teeth, showered, and was sitting on the verandah drying her hair when the subject of her angst calmly walked up the path and presented her with a bunch of wild orchids.

"I know these grow everywhere but I thought you might like some for your cottage." Warm hazel eyes held Olivia's in a steady regard.

Flustered, Olivia took the flowers and thanked her. She could feel color seeping into her face and hoped Merris would attribute it to the shower. "Would you like to come in?" she invited in a tone she hoped was relaxed. "I was about to make a pot of tea."

"Sounds good." Merris followed her indoors, looking around with interest. "This is nice. Yours is bigger than mine."

Olivia stifled a small gasp. "I love this place," she managed. What was the matter with her, reading innuendo into a comment about their rooms? "It's so authentic and unpretentious. Simple décor, and these decorative quilts are fabulous. They must take weeks to make. I was thinking I'd look for one to take back home. Cody says they sell them at the Punanga Nui market in Ruatonga so I'll probably take a ride with Annabel one day and—" She broke off, aware she was chattering inanely.

Merris was staring at her with unnerving intensity, those laser-sharp eyes combing her face for what was not being said. Olivia found herself unable to look away. It was as if she had never really seen Merris until that moment. She hadn't noticed her straight, determined nose, her equally straight mouth or the small dimple that played in one cheek when she spoke. Today, her eyes looked more green than hazel. Short, thick lashes lent a sensuality to them that was echoed in her body language.

In a loose white linen shirt and lightweight chinos, she

looked both polished and completely at ease. Merris struck her as the kind of person who chose what she wore, where she dined, how she lived, based on common-sense principles like quality, value and functionality. Olivia could imagine her unmoved by designer labels, buying something for no reason other than that she liked it. She paid attention to detail. Her hair was short and perfectly cut, her nails were neatly manicured, her clothes were immaculate. It wasn't about presenting any particular image, Olivia sensed. She was simply being her well-groomed self.

"Is something wrong?"

Olivia realized she had been completely transfixed. "No, not at all." Summoning a bright social laugh, she said, "I guess I'm not really awake yet. I need that tea."

She set the orchids down on the kitchen counter and found some cups, conscious all the while of Merris watching her with frank appreciation. Automatically, she checked the knot at her breasts, feeling entirely too aware of her nakedness beneath the flimsy cotton. Hot water spilled across the top of the teapot onto the counter, and Olivia stared down at it, befuddled.

"Let me do that." Merris took the teapot from her and carried it over to the sink. She drained the excess then poured their tea. "Want to sit outside?"

Olivia nodded, feeling stupid and cross with herself. Why was she so affected by this woman's presence? It made no sense, even if she had spent the past hour contemplating the possibility of a holiday fling with her. It must be a rebound thing, she decided. Merris was the first woman she'd felt drawn to since Hunter. These feelings were proof that one day she would be able to move on. Until now she had wondered if Hunter had destroyed all hope of that.

If she could, she would make love with Merris right now, she realized with disquiet. Not because she cared for her or even truly desired her. Not because she thought something might develop between them. If she were honest, it was all about proving she still existed as a woman and she could get beyond Hunter. Ashamed of herself, Olivia inspected her tea. She barely knew Merris but she seemed like a good person. She deserved better than to be used as self-esteem therapy for a woman who was an emotional basket case.

They were both waiting for the other to speak. Reaching for her self-respect, Olivia said, "I was thinking. Maybe we shouldn't meet tonight."

Merris sipped her tea. "Why?" she asked in a neutral tone. "What's on your mind?"

Olivia was torn. She had an urge to trust Merris with the

truth, or at least part of it. But she was loathe to reveal herself to a person she barely knew.

"I like you, Merris," she said eventually. "I wish some things were different. I broke up a while ago. It was one of those scorched-earth relationships, and I feel like it colors everything for me. I guess what I'm saying is that I don't think I'm good news for any woman right now."

When Merris finally spoke, she sounded very matter-of-fact. "This is when I say I can respect that and some bullshit about how we can be friends. Right?"

Olivia swallowed. Her companion was nothing if not direct. "I'm trying to do the right thing," she said quietly. "I know we're meeting just to talk, but things have a way of getting complicated."

"What is it you're afraid of? Getting hurt again? Hurting me?"

"All of the above."

"I'm a big girl. What's the worst thing that can happen? I get a wounded ego because you don't answer my calls?"

"I would never be so rude," Olivia said.

"Let's stop a second." Merris's tone was gentle. "What are we discussing here? No one said anything about getting married, or even getting laid. We're just going to get together and shoot the breeze, like people do."

"Let's not pretend people always stick to the rules they make for themselves. I'm trying to be realistic."

"I can respect that. But we're not powerless pawns in some mysterious cosmic game. We're in charge. We choose what we do or don't do." Her face serious, Merris continued, "Forgive my saying this, Olivia, but you're second-guessing yourself way too much. I can see your ex has left you with some baggage, and I'm sorry you've been hurt. But it's up to you to decide whether you're going to allow the past to control you forever, or not."

Olivia felt her eyes prickle. Merris was right. But it was all very well in theory. Emotionally, she felt utterly stuck. "I understand what you're saying..."

"But?" For a moment it seemed Merris was going to get up and walk away. Instead she lifted a hand to cup Olivia's cheek. "I know it's not that simple, but I can help if you'll let me."

"Why? I mean, why would you bother?"

"Do I need an agenda? I'd like to get to know you. No drama."

Her touch was comforting, her gaze tender. Olivia placed her own hand over Merris's and closed her eyes briefly. Her throat was tight. She felt a tear trickle down her face.

Merris brushed it away, then slid her fingers through Olivia's hair. "You should wear it out more often," she said, caressing the back of Olivia's neck.

Something in her expression altered and she drew closer until with each breath their bodies almost connected. There was a frank question in her eyes. Olivia hesitated, leaned forward, and answered it with her mouth. First a tentative kiss, a recognition of the inevitable. Then a second, soft and curious, inviting a more urgent third.

Olivia believed in kissing. When real kisses cease, you know your lover has secrets to hide. Hunter's kisses, once so honest and passionate, had become automatic, bloodless, sometimes punishing. Olivia was a specialist in their shades of meaning. There was the guilty kiss, tender and tainted with betrayal; the dutiful kiss, the resentful kiss, the grateful kiss, the payoff, the blow off. Finally, there was the last kiss. Hunter didn't know it, but Olivia did.

Life took curious turns. Sometimes you had no idea you were kissing a lover for the last time. Olivia knew she would never kiss Hunter again. They would never make love, and if she had any say in the matter, neither would they see one another again. There would be no transition to friendship, no revolving door flings for old time's sake. It was over. Period.

And now, here in this far away world, was a first fledgling kiss — mouths meeting as strangers: cautious, a little formal, still bearing the sense-memory of other lips, hovering and tasting like hummingbird to flower. It felt new and good and real. Breathless, both women drew back at the same time, checking in with one another like two innocents sampling the forbidden. Merris smiled. Olivia smiled back. They kissed again. It was that easy.

Olivia was flooded with relief. A kiss was just a kiss, but even a day ago she could not have conceived of this. Lightly, with her fingertips, she explored the contours of Merris's face — her smooth wide forehead, the square set of her cheeks and jaw line, her straight determined nose. Their kisses deepened. Olivia felt herself sinking back into the sofa as Merris's weight shifted over her. She was aware of her sarong loosening as Merris's hand slid beneath it.

"I want to make love to you," Merris murmured against her mouth.

"I can tell."

Merris's mouth moved to her throat. "Is that a yes?"

"I don't know." Her body did, skin prickling, nipples tight. Olivia shivered.

Merris took her shoulders and drew her up so they were sitting once more, facing one another. Tenderly kissing her cheeks and forehead, she held her close, arms strong and possessive. Her body felt warm and solid, well exercised. Olivia all but sagged against her. In that moment, her mounting desire was overtaken by an intense craving for comfort.

Merris must have sensed her mood change, for she pulled Olivia onto her lap and cradled her as naturally as if they'd done this a thousand times. For the longest time, Olivia took refuge in her embrace, content simply to breathe. Merris smelled as clean as salt air, her skin tinted with the faintest trace of sweet lime. Beneath the weave of her shirt, her heart beat against Olivia's cheek, robust and full. Olivia was certain her own heart must sound quite different, pounding with the uneven gait of a cripple.

"Let me stay with you tonight," Merris murmured.

Another woman inside her body. New hands wiping her clean of Hunter's touch, making it safe for the exiled self to return. Olivia opened her eyes. It had to be more than that. She studied Merris anew and saw a real person, someone who could see her too.

"Yes," she answered.

YES! MERRIS THREW open her cottage door and paced back and forth through the small rooms. She had twelve hours to fill. It seemed like an eon. She had no idea how she had managed to leave Olivia on that sofa, flushed and yielding, when every competitive instinct said there was a deal on the table and she should close it.

It struck her that when she was with Olivia, she was tuned into a frequency that was theirs alone. She could sense Olivia's shifts in mood and found herself responding to her emotional needs whether or not they were articulated. Moments ago, holding her, something had told Merris it was not the right time to make love. Innately, she knew that, more than anything, Olivia needed to be able to trust someone...to connect with another person.

Merris could never have imagined having this unconscious rapport. With previous girlfriends, she'd always felt they occupied two different planets. Communication involved carefully negotiating a minefield littered with misinterpretation and flawed assumptions. Merris was eternally on tenterhooks, certain she would put her foot in it at any moment. She thought about Allegra. It had become too much effort for too little reward.

With the benefit of hindsight, she could see they had never really been in love. She had been in lust for a time, which was followed by a period of adjustment in which she rationalized her loss of interest as part of a natural cycle in any relationship. She had been in love with the idea of building a stable home and family. Having grown up an only child and hating it, she wanted several children. It had never bothered her that Allegra had no career ambitions. Merris supposed she was a little old fashioned. She wanted a wife who would be happy to be at home with the family when that day came.

Allegra had seemed to want that role too—Merris now suspected it made no difference with whom, so long as there was money. Allegra was in love with the idea of living the life her mother never had, with the big house, the status-symbol cars, designer clothes and showy jewelry. When they were first together, Merris had been puzzled but mildly entertained by her obsession with photographs. It was as if nothing was real to her unless there was a frame around it. Eventually she understood that Allegra was an actor in her own life. Photographs authenticated her carefully constructed reality.

As a consequence, their home was awash with narcissistic portraits. Some included Merris or the twins, arranged like accessories, for effect. Lately, like any proud parent, Allegra had started a wall for their daughters. Merris couldn't think of a single picture she liked. To her, they all looked like greeting cards, the twins, usually in theme costumes, posing for the camera like tiny professionals. Merris felt sure they would already be singing "Wind Beneath My Wings" at the Little Miss Kentucky Cuties pageant if Allegra were not at such pains to reject her roots.

Not only did this obsession involve a change of name from KarleeBeth, but also speech therapy to 'redesign' her accent. And it meant their home was generically stylish and wholly devoid of personality. Allegra had systematically redecorated to remove all trace of the mundane comfort Merris had grown up in. Her parents' solid but dull furniture was banished to a storage facility, with the exception of a few antiques singled out because the decorator said they were valuable. In most of the downstairs rooms the wood flooring had been replaced with a sea of pale marble that made little sense in the Colorado climate, besides being dangerous for small children. Original art deco bathrooms were ruthlessly gutted and replaced with black granite and gold fittings; brothel décor, Merris's friend Sam had termed it. What the house had lost in cohesive style and charm, it made up for in self-aware opulence.

Merris should have put a stop to it, but she had been a coward. Allegra considered their home a testament to her personal good taste, rather than the design literature it faithfully mimicked. She saw nothing absurd in a modernist bar adjoining a dining room furnished in mock Italian rococo. Any tactful suggestion Merris made about change led to hysterics, so she avoided the topic entirely. When Allegra left, Merris said she could take all the furniture she wanted. Most of it was now crammed into the apartment she occupied with "Romeo" and the twins. Recently, Romeo had walked right into a chandelier that had once graced the Randall entrance hall and had to go to the hospital. Pity.

It was disturbing to acknowledge that she had been willing to make a life with a woman she did not love, in fact barely liked. Instead of asking why Allegra had had children when she really didn't want them, the real question was, why had *she* pushed Allegra to get pregnant when she knew in her heart their relationship was never going to work? It wasn't pleasant to take a good hard look at herself and realize she had been both selfish and cowardly. She should have had the guts to end her relationship long ago, instead of making Allegra so miserable she was driven to look elsewhere. She could be as judgmental as she liked about her ex's pretensions, but at least Allegra had honestly tried to be the best partner she was capable of being. It was more than Merris could say.

Feeling very sober all of a sudden, she poured herself a glass of fruit juice and wandered onto the balcony outside her bedroom. The sky seemed a little darker than usual on the horizon, she thought absently. Perhaps it would rain later in the day. She conjured up a delicious fantasy of herself and Olivia in one another's arms, lulled by a rainstorm after hours of profound lovemaking.

This time it would be different, she promised herself. She was not going to screw up. She would never give Olivia the slightest reason to doubt her.

Okay, so she was getting ahead of herself. Merris finished her juice and wiped her mouth with a paper napkin. She barely knew Olivia and maybe it would come to nothing. But tonight was a sure thing. For now, that was more than enough.

Chapter
Twelve

CHRIS BLINKED AND rubbed her eyes with hands she knew were filthy. Groaning, she stretched her cramped limbs. At forty, the body did not take kindly to a night of broken sleep on a slab of rock. Chris had fashioned a makeshift bed by removing her clothes and piling them onto the stiff suede pants and leather boots that had belonged to the long-dead sailor.

She wondered what the time was and wished she had worn a watch with a luminous dial instead of the dressy one Elaine had given her for her birthday last year. She felt sure it must be dawn by now, not that it would make any difference. The cave was pitch black and she could see only one route out, back the way she came. Getting through the fissure was the easy bit. Chris had no idea how she was going to climb the narrow chimney up to the main cavern.

Reluctantly, she flicked on her flashlight. She had been conserving the batteries for her big push and now was the hour. Slowly, she panned the cave looking for any indication of another exit. Something caught her beam, and she jerked to her feet. Just yards away, coated in a pall of dust and cobwebs, lay an antique sword alongside some kind of dagger.

Chris's heart accelerated and she licked her dry lips. The sword was heavy, and she doubted it would be of any use to her. But the dagger was another story. A solid weapon, its blade was straight and fairly thick, like the heirloom Scottish dirk Elaine's father had once showed her. Chris cleaned the knife and dragged it experimentally along the cave wall. Its point found the first available groove; she pushed hard. The blade did not snap and remained in position. It wasn't a rock anchor, but Chris figured it could provide some much needed leverage if she could wedge it into cracks and pits.

Charged with optimism, she stuffed everything into her backpack, careful not to damage the treasure map. Instead of changing into her spare t-shirt, she tore it in strips and used these to bind her hands and knees.

"Okay, I'm out of here," she informed the grinning ancient mariner. "Nice making your acquaintance. Sorry it was a couple of hundred years too late, pal."

CODY OPENED MELANIE'S door, balancing her breakfast tray. "Good morning," she said, knowing her cheerfulness sounded fake.

Melanie was sitting up in bed, brushing her hair. She gave her usual sweet smile and set the brush aside. To Cody's horror, it was choked with hair. "I know," Melanie said, catching her shocked expression. "At this rate, I'll be bald by Christmas."

"Why is it coming out?" It was better to be forthright. Melanie said it made her feel invisible when people pretended nothing was happening. "Did you have chemotherapy?"

Melanie shook her head. "It doesn't usually happen with ALS, but I guess I just got lucky. My doctor thinks it's a reaction to one of the drugs."

Cody set down the tray and poured a cup of tea. "I'll draw a bath for you. Annabel will be in to help as soon as she's fed Briar."

Melanie's soft brown eyes fixed on her. "This must be pretty strange for you. The baby...me being sick like this. I shouldn't have come."

Cody felt like kicking herself. Obviously, she had done something to make Melanie feel unwelcome. "Annabel's thrilled that you're here. And I'm really glad, too. If I've said anything to make you feel I'm not, then I didn't mean to."

"Oh, no." Melanie touched her arm. "Quite the opposite. You've both been wonderful. It's just, I had been managing fairly well, and all of a sudden I'm like this. I know neither of you has time to look after a baby, let alone run around after me."

"Mel, you're family. You can stay with us as long as you want."

Melanie's expression was suddenly beseeching. "Cody, I need to ask you a favor."

"Anything."

"Don't send me to the hospital." Her fingers closed weakly around Cody's wrist. "I don't want to die by myself."

"Now stop talking like that." Cody was alarmed. "That's a long way off. You don't have to think about any of that now."

"Please listen," Melanie begged. "We can bring all the equipment I need here. The oxygen. The drugs. I'll hire a nurse."

Cody sat on the bed. She felt profoundly inadequate.

Melanie was trying to deal with her situation like an adult, and she was being no help at all. "I'm not sure if we can do that. I mean nothing we could fix up would be as good as a hospital."

"Cody, I don't want to be kept alive on machines. Do you understand what I'm saying?"

It was time to get Annabel, Cody thought. It wasn't right that Melanie should be having this conversation with anyone but her own blood relative.

Melanie must have guessed what she was going to say. "I can't talk to Annabel about this." Her voice shook. "We're too close. I need you to do this for me. Can I count on you?"

What was she supposed to say to a dying woman who asked for help? "Absolutely. Whatever it takes," Cody promised.

Melanie closed her eyes and relaxed back into her pillows. "I'm so glad Annabel has you. The two of you are perfect."

"SLOW DOWN." ANNABEL pulled the nets closed around Briar's bassinette. "What do you mean you're worried? She seemed fine in the bath. A little short of breath, maybe."

"It's not her breathing." Cody looked stressed, fingers erratically combing her dark hair back from her forehead.

The unconscious gesture always told Annabel something was bothering her. "You two seemed to be deep in conversation when I went past the room earlier," she remarked.

Cody shot a look at her. "You heard?"

Annabel had only caught a word or two, but she had seen Melanie's eyes, full of desperate appeal. "I think I know what she's asking."

"You need to talk to her," Cody burst out. "Tell her the hospital is the best place. We can't look after her when it gets really bad. I was reading this booklet she has. People can't breathe. They have to have an oxygen ventilator, and eating is almost impossible so they have to be tube-fed. We can't do that."

Annabel stilled her with a touch. "I know, sweetheart. I will talk to her. There's a doctor in Avarua I want her to see. We can arrange some equipment to make her more comfortable if she takes a turn for the worse. Meantime, I thought I might go fetch Violet. If I fly out this afternoon, I could be back by tomorrow."

Cody cringed as she always did when Annabel mentioned Solarim Atoll. It was hardly surprising, considering she had crashed a plane there not so long ago. Cody seemed to have convinced herself that the island was responsible for anything and everything that went wrong on the rare days Annabel traveled there.

"Do you think she can cure her?" Cody looked dubious about the whole idea. "It would be wrong to get her hopes up if...you know."

Annabel tucked her arm into Cody's and walked her out the French doors to the verandah. "There are people who live with ALS for many years. No one knows why the disease is worse for some than it is for others. I want Mel to believe it's possible to hope for more time, and I think Violet could help." The old lady was a trained nurse, but she also possessed a gift for healing that went well beyond conventional medicine. The way Annabel saw it, they had nothing to lose.

She glanced up at the sky. There was a strong breeze and a few dark clouds had collected to the north. She would need to leave soon if she was going to have time to get to Solarim before sunset. First she had to fly to Raro, collect Dr. Glenn Howick and her team from their hotel, and take them to meet the *ruahine* who would be conducting the rituals on Moon Island at the end of the week. Dr. Howick would then fly back to Moon Island with her, leaving her team on Rarotonga to interview participants ahead of time.

Annabel felt uneasy about the entire process, but the women she knew were quite capable of telling some UCLA academics to go to hell if they were out of line. It was going to be fine. Her main worry was making sure no one fell off the cliffs on the day. Right now, however, she had more pressing concerns.

"Is it the power of positive thinking?" Cody asked. "You know, with Violet."

"I'm not sure," Annabel replied. "But I refuse to accept that Mel is just going to fade away and die within a few weeks, so I'm willing to try anything."

Cody planted an impulsive kiss on Annabel's cheek. "You're right. You're always right about stuff like this. I can come with you if you want." As soon as she said it, she remembered, "No, I can't. Someone has to be here with Melanie and Briar."

"Do you want me to show you how to change her diapers again?"

"No. I think I got it." Cody hesitated. "What's going to happen to her when..."

"That's another conversation I need to have with Mel," Annabel said, with a quick glance at her watch. "It'll keep."

She collected up her flying gear, and they strolled through the mango trees to Passion Bay. Cody kept a small outboard in the boatshed below Villa Luna. Kahlo would soon be too old to carry them both, so these days they used the boat for transport to and from the airstrip that lay on the western promontory of

Marama Bay.

"What time do you want me to pick you up?" Cody asked.

"Three o'clock, assuming I can drag Dr. Howick out of the meeting in reasonable time. I'll leave for Solarim after I've refueled."

"I wouldn't hold my breath. You'll never get those academics out of a meeting with a genuine priestess."

No matter how hard Cody tried, she couldn't conceal her disapproval of the UCLA team's project. Her complete transparency was one of the things Annabel loved about her. With Cody, you always knew exactly where you were. It made no difference who a guest was; rich, poor, black, white, jane doe or movie star, they always received the same treatment. Cody had been horrified when Annabel introduced a special package for celebrities so that they could deal with security arrangements.

With a smile, Annabel watched her lover meticulously ready the boat. Cody had grown up in a country where not the even the police carried guns, and celebrities could wander around in public without attracting more than a second glance. But the rest of the planet was not like innocent little New Zealand. Even on Moon Island, the outside world could intrude when you least expected it.

CODY WATCHED THE *Lonesome Lady* soar overhead and wished Annabel would delay flying to Solarim. The weather looked changeable and the trip was a pain the ass. There was no landing strip on the atoll, so Annabel had to leave the B-17 on another island and pick up a twin engine Seabee to make the final leg. Cody had only made the trip once. There was nothing quite like landing on the ocean and anchoring your plane just offshore.

Dragging the outboard onto the beach, she tied it down and thought about Violet Hazel. The woman was seventy-something and basically nutty. She used to work as a nurse on Rarotonga and had known Annabel's birth mother and her lover Rebecca all those years ago when they had lived on Moon Island. Eventually she had moved to Solarim, a tiny atoll in the middle of nowhere where she lived like a hermit with a couple of cats and a parrot that spoke five languages, including Latin. And she had saved Annabel's life. As far as Cody was concerned that meant Violet could see dead people and hey, not a problem. Maybe the eccentric old woman could do something for Melanie. It was worth a try.

Hearing her name called, she glanced up as she approached the Villa.

"Thank God!" A woman plunged down the verandah steps looking like she'd been shipwrecked. There was blood all over her and a lump the size of a golf ball above one eye.

Evidently Chris Thompson's hike hadn't worked out quite the way she'd planned. Cody grabbed their guest before she could faint. "Crikey. What happened to you?" she asked.

"I fell." Chris was panting and bleeding all over Cody's clean white shirt. Color fled her face, and she added weakly, "I need to sit down."

"Cody? I thought I heard something." Melanie stood, propped in the doorway, eyes wide.

"Stay put, Mel." Cody half-carried Chris up the steps, muttering, "Jesus, you weigh a ton."

Chris made a wheezing sound Cody took for laughter. "You have no idea how happy I am to see you."

"I'll get a facecloth." Melanie started back indoors.

"No. Stay here with her." Cody deposited Chris on the chaise lounge and pulled a chair over for Melanie, instructing, "Talk among yourselves, you two. I'll be back."

It was like some bizarre jinx, she thought, as she marched along the hallway to the kitchen. *Annabel decides she'll go to Solarim and ten minutes later everything goes all to hell.* It happened every time that wretched island was mentioned. Cody filled a bowl with warm water and grabbed the first aid kit and a couple of towels. Chris probably needed a doctor and Annabel wouldn't be back for hours. Maybe she should radio Rarotonga. They could send out a medical chopper if it seemed Chris was badly injured.

To her dismay, she returned to find Melanie on the chaise lounge, struggling to support Chris. The woman looked half dead.

"Is she conscious?" Cody asked in a panic.

"I'm fine." Chris lifted her head. "Just a knock on the head, and I think I broke a couple of ribs."

Melanie held a glass of water to the patient's lips. "She found a dead body," she informed Cody breathlessly.

"What? In the Kopeka Cave?" No one else had said anything about going caving, and apart from Chris, there were only four other women on the island. Cody dragged her fingers across her head. This was a nightmare. "You're sure she's dead?"

"Extremely dead," Chris said.

Cody sank down in her chair. The Solarim jinx was working today! "I better get out there."

"There's no rush. He's not going anywhere." Chris reached for her pack, yelped slightly and clutched herself around the middle. "If you want to pass that over, I have something to show you."

Cody fetched the pack, her head spinning. "Did you say *he*?"

"Well, it's not one of your guests."

"Now you tell me."

"Oops." Melanie giggled. "I guess I should have said skeleton, not body."

Chris opened the pack and upended it on her lap. "Check these out."

She handed Cody a pair of boots that looked like something out of the Brothers Grimm fairy tales. There was also a strange old pistol, a dagger, and some heavy gold coins. Finally she found what she seemed to be looking for: a roll of paper so stiff she had trouble flattening it out.

Melanie held a curling edge so they could all examine it. There was a breathless hush, like the ones you see in action movies. No one said a word, but they all exchanged significant looks.

"I think it's Moon Island." Cody stated the obvious.

Melanie touched the X like maybe no one else had noticed it. "I wonder what this means."

"If it's buried treasure, I get a finder's fee," Chris said.

"If it's buried treasure, you should have kept this to yourself!" Cody bent lower to study the paper more closely. Melanie's fingers were shaking with the effort of holding the edge. Cody took over from her without fuss.

"I won't say I didn't consider it. But I'm one of those lawyers who thinks the law is actually important, damn it." Chris started to chuckle, then moaned and clutched her sides. "Don't anyone make me laugh. Okay?"

"You're a lawyer?" Melanie's eyes were very bright all of a sudden. "That's wonderful."

"Not a reaction I'm accustomed to," Chris remarked.

"Occupational profiling. Fuck them," Melanie said.

Startled to hear this kind of talk from Annabel's ladylike cousin, Cody shot her a look. Her cheeks were pink, and the dullness had fled her eyes. Chris was obviously charmed by her, Cody observed. She wondered if she should let their guest know Melanie was not gay, just gay-friendly. At least that's what Annabel said.

Cody rolled the map up and read the inscription along the edge. Puzzled, she said, "It's in Cook Island Maori."

"I wonder how our dead friend from the eighteenth century

came to acquire the language," Chris mused.

"Even if he could speak it, he couldn't have written it down like this. It was the missionaries who first started writing the language down so the locals could read the Bible in their own tongue. And that wasn't until about eighteen-thirty." Cody squinted harder. After the inscription, in tiny letters that had almost faded away, were the initials R.J.G.

"Do you know what it means?" Melanie asked.

"My Maori is not that great," Cody admitted. New Zealand was officially bilingual, but Maori hadn't been taught in most schools until after Cody had started college. Ironically, she'd picked up more of the language living in the Cook Islands than she had at home. "I think it means something like...keep it a secret."

Chris wiggled her eyebrows. "The plot thickens."

"You know what's strange," Melanie examined the wax seal, her black eyebrows drawn together in an intent frown. "It looks like there were two wax seals, not just one." She pointed out a small violet blob within a wider perimeter of faded red. "I think someone broke the first seal, then added new wax to seal it again."

"Quite the CSI, Melanie." Chris clapped her lightly on the shoulder. "If you're ever looking for work as an investigator, just give me a call."

For two people who had just met, there was a cute rapport between them, Cody thought. Melanie was glowing and Chris, who struck Cody as your average hardened cynic, handled the younger woman with surprising sensitivity. Maybe Mel was not as straight as Annabel thought. She stole another look at them, then had a sinking feeling. Chris would have to be told.

"What if someone else wrote the Maori? The ink is a different color, too." Melanie's expression was apprehensive, as if she expected them to scoff at this theory. "Maybe someone read the map, then sealed it again and wrote the warning."

Cody exchanged a look with Chris. "I think she's onto something."

"You're a genius," Chris told her.

Melanie's smile eclipsed her pale elfin features and she grabbed both of them, declaring, "This is so exciting, I could die!"

Cody froze in mortification at the choice of words. She could tell from Chris's face that she was equally aghast. Obviously she had already guessed that Melanie was very ill.

Melanie shook the both of them by the arms and hiccupped with laughter. "Just look at the two of you. Get over it, for goodness sake! I'm not dead yet."

"No, you're not," Cody reiterated, relieved to hear Melanie talking in positive terms.

She was on a roll. "We have to go there. I want to find that treasure. I'll take all my pills, and if we go slowly, I'll be able to do it."

"We'll do whatever it takes," Chris said, eliciting a happy squeeze from Melanie. "If we have to carry you, we will. And trust me, if there's anything there, we'll find it."

"Sounds like a plan. Meantime," Cody opened the first aid kit, "let's see about those cuts.Then you better take a shower, mate, because frankly, you don't smell too fresh."

Chapter
Thirteen

A HALF-HEARTED RAIN pattered against the windows, dissolving the twilight view. Being prepared too far ahead of time was unwise on these occasions, Olivia reflected. It meant waiting. And waiting meant wondering. Once upon a time, anticipation had charged these countdowns with giddy hope. Life was an adventure eagerly sought. The weightlessness of consequence prompted risk-taking. Now the tick of her clock measured an ever-shrinking option to escape complications before they arose.

Olivia poured herself a shot of vodka. If she was going to go through with this, she had to steady her nerves. What was the worst thing that could happen? *You could throw several years away on a romantic delusion and end it, robbed of all sense of yourself as an attractive, interesting woman.* Not this time, Olivia vowed. This time the worst thing that could happen was one of those uneasy sexual encounters where nothing quite gels and you both agree not to go there again. No hard feelings.

She tried to imagine making love with Merris. The idea felt like algebra, abstract but strangely compelling. Who knew how the equation would map out, what it would prove, where it would lead? The possibilities were exciting, yet uncertain outcomes bothered her these days. The part of her that had once thrived on chance had fled. In its wake, she was riding out her life like a nervous passenger. Olivia concentrated on finishing her vodka instead of listening for the inevitable knock on her door. It was too late and too cowardly to phone Merris and cancel. If she was going to change her mind, the least she could do was tell her to her face. Maybe they could just go back to their original plan and have meaningful conversation on the beach.

Dubiously, she examined herself in the bedroom mirror. The low-cut green dress she was wearing made a lie of her ambivalence. Deciding to change into something less enticing, she unzipped it and returned it to the closet. She had brought very few dressy clothes with her, anticipating little necessity for them. Hastily, she donned a pair of flimsy, dark burgundy drawstring pants and a demure butter-yellow tunic top split up the sides. Knotting her hair loosely at the nape her neck, she blotted off most of her lipstick. Now Merris could knock, she thought.

And Merris did. Summoning her breeziest social smile, Olivia opened the door and invited her in. The scent of bougainvillea and damp jungle drifted through the open door. Soft golden light pooled from every corner, setting the perfect scene for a seduction that would probably not be happening. She should have blown the candles out, Olivia thought, with a distracted glance around the room.

Merris's eyes were warm. She said a simple hello and took Olivia's hand. "You look beautiful."

What to say? Olivia opted for the truth. "I'm not sure if I can do this." The words spilled out in a rush.

"You're sending me home without inviting me in?" Light and teasing. "Too cruel by far."

"Well, since you put it like that." Olivia stepped back from the door. "Come in. Make yourself at home. I have food. Wine. Music. Intelligent conversation. No guarantees of anything more exciting."

"That's the best offer I've had in a while," Merris said. "Actually, the only offer."

"I find that hard to believe." Olivia held up a couple of wine bottles. "Red or white?"

Merris chose red and took the bottle from her. "Annabel keeps a decent cellar," she noted, reading the label with evident approval. "Penfolds Grange. What a treat."

"I thought you might enjoy it." Olivia congratulated herself on picking a winner.

She'd phoned Villa Luna late that afternoon to request a dinner selection for two, and Cody had dropped the food by along with some suitable wines. A beer drinker herself, she said she had no idea what any of them were like. But she knew the wines Annabel usually recommended. Despite Cody's feigned disinterest, it was obvious she was busy adding two and two. Smiling to herself, Olivia located some respectable Bordeaux glasses.

Merris poured a small measure into each, swirling the wine for a short time before handing a glass to Olivia. Looking like someone who actually knew what she was smelling, Merris sampled the bouquet. "Sensational. And it's barely breathed." Meeting Olivia's eyes, she raised her glass and said, "To the unexpected."

They sipped in silence for a minute or two. The wine was delicious. Olivia drank very little red, but this one was far superior to her usual pedestrian choices. "So, how was your day?" she asked, gesturing for Merris to sit down.

"Interesting." Merris chose one end of the sofa. "I took a walk in the jungle. It's not Central Park."

Olivia sat on the other end of the sofa, wanting to be friendly, but not *too* friendly. "Cody leads an organized hike once a week," she said. "I thought I might go on the next one."

"Makes more sense than wandering around in circles like I did. The jungle gets pretty dense once you head inland, and it all looks the same."

They fell silent again. This time it was an awkward silence burdened with the unspoken. *This is going well*, Olivia thought with irony. "Strange, isn't it." She fell back on small talk. "It's probably snowing in Cherry Creek right now."

"And it's morning."

"Is this the farthest you've traveled?"

"In this direction, yes. I've spent a lot of time in Europe. We...I vacation there most years."

"I'm sorry about your girls." Olivia immediately felt bad that she had raised the topic. "Forgive me. My friend Polly is a gossip. She ran into your ex and got talking and...you know how it goes."

Merris shrugged. "Don't worry. The entire state knows every detail of my personal life. I get to see my daughters twice a month. At this rate, all I'll ever be to them is a visitor."

"I think that depends. Parenting is more than mere proximity."

"Do you have children?"

Olivia smiled. She could feel her knees relaxing. The wine was starting to work. "No. But I was brought up by unconventional parents. They weren't always around, but when they were, they gave me their complete attention."

"You're an only child?"

"Yes."

"Me, too. My folks wanted more, but it never happened."

"Mine didn't plan on having me, but they came to terms with it. You know, the world needs more Marxists."

Merris grinned. "Your folks are—"

"Commies."

"No kidding? How do they feel about the *former* Soviet Union?"

"The poor things are horribly disillusioned. Bad enough Stalin. Now there's North Korea, that flower of the people's revolution. They're idealists."

"In a world run by ideologists. I feel for them." Merris refilled Olivia's glass. "You know, of course, that I thought about you all day."

Olivia studied her wine. "I thought about you, too. I still can't believe we're both here. It seems — "

"Meant?" Merris suggested.

"Well, you're full of surprises," Olivia remarked. "I didn't have you down for a fatalist."

"Never judge a book by its cover," Merris said solemnly.

"Quite right," Olivia played along. "I could be a serial killer for all you know."

"I'll take my chances."

"I promise I have no plans to eat your liver."

"Well, that's a start." Merris relaxed into the sofa, legs crossed, one arm casually draped along the back. Again Olivia was struck by her self-assurance. Merris was not about impressing anyone. She was not playing to an audience. There was no hidden agenda. "Do I pass?" Merris enquired with a trace of mockery.

Olivia felt her color rise. Attempting to lower the heat that simmered suddenly between them, she said, "Actually, I was wondering what line of work you're in."

Merris regarded Olivia with sensual good humor, as if she saw right through this ploy but was willing to indulge her. "I had an IT company. We were taken over a few months ago."

"Is that good or bad?"

"I don't know yet. It feels strange not to be working eighteen-hour days. Strange in a good way. How about you?"

"I'm in the music business. Specifically, I write songs."

"I *see*," Merris intoned, as if this explained a good deal.

"Oh, do you now?" Olivia laughed. "What exactly is it you see?"

Merris topped up both their glasses. "I see a sane woman working with crazy people. This is why you turned to serial killing. It was that or — "

"Politics," Olivia confessed. "I was desperate."

"Misdirected rage," Merris sagely pronounced.

"Write another hit, Olivia."

"Who wouldn't have performance anxiety?"

"Looks like you got my number."

"Actually, now you mention it, I'd like your number."

Olivia laughed. "You're good."

"Come here." Merris patted the sofa next to her.

Against her better judgment, Olivia shifted across the sofa.

The wine was definitely working.

Merris set their glasses down on the coffee table. She took Olivia's hands and slowly drew them to her mouth. "So, you've been having second thoughts? Why?"

"Because I said yes for all the wrong reasons."

"Such as?"

"It's a long story. What you said about not thinking like a victim. I guess I'm having trouble with that."

"So, you're not saying my kissing sucks and my charm will never win you over?"

"No, of course not. I mean—" Olivia started to laugh. "You can't make fun of this. It's serious." She tried to tug her hands away, but Merris kept hold of them.

"So the kissing was okay?" Her warm expression left Olivia in no doubt the memory worked for her. "That's a relief."

Olivia made a nervous sound halfway between a giggle and hiccup. "I'd better stop drinking this. It's gone straight to my head." And because it had, she added, "For the record, I think you're a good kisser."

Merris raised an eyebrow. "But, you're going to make me work for it tonight? Seems reasonable." Her teeth found the inside of Olivia's wrist, and she bit down softly.

Olivia suppressed an urge to withdraw. Instead, as if illicitly through a crack in the door, she watched Merris enjoy her. Close up, she had tiny freckles sprayed across her nose. At her temples, a few strands of silver lightened the ash blonde. Her jaw line was smooth and strong above her solid throat. Succumbing to sensual temptation, Olivia bent forward, brushing her mouth across that strong neck, tasting Merris's skin with the tip of her tongue.

Merris drew her closer, releasing her hands. Small shocks of pleasure played across Olivia's throat and collarbone, where Merris's mouth made contact. She slid her hand over the short, sleek hair to cradle the back of Merris's head. Desire stampeded through her veins. Only the thin cotton of her top diffused the heat of Merris's body, hard against hers. Olivia's breasts felt full and heavy, nipples tugging the surrounding flesh tight. She wanted the flimsy garment out of the way. She wanted skin. Common sense could wait until tomorrow.

When they finally kissed, it was without caution, their mouths demanding much more than a curious taste of one another. Olivia felt herself give in to the sweet trespass of tongue and breath. It was a kiss they were meant to have, intense and unhampered by reason, sweeping aside boundaries and histories. She could hardly bear it when Merris drew back to stroke the wet swollen flesh of her inner lip with a finger, teasing her mouth wider. Opening her eyes, she read what was starkly written on Merris's face, took the finger deep inside, and slowly sucked. Her thighs felt damp. She wanted to part them. Merris slipped from her mouth, trailing her wet finger down to the hollow of Olivia's throat.

By some unspoken accord, they stood but didn't speak, as if words might tear the delicate web that ensnared them.

A single candle lit the bedroom. Merris lifted Olivia's hair from her neck and unzipped her tunic. Olivia slid it from her shoulders and unfastened her bra. Standing behind her, Merris cupped her breasts and bit firmly on the tendon at the base of her neck. Her hands tugged the ties at Olivia's waist undone and the pants slid down. Olivia stepped out of her clothes and turned to face the woman she had planned to send home.

With shaking fingers, she unbuttoned Merris's shirt. She wore no bra. Her breasts were firm and not especially full, the nipples small and dark brown like her freckles. She progressed to Merris's belt, unfastening it then unzipping her slacks. They slipped to the floor. Merris's belly was firm; the flesh flinched to Olivia's touch. Before she could explore any further, her wrists were caught. Drawing Olivia firmly down onto the bed, Merris studied her at length.

Olivia was suddenly self-conscious. Even the candle seemed too bright. She closed her eyes and felt Merris lean over her, pull back the covers, lie down beside her. Firm hands removed Olivia's panties and denied her the sheets she reached for.

"I want to see you." Merris looked her square in the eye. Her hands moved slowly over Olivia's shoulders, past her breasts, down her torso to her thighs. These she parted as if it were already her right. Her breathing altered, and for a split second there was a question in her eyes.

Olivia moved her legs a little wider. Her mouth felt so dry she could hardly form words. "Touch me," she invited.

Merris stroked a fingertip from Olivia's throat to her pubic bone. "Show me how you like it."

A small, sharp thrill caught at Olivia's chest. Taking shallow breaths, she slid her hand between her legs. It had been so long since she'd touched herself, she was almost surprised at how she felt. Her wetness, the soft straight hairs that caught at her fingers, the fleshy arch of her clit. She wasn't certain quite when Merris took over from her, only that she was so aroused she could no longer think beyond her own pleasure.

Merris slid one arm beneath her, turning her so their faces were close. Her mouth was warm and sensual on Olivia's, her kisses increasingly fierce. Answering her body's own emphatic demands, Olivia reached down and guided Merris's hand where she was welling and craving. She felt Merris's weight descend on her. Their thighs entwined and, at last, the yearning space inside her was filled. Merris was sweating, her back slippery beneath Olivia's fingers.

Hoarsely, against Olivia's cheek, she said, "I've wanted this since the moment I saw you."

Olivia responded by lifting her hips, increasing the exquisite pressure. Merris pushed harder, moving deeper inside. For a long while, their bodies rose and fell in a primal rhythm over which neither exerted will. Eventually, Olivia felt herself brimming, contracting, releasing, and she could not distinguish her own cries of pleasure from Merris's. Lost in a flood and ebb of exquisite tension, she knew there were tears on her face only because Merris licked and kissed them away. Their bodies rocked together, but more slowly. Only when they were finally still and their breathing had slowed did Merris ease herself from between Olivia's legs. Tenderly she took Olivia into her arms and they lay, sweetly entrapped, facing one another. For hours they slept that way until they woke to the final stuttering flicker of the candle. In the darkness, they made love again as the clouds burst over the island and a tropical rain beat down.

Chapter
Fourteen

"THIS WAS A great idea," Chris remarked as she and Annabel rigged up hammocks on Violet Hazel's enclosed front porch. They had spent a fascinating evening on Solarim with the old woman, who obviously adored Annabel. Violet had finally agreed to return with them to Moon Island to help with Melanie, provided they could bring her cats and parrot.

"I'm happy you were up for it." Annabel smiled, her eyes dark amethyst in the low light of dusk.

"I'm a terrible patient," Chris confessed. "I couldn't wait to get away from those two."

"Mel's taken quite a liking to you." Annabel said it in a neutral tone, but Chris could tell she was fishing.

"Your cousin's a very special person. We got talking a couple of days ago when I dropped by." She jammed a couple of pillows into the hammock's head end, adding with difficulty, "We have some common ground. I lost my partner recently."

Annabel made a small sound like a stifled sigh. "What was her name?"

"Elaine. She would have loved this...the island, the adventure...a treasure map, no less."

"I'm so sorry, Chris. I can't imagine how hard it must be." Annabel's face was full of emotion, yet she did not press hugs on Chris, or start talking about someone she knew who had died. Instead, she pulled a flask from her bag and said, "I don't know about you, but I could use a stiff drink."

Chris could not completely hide her surprise. Annabel, with her ethereal beauty, was the last person she could imagine drinking single-malt Scotch. But then, the woman who owned Moon Island also flew a bomber and was some kind of local legend for surviving a plane crash. Clearly there was more to her than met the eye. Chris took a swig of the smoky liquor. At first it was a shock to her palate, dry and redolent with peat. A second sip changed its character completely and Chris savored the smooth, musky sweetness. A slow tide of warmth spread across her chest and through her limbs. Annabel was right. A stiff drink was exactly what she needed.

Handing the flask back, she said, "Well, that's me knocked out for the night."

"Beats Tylenol. How are those ribs, by the way?"

"I'll live." Chris ran her hand across the straightjacket of strapping Violet had constructed after they arrived. "Besides, my posture could use some work."

Without a trace of diffidence, Annabel removed her boots and stripped down to her t-shirt and panties. She was a babe, Chris reflected. The observation was strictly academic. She was almost sorry about that. It would be a nice change to feel something other than complete disinterest in an attractive woman.

"I still think we should get you X-rayed in Raro tomorrow," Annabel said as she got into the hammock and dragged a light cotton throw over herself.

Chris performed the same maneuver, but more clumsily, emitting moans of pain. Seconds later, swinging in her hammock like a lumpy pendulum, she gasped, "I don't need to see a doctor."

"Uh huh." Annabel dissolved into infectious laughter.

Chris joined in, clutching her sides. She felt like a twelve-year-old at summer camp. She must have looked ridiculous wrestling the hammock into submission, she thought. And God it hurt. When she'd recovered enough to speak, she said, "Seriously. Violet's opinion is good enough for me." Their host had pronounced her ribs unbroken and had applied a poultice for the extensive bruising.

Annabel peered over the edge of her hammock. "If you were my attorney, I'm sure you'd advise immediate hospitalization for any guest who injured herself on my property."

"If I were your attorney, I'd have all your guests sign waivers before they ever set foot on that island of yours. Second thoughts, before they board that B-17. You folks have left yourselves wide open for a lawsuit."

Annabel rolled onto her side and propped herself up on an elbow. "This is the Cook Islands. No one in their right mind wants to litigate here."

Chris could imagine. She was aware of the Cook Islands as a tax haven made to order for wealthy clients who needed to protect their assets. The government was stable, the statute of limitations was virtually a joke, privacy laws were extensive, and the court system took a dim view of foreigners stirring up trouble. Any tourist mounting a physical injury lawsuit would almost certainly face lengthy delays and an unrealistic burden of proof, assuming they could find a law firm crazy enough to take their case. Annabel was no slouch. She had probably thought the whole issue through long ago.

"I take your point," Chris said. "I'm curious about something. I thought foreigners could not own land here."

"That's true these days. But Moon Island is a unique situation. After missionaries took over the Cook Islands, they made it a crime for anyone to visit the island."

Chris was astonished. "Missionaries were the government here?" It was a right-wing wet dream.

"Theoretically the tribal chiefs were in charge, but they had no power. The missionaries took over the land and ran a police force that was like the KGB. Their job was spying on people and reporting on their morals. There were hundreds of them, and only a few thousand islanders."

"Hence all the churches on Rarotonga."

"They never built one on Moon Island," Annabel said. "The only people living there were *ruahine,* and the missionary police were afraid of being cursed, so they refused to set foot on the place. Eventually all the women who lived on the island either died, or were taken by slave boats from Peru, and the place was abandoned. My Aunt Annie's partner bought it before the modern laws about land purchase were passed."

"And you inherited?"

"Five years ago."

Chris tried to imagine a life without television, cars, the mall, pizza delivery. "You don't miss home?"

"I get a consumer-culture fix every so often, when I visit my mom in Boston. I have no regrets."

"That must be a great feeling." Chris felt bitter all of a sudden. She reached for the flask and took another sip. "I can't think of anything worse than being on your death bed, knowing you could have led another kind of life and wishing you had. But we don't always have the option."

"I disagree," Annabel said. "I think we all make life choices at certain times. We can carve out opportunities or seize them if they fall into our laps. But most people would rather plod along in a situation they know than risk doing something different. It's human nature. No one likes change."

For a woman like Annabel, who had grown up in privilege, life did offer a smorgasbord of choices, Chris thought. Trying not to sound patronizing, she said, "People have to eat. They have children and responsibilities. Even most middle-income families live from paycheck to paycheck."

"Whose decision is it to have four children and a house they can't really afford, two cars instead of one, ten credit cards, a television in the kitchen? If material comfort is so rewarding, why are millions of middle-class Americans on anti-depressants?"

Chris could see what Annabel was getting at. She knew plenty of people whose material possessions seemed to be consolation prizes for a life devoid of real satisfaction. Maybe she was doomed to become one of them, working her ass off in a job she loathed to support a lifestyle that didn't make her happy anyway. She could see why Prozac was such a hit in the land of the free. Drug companies had trained the public to expect an emotional spectrum that began at fine and ended with deliriously happy. Pain, unhappiness, and grief had no place in this sunny vision of the human condition.

Recently, Chris's doctor had prescribed an anti-depressant for her, as if it were somehow aberrant to mourn the loss of her partner as profoundly as she did. Chris had not picked up the prescription.

"I mean, what would you do?" Annabel was asking her a question. "If you could just throw it all to the wind right now?"

"In a way I did that by coming here," Chris said. "I'm a senior associate in line for a partnership, and I just opted out of a big case. There won't be any corks popping when I get home."

"Do they know about you?"

"It's a don't ask, don't tell situation. I was lucky to get the time off for Elaine's funeral. The day she died, I called in sick. My boss phoned back and gave me all kinds of shit."

"But you're still racking up billable hours for these assholes." Annabel said it lightly, without judgment.

"What can I say? I could change firms, but it wouldn't be any different."

"I'd almost forgotten what it's like to take a homophobic culture for granted."

"Well, you live on the next best thing to Sappho's Lesbos." Chris pointed out.

"Minus the nubile hetaerae." Mock wistful.

Chris reached up and turned the screw to extinguish their kerosene lamp. "Sappho must have been a patient woman."

"And a busy one." Annabel sounded absent, all of a sudden, as if her mind had wandered elsewhere. A few moments later, she said sleepily, "Chris, I need a lawyer."

"Right now?"

"This is what I love about your profession. So eager."

"Strike while the client is hot."

Annabel yawned. "Breakfast tomorrow?"

Chris grinned. "Twist my arm, why don't you." As she was drifting into sleep, she started thinking about the treasure map again. After these goddess-worship ceremonies were over at the end of the week, she and Cody could excavate the spot without attracting attention. It would probably turn out to be another grave, she thought glumly. "Annabel?" she called in a low voice.

"Mmm..."

"We have to tell the others not to talk to anyone about the map." Chris could picture treasure hunters parachuting onto the island under cover of darkness. It happened. "Annabel?" she whispered again.

"Go to sleep, Chris," Annabel mumbled. "The treasure will still be there tomorrow."

DAWN WASHED THE morning sky bright scarlet. Rosy light filtered into Olivia's bedroom, tinting the walls pale pink and casting a mantel of pastel hues across the bed. Olivia still slept, one arm flung sideways, the other resting on Merris. Sometime in the night, she had kicked back the covers, and they were crumpled around her legs. In the innocence of sleep, her mouth was softly parted, and her hair, free of its customary restraints, spilled in a silken tangle across her pillow. Merris lifted a strand. It was Irish black, true raven's-wing, as if a little sky were blended in.

She was one of those women who had missed being conventionally pretty, but was instead striking. In another age she would have been called handsome. Sprawled on the bed, she was still flushed from their lovemaking, her skin impossibly luminous, eyelids fluttering, held captive by her dreams. Olivia was ravishing, the most gorgeous woman Merris had ever set eyes on. She knew beauty was in the eye of the beholder, but decided this was unbiased. If only she were a painter, she could capture this image for all time. A photograph could not do Olivia justice. In the absence of flesh, only oils on canvas could feel somehow alive to the touch.

Recalling that painting in Olivia's library, Merris felt a hot stab of jealousy. Was it the work of one of her lovers? If so, she could understand what had driven the artist. Olivia was the kind of woman you wanted to possess, but never could. There would always be an elusive part of her you could glimpse but never know, a self she shared with no one. Whoever had painted the nude above her fireplace knew this about her and had conveyed it like a warning to the would-be lovers who would one day gaze darkly at that portrait.

Merris had never thought of herself as the jealous type. She expected her partners to be faithful only if monogamy was what they had agreed upon. Her anger over Allegra's betrayal had been about dishonesty, not jealous rage. Yet here she was, having what might be nothing more than a holiday romance, and the very idea of Olivia being with another woman made her crazy. All kinds of irrational, not to mention politically unsound, urges presented themselves as reasonable ideas. *Never let Olivia out of sight. Lock her up where no one could steal her.*

Embarrassed, but also entertained by these caveman inclinations, Merris stared at the body she had come to know so well in just a few hours. Olivia's taste was still in her mouth, the smell of her skin just a breath away, her curves and contours a map Merris's hands would remember always. A rosy bruise above one nipple marred the perfection of her breast. Dull purple fingerprints dotted her thighs and shoulders. Merris was shocked; she thought she had been nothing but gentle. Yet she was oddly pleased, as if these marks somehow staked a claim.

Lightly, she stroked the bruise on Olivia's breast and watched her nipple harden. Olivia stirred, a soft sigh escaping her. Merris knelt over her, inhaling deeply. She eased the tangled covers from Olivia's legs and moved her knees gently apart. Very delicately, she opened her, kissing the dark wet pink flesh. It was all she had meant to do, but Merris could not resist the ripeness before her. With her tongue, she collected some salt-sweet fluids, burrowed a little further, and took Olivia in her mouth.

On either side, Olivia's thighs moved against her. Merris stilled them with her hands. Olivia said something, but Merris did not raise her head. She could feel Olivia swelling in her mouth, her juices flowing, her body quivering. Placing one hand on the rounded rise of her belly and sliding the other beneath her ass, Merris held her firmly, demanding her compliance.

If their night had to end, she wanted their day to begin with Olivia knowing she had a lover. There would be no pretending it didn't happen, no compartmentalizing night from morning, as if sunlight nullified all that occurred in the darkness that preceded it. She wanted to be more than an interlude in Olivia's life. She wanted this to mean something. As Olivia's womb fluttered against her hand and release broke across her body, she thought, *I want to be your person.*

OLIVIA SAT ON the steps of her verandah, combing her wet hair dry. Her body was tender. She liked that. For too long she had felt homeless in her own flesh, so numb she had all but stopped enjoying the sensuality of her body. It was as if she had been switched off at the mains and now, suddenly, there was voltage again. Tingling, she flipped her hair back and stretched her arms above her head.

Merris was a very different sexual partner from Hunter. They were both dominant, but Merris was the more generous lover: sensual, attentive, nurturing. It occurred to her that with Hunter, she had never felt cherished. Their sex life had been exciting by any standards — an intense exploration of boundaries, the kind of sex most people wished for. Theirs was a private, erotic conspiracy, a dimension they had occupied even when they were surrounded by other people. For Olivia, it became the one place they could be truly alone with one another, the only place she did not have to share Hunter with the rest of the world. Its violation had changed everything.

Instinctively she knew Merris would never cheat on a woman she loved. For that, Olivia liked her. She liked her a great deal.

"A penny for them," Merris said so close Olivia jumped.

"I didn't hear you."

Merris slid her arms around Olivia's waist from behind and kissed her nape. "I'd drag you back to bed right now if we weren't about to be invaded."

"It can't be that late." Most mornings, Cody dropped the snack delivery off at around 10 am.

"Time flies when you're getting laid."

"They must see this all the time. People pairing off for a holiday fling." Feeling Merris stiffen slightly, Olivia slipped a hand beneath the arms encircling her and leaned back a little, inviting another kiss.

Merris turned Olivia to face her. It seemed she was about to say something, but she didn't, instead kissing her on the forehead then the cheeks.

Smiling, Olivia touched Merris's cheek, her hand lingering. "I was just thinking...I'm so glad you're here."

Merris looked touched and pleased. They kissed. It was a contented kiss, the kind people exchange when they feel safe with one another. Its intimacy affected Olivia strangely. First she felt happy, then a terrible unease gripped her. It was too soon to feel safe. Feeling safe could mean she was already losing her grip on common sense. She didn't want to find herself on that slippery slope again.

"Let's elope," Merris murmured.

Because that sounded like a good idea in her weakened mental state, Olivia said, "Absolutely not."

"I'm crushed. Is it my oral sex technique?"

"Um." Olivia made like she was thinking about it.

Merris laughed. "You know something I really like about being in my thirties?"

"Other than fast cars and loose women?"

"Seeing the funny side of things. I never used to. I had a stomach ulcer by my mid-twenties."

"Seriously?"

"The doc said if I didn't lighten up, I'd be a heart attack candidate by the time I was forty."

"Well, you're pretty funny these days. Congratulations."

"I like your sense of humor, too. It's very English. Deadpan."

"It gets me in trouble sometimes," Olivia confessed. "Americans tend to take my form of irony literally."

"Why did you leave England?"

"I never intended to. My agent convinced me to stay in the US. In my business you have to be around to suck the right dicks."

"What an opening," Merris lamented. "Notice how I'm not taking it."

Olivia tucked her hand over Merris's waistband. "Maybe we should revisit this conversation tonight." Catching a flicker of surprise, she added, "That is, unless you gave up toys for Lent."

"Actually, I skipped Lent this year." Merris took Olivia's hand captive and twisted it gently behind her back, compelling her closer. "I showered and you're making me sweat. Want to come back to my place?"

Olivia was tempted. This felt so easy and natural. So had every disaster she had ever walked into. Determined to give herself time to process what was happening, she said, "I need to do some girl stuff today. You know, the nails are a mess...there's waxing..."

"A fumbling assistant is not part of your vision?"

"Tempting. But, no." Olivia softened the edge in her voice with a smile. "What say I promise to be nice to you at dinner instead?"

"How's seven o'clock? Enough space?"

"Sounds perfect. Now kiss me again."

Chapter
Fifteen

DID LOVE JUST die? Olivia poked her feet into the warm, glittering sand and watched history pour through the cracks between her toes. Every grain was once part of something larger — a creature that made its home in the reef, the living coral that sheltered it, the shells of tiny mollusks, lava from an ancient volcano. Time and ocean rendered mineral to particle, organism to matter. Was love transformed, too? Could it be swept into oblivion as if it never existed, or did it pile up on the beaches of the subconscious, the debris of happiness lost?

Would the day come when she could deceive herself that she had not loved Hunter? She could see their love was made of mirrors that had magnified her feelings. Hers was a passion that had fed itself on delusion and denial. Truth had smashed her house of glass to dust. Was love any less real if you were alone in it? Should she be unhurt because her feelings had been rooted in mirage?

Lost in thought, Olivia climbed over the jetty and contemplated the dinghy tied nearby. She had some hours to kill and a race to prepare for. The little red boat was in excellent condition; sturdy, fresh paint, decent oars. She surveyed her surroundings. The lagoon was as calm as a millpond. A few darkish clouds hovered, promising more rain. She didn't know these skies, but a weather change did not seem imminent. Besides, she would not be out for long.

Grabbing her camera and towel, she dropped her shoulder bag near the jetty so Merris would know she'd be back soon, if she came looking. The dinghy was not heavy, and Olivia turned it over onto the wooden ramp without much effort. Tossing the oars on board, she launched.

Moon Island looked even more beautiful from the sea. The beach was idyllic, a long belt of white sand embossed with dark shiny palms. Huge hibiscus flowers rioted beyond the sand line in an artist's palette of red, pink and orange. Hibiscus Bay was well named.

Olivia belted on a life jacket she found under the bench, wrapped her camera in the towel, and took up the oars, rowing north. It had been a few years, but she soon fell into a relaxed stroke. Her muscles might be sore tomorrow, but they were welcoming the work now.

As she rowed, her mind drifted once more to Hunter. She would never love that way again, she thought. Perhaps that was a good thing. In such love, common sense was handed in at the door. Doubting friends were branded envious. Trust was squandered. It took a certain kind of nerve. Had that, too, died in her? Had she lost the capacity to love without limit? It seemed so, and that was also a good thing, she decided. If passion could find nowhere to reside, she was safe. Never again would she find herself pegged out for carrion to gnaw her insides. There could be no betrayal without trust, no disappointment without hope. She expected nothing of love now. And yet, she said yes to Merris.

Olivia increased her stroke rate. That was not about love. She had said yes to sex as first aid, yes to living life as a scarred person did, within limits. It seemed possible that she could do this with someone like Merris. She liked the honesty of their communication. There were no games. They both knew where they stood. And Merris had a sense of humor. She was a grown-up. By contrast, Hunter seemed increasingly immature and self-centered.

Maybe she and Merris could have more than a holiday dalliance. No one wanted to spend their life alone; she was no exception. Olivia tried to imagine what it would be like to live with a woman she loved in a tepid, uncomplicated way. It would be comfortable, she thought. None of the untidiness of passion. They would be companions and friends. Like any sensible long-term couple, they would have sex because it sustained good health and provided insurance against the risks of infidelity. It could become an interesting hobby or a dull routine. The former would be a plus, the latter no less than most women settled for. So far they were off to a promising start in that department. But compatibility was what really counted in the long run—similar values, ideas, and domestic habits. It sounded dreary but sane.

She rested on her oars for a moment, allowing the momentum of the boat to carry them along. Saying yes to Merris could well be the first victory of pragmatism over romance for her. It meant she was doing something different. Her head was ruling her heart for a change. This was a situation she could control. Abigail would be proud of her. And yet... Olivia was aware of a lingering doubt. Something about Merris stirred her feelings. It was like having emotional pins and needles. Was this a good thing? She had no idea.

Unsettled, she gazed over the side of the boat. It was hard to guess the depth of the lagoon. Directly below, a fortress of coral bejeweled the ocean floor. Shoals of tiny fish navigated their way through this forest of brilliant pink, yellow and blue antlers. Every now and then a larger fish materialized, dispersing its tiny counterparts in shimmering cascades. Olivia recognized a barracuda and a long silvery cod. The water was so clear visibility extended hundreds of feet. It was probably too shallow for sharks, she decided with a quick rush of relief. Maybe she would go snorkeling in a few days' time. Her package included complimentary lessons.

Olivia picked up the oars and pulled briskly for ten minutes or so, rounding the rocky promontory where the airstrip was located and passing several small cottages. She slowed as she reached Villa Luna, a long wooden dwelling with deep verandahs and a thatched roof of five gables. Set among huge mango trees, it looked like a true South Seas plantation home. She toyed with the idea of dropping by, but she was not in the mood for meaningless conversation.

Circling slowly, she jumped with fright. About six feet ahead of the bow a dorsal fin skimmed through the water towards her, then vanished. A split second later a glistening body sliced the surface right next to the boat, and a smiling face turned to stare at her: not a shark, but a dolphin. And this was hello, Olivia thought, captivated. The dolphin regarded her with candid interest. She was *other*, a graceless alien suspended above its watery world in her flimsy wooden vessel.

The dolphin floated alongside, the sky spilling across its dark back as if reflected in oil. They found pregnant women interesting; Olivia recalled a random fact. She could feel the creature assessing her and wondered what it knew that she never could. To see as a dolphin did, human beings needed multi-million dollar technology. Yet we had the arrogance to murder their kind for the sake of a tuna fish sandwich. Was it really so hard for the world's fishing industry to switch to dolphin-safe nets?

I'm so sorry, Olivia wanted to tell it, *for what my kind does to your kind.*

The dolphin rolled onto its back, displaying a belly that was almost pink. It whistled softly at her and Olivia had the oddest sense that it understood. She wished she could get out of the boat and float alongside it. By some strange telepathy, she knew the creature was inviting her, yet just as she was contemplating dropping anchor, it suddenly twisted and vanished beneath her boat. Water erupted twenty feet ahead as her new friend flung itself into flight. For an inch in time, the dolphin hung suspended, as if its pectoral fins were wings, before freefalling back into the sea.

Startled and thrilled, Olivia pulled hard, trying to gain some ground on the dorsal fin as it cut through the water away from her. Maybe her visitor was accustomed to humans. She remembered reading that on some of the Cook Islands you could swim with local dolphin pods. As she drew nearer, the dolphin circled back around her boat, then sped ahead and leapt from the water like a child showing off. It did this several times, getting closer and closer, until with the last leap, Olivia was soaked in seawater. As if it knew, it popped its head up beside the boat to inspect her. Apparently, she looked hilarious. Mouth parting in a huge grin, her pal made a long clicking screech that sounded like dolphin laughter.

Olivia located her camera and continued rowing after the slick gray form, along the length of Hibiscus Bay toward the jetty. She was rapidly approaching the outer rim of the reef where the water was choppier. Exercising caution, she steered herself back within the tranquil confines of the lagoon. Ahead of her, along the reef's edge, lay a tiny islet separated from Moon Island by a narrow neck of water. Her escort raced through this channel, then lifted its head emitting a series of loud clicks.

Olivia snapped a few pictures and was about to wave good-bye when several other dolphins converged on the scene, cavorting and screeching as if they'd just run into a long-lost friend. Captivated, she rowed over. They had moved ten or twenty feet out to sea and were joyously gamboling, their bodies supple and gleaming. Among them she recognized her friend from a distinctive featherlike stripe that cut across its dorsal fin. The water looked perfectly calm, so Olivia rowed through the channel and along the coastline a few hundred yards for a closer view of their antics.

The southern side of the island was completely different from the beaches. Land rose up from water that was deep and sapphire blue. Olivia could still see the bottom, but it seemed a long way from her hull. A huge frigate bird with a bright red breast alighted nearby, snatching a fish from several startled, screeching gulls. The dolphins had moved farther along the shoreline and were playing below a rocky outcrop. Olivia hesitated, unsure whether it was wise to continue.

The water was distinctly choppier on this side of the

channel, and there was a swell of a couple of feet. But the skies were clear. She was wearing a life jacket and was close to shore. She felt strong. How often did a chance like this come along? Lots of people would give anything to see a pod of dolphins in the wild. What was the worst thing that could happen? They might disappear out to sea before she could get a decent photo and she would have to row back empty-handed?

Olivia stepped up her stroke rate and pulled her oars in about forty yards from the cliff wall. There she dropped anchor and took a long drink. Some ten or more dolphins had gathered around the boat and, standing out of the water almost half their body-lengths, they seemed as excited by her as she was by them. Olivia photographed them airborne in sun-kissed somersaults, in groups swimming beneath the surface, and close-up as they gazed at her with their dark, profound eyes. She was aware that her anchor was dragging slightly, but there seemed little point dropping it all over again. She would be leaving soon anyway.

She hung over the side of the boat to get a picture of a mother and her baby and was again tempted to swim. She gave the anchor a sharp tug, hoping to bed it more securely. It held firm enough. Impulsively, she removed her life jacket, shirt, sneakers and shorts. To avoid scaring the dolphins off with a big splash, she lowered herself gently over the side of the dinghy into the crystal blue water. It was not as warm as the lagoon, but just as clear, and felt smooth and fresh against her skin.

Olivia kicked out from the boat in a slow breaststroke before diving down a few feet below the surface. There she held her breath, and with her arms at her sides, kicked her way toward the most inquisitive members of the pod. The constant click and chatter of the dolphins was amplified beneath the water. She wondered what they were saying. Probably *look at this atrocious swimming technique.* Perhaps, like foreigners who appreciate when you make an effort to speak their language, the dolphins knew she was out of her element.

They drew closer, and one cruised alongside her as if in approval. Olivia surfaced for air and immediately dived down again, this time kicking a little deeper. She could see the mother and baby about ten feet away but refrained from approaching. Instead, she managed a small underwater somersault of her own. This was instantly matched by the dolphin that had first befriended her. The chatter grew more excited. Spellbound, Olivia performed the trick a second time and several dolphins followed suit, adding graceful embellishments of their own.

If only she could hold her breath longer, she thought, scrambling back to the surface and gulping air. Slightly disoriented by her spell beneath the water, she kicked for flotation, and glanced around,. The shoreline was not exactly where she had expected it to be. The current had carried her back some distance in the direction she had come. Her boat seemed closer to the cliffs, but it was all a matter of perspective. She was actually further out to sea, by about ten or twenty yards. The distance was nothing. She still had plenty of energy. Swimming back to the boat would be no problem. Just a few more minutes, she promised herself. Then she would say farewell to the beautiful creatures who had welcomed her to their world.

Time slid by all too easily when you could hardly bear for an experience to end. Kicking toward the sunlight a short while later, Olivia felt sad to be leaving. It seemed the dolphins knew she had to say goodbye. The pod was already swimming away from her when she surfaced for the last time. Olivia waved at them and turned back toward the cliffs. Again she felt disoriented. The dinghy had moved, only this time it was no illusion. Olivia cursed beneath her breath. The boat was adrift and heading around the cliffs toward the forbidden south of the island.

She could catch it; Olivia felt certain. Her legs were starting to feel tired, but she was quite capable of swimming the hundred or so yards that now separated them. She would hate to have to report to Cody that she went out training for their race and lost the boat. Laughing to herself, she swam strongly toward the sharp vertical cliffs. She could feel the current changing as she drew nearer. The water itself had a different consistency, thousands of tiny bubbles ascending as if from some distillery far below. It was like swimming in blue champagne.

She rested her legs momentarily, then changed to a slow breaststroke. The boat was just twenty feet from her now and she knew she would make it. On the leeward side of the cliffs lay a small, secluded beach the shape of a half moon. Completely encircled by towering limestone, it was accessible only by sea, she guessed. A rocky outcrop on the far side looked like the perfect place for mermaids to sing. Smiling, Olivia grabbed the dinghy's anchor chain. It was floating free, well above the ocean floor.

Thankful for the chance to rest, she kept hold of the chain, allowing herself to drift with the dinghy while she caught her breath. The bubbles were larger now, she noticed, bursting across the ocean's surface in a foam that formed distinct swirls ahead. Uneasy at the sight of this, Olivia began to move around the boat. It was rocking a little, and slowly turning in a semicircle. Her fingers locked onto the rim and she kicked around to get herself square with the side. She could probably get one leg over, she thought, alarmed by a dragging sensation. It was as if someone had just tied concrete to her feet.

Olivia tried to hoist one leg up, but the boat was circling more rapidly. It was all she could do simply to hang on. Adrenalin surged and she threw herself up hard, managing to get her elbows over the rim and her body partially out of the water. The oars were banging an erratic tattoo on the hull. The dinghy jerked and picked up speed, heading straight for the cliffs. Olivia felt herself being ripped away from the side as if she were little more than seaweed. Locking her arms tight, she clung to the tiny craft but her weight acted as ballast, dragging it down in the water. Desperately, she scrambled for a better grip, kicking and elbowing. She could see her life jacket in the bottom of the boat and tried fruitlessly to reach it.

The ocean rose and fell as if some gigantic creature had stirred below. Above her, ever closer, the cliffs loomed, and Olivia knew with sinking certainty her boat was going to be dashed into them. With each rocking motion, they were flung forward and sucked back with increasing violence. Her strength was failing. If she swam now, she could just make it to the beach, she thought, and took a deep, calming breath. It was the hardest thing in the world to let go, but as the next wave receded, Olivia did just that.

She was immediately sucked back but threw herself sideways and kicked with all she had, trying to propel herself beyond the cliff walls toward the sanctuary of the beach. She made it no more than a few yards into a choppy stretch of water, boiling and dark with sediment. There was simply no way she could swim, Olivia realized. She was pulled into a current that heaved her away from the beach with such force she felt winded.

Terrified, she tried to change direction, but sank below the surface as she attempted to kick away. Water flooded her nose and mouth. She gagged and choked, trying to keep her head above the surface. The sea was rougher and colder now, waves breaking over her head. In shock, Olivia made one final desperate attempt to steer herself toward the beach. She couldn't even get horizontal to swim. Gasping and swallowing water, she began to sob. The beach was receding with every stunted breath she drew, and she knew with harsh clarity that she would never make it. She was drowning, her flailing body demanding more oxygen than her lungs could supply.

Exhausted, she stopped struggling and relaxed into the limitless might of the ocean. There were worse ways to go, she thought. This was a beautiful place. It had been a wonderful day, and a wonderful night before with Merris, whom she would now never get to know. The thought saddened her and she made a final, desperate attempt to restore buoyancy. But her arms and legs were spent. She could see the sun glinting behind a veil of water as she sank beneath another wave.

This time she did not surface in the trough. Stretching her arms above her head, she grasped air with her fingertips, then slid down into the blue silence. Releasing a little air from her bursting lungs, she watched the bubbles rise with an odd sense of déjà vu. The Fates had sent her here, and now Olivia knew why. It was all over, she thought, and slowly released the breath she could hold no longer.

Chapter
Sixteen

"I SEE THE problem." Glenn Howick peered at Riley over her sunglasses. Her eyes were the same cool marine blue as the ocean.

"I've tried the paths with the yellow markers." Riley explained her coding system. "All dead ends. And I walked east to look back, just in case there was an obvious route. It's tough through there. The jungle is like Vietnam or something."

Glenn made some notes and asked for the binoculars, removing her glasses and dropping her backpack. "Which one goes farthest down?" she asked, and took the path Riley indicated, telling her to stay put.

Wracked with nerves, Riley watched her descend.

Glenn was very sure-footed. Glancing up at one point, she called, "Relax. This is child's play. I climbed Antisana last year." She surveyed the beach and the cliffs at length, then lowered the binoculars and retraced her steps.

"I didn't know you climbed," Riley said, awed.

Glenn was the kind of person who could win the Iditarod, and no one would have a clue until they saw her in the newspapers posing with her sled dogs. It was hardly surprising that she mountaineered in her spare time. She was born to stand on a summit, Riley thought, both metaphorically and in practice. Undisguised by her usual professional attire, her athleticism was apparent. She had the lean-hipped frame of a long-distance runner coupled with a muscularity of shoulders and thighs that spoke of grueling hours in the gym. Then there was what you couldn't see. Glenn Howick had the strength of will to risk her life. She was the real deal.

Aware she probably had her mouth open, Riley stopped staring and handed Glenn her water flask.

"Thank you." Glenn gave one of her rare smiles and took a long drink, head tilted slightly, the sea breeze catching her dark honey ponytail.

Riley could almost feel her mouth on that tanned throat. Glenn wore a thick gold chain, she noticed. Suspended from it a diamond-studded butterfly beamed like a tiny laser in the sun. It struck Riley as an odd choice for such a powerful woman. Butterflies were what several nitwit lovers of hers had tattooed above their butts because they thought it was more original than a rose. It was hard to imagine anyone who knew Glenn giving her such a girly piece of jewelry. Riley decided it was from her mother, and she wore it for sentimental reasons.

"So let's concentrate on that today." Glenn said, reorganizing her pack.

Reminding herself to listen instead of daydream, Riley made like she had some idea what Glenn had been saying. "Shall we leave the stuff here?"

Glenn shook her head. "There's no point having to circle back for it. You're not tired, are you?"

"No way," Riley said emphatically. "I could do this all day."

"That's what I thought."

Riley's heart pounded. The tone was almost flirtatious. She gazed at Glenn's fingers, at work retightening the laces on her hiking boots. Hers were not the delicate, wafty hands people termed beautiful. They were sculpted and expressive, hands Da Vinci might have sketched: musician's hands, a marriage of art and discipline. Despite the oozing afternoon heat, Riley goose-bumped at the thought of those hands on her body.

"The women I spoke with are unable to recall how they arrive at the cave, and of course the associated *tapu* prohibits them from describing their experiences inside it. They all agree that it's small and there is a pool of water. This must be fed somehow." Glenn consulted a geological survey map she had brought with her from Rarotonga. "There is a stream here and a waterfall."

"That sounds promising," Riley said, trying to concentrate on the maze of fine lines instead of the glimpse of breast as Glenn leaned forward. "I can mark out a grid this evening if we don't find it."

"Good idea. This terrain is much more difficult than I expected. I think I'll arrange for one of the team to come over tomorrow."

Riley managed not to protest out loud. Instead she said, "Why not recruit the owners? They know the island better than anyone, and they did agree to provide every assistance."

"I'll speak with them over dinner tonight," Glenn said, dashing Riley's hopes of an evening alone in the cottage, just the two of them.

Apparently Glenn planned to socialize while they were here. It was diplomatic, Riley supposed. Cody and Annabel could have refused to allow the research team onto the island at all. Obviously Glenn needed to keep things sweet.

"It would be ideal if we could boat in and explore the cliffs from the base," she said.

"Cody says we can only get in if the tide is right," Riley said. "The currents are incredibly dangerous."

"Hence the wreckage on the beach."

"What wreckage?" Riley was embarrassed as soon as she spoke the words. It seemed she had missed seeing something blindingly obvious.

"It looks like some type of small boat. There's a smashed up hull and some planks piled up on the rocks over there." Glenn waved a hand toward the western end of the cliffs.

"Oh, *that* wreckage." Riley covered herself. "That's part of a boat? I didn't realize."

"Shall we?" Glenn checked her compass and started into the jungle. Shoving a young banana palm aside, she remarked, "Why is there never a machete when you need one?"

MERRIS KNEW IT was probably too early to knock on Olivia's door. But the champagne was cold, and she thought she could probably sell Olivia on the idea of an outdoor aperitif before dinner. It was a safe bet that she would be wearing something more civilized than shorts, so Merris had carried a couple of deck chairs down to the beach. Unusually for her, she had changed her own outfit several times before settling on cream pants in a chunky linen weave, and a black rayon shirt. She hoped her look said casual but tailored, as opposed to Miami mobster on vacation.

It was the hair, she thought, just before her knuckles connected with the door. She often wore it combed back, but this time she'd used more hair stuff than usual. It was not too late to go back home and shower all over again. Merris considered the possibility seriously for several seconds before she came to her senses and reminded herself she was not eighteen.

She knocked, her entire body prickling with anticipation. She still couldn't believe she and Olivia were lovers. It had been so much easier than she'd anticipated. She half expected to find her waiting, embarrassed and awkward, having had a change of heart. She had already planned how she would handle that. Gallantly. No pressure. But neither would she simply accept it and walk away. You didn't win a woman's confidence by behaving like a sap. If Olivia needed time, that was okay. In fact, Merris wanted to court her properly.

She knocked again more firmly and wondered if Olivia was in the shower. Perhaps she was one of those women who loathed early guests catching her unprepared. Maybe Merris should leave and come back later. She tried the door handle. It was unlocked. Leaning into the room a little, she listened for the sound of water running, and called, "Olivia?"

The cottage was silent and unlit, with no indication that Olivia was present, let alone expecting company. Puzzled, Merris entered and called again, then walked through the cottage opening each door. Olivia's bedroom set her pulse racing. Laid out on the bed was a simple silk dress in emerald green. The front was cut low. Olivia was planning to look gorgeous for her. A woman having second thoughts would not be doing that. Raw lust made her clothes feel too hot, and Merris returned to the kitchen and stowed the champagne in the fridge, pausing in the doorway for a moment to cool off.

Olivia was probably on the beach. Perhaps she had fallen asleep in the sun. Suddenly concerned, Merris strode out into the early evening and followed the path down to Hibiscus Bay. She called Olivia's name a few times and strolled out to the water's edge, scouring the beach left and right. The sky was brooding, the ocean slate blue-gray beneath a heavy veil of clouds. Beyond the lagoon, the white caps were bigger than she'd yet seen them. Compressed between cloud and earth, the air felt heavy and hot.

Starting to perspire, Merris climbed the jetty and checked the surroundings again. Right in front of her, on the opposite side of the white wooden structure, lay a towel and a colorful cotton bag. She jumped down and picked these up. Inside the bag were a Margaret Atwood novel, a bottle of sunscreen, and a thoroughly cooked banana. Clearly Olivia had left this stuff on the beach hours earlier. She must have forgotten all about it. Something jarred, and Merris stared down at the narrow boat ramp a few feet away. Where was the little dinghy that was usually here?

PROPPING BRIAR AGAINST her shoulder, Cody picked up the telephone and tried not to yell *What?*

Bad enough Annabel had barely got home yesterday before she set off again for Solarim. Now Cody had discovered she was supposed to entertain those UCLA women for dinner tonight. This she would have to do alone because Annabel had talked Chris into taking the joyride to Solarim with her, and all the other guests had their own plans, except for Trudy. That bimbo had phoned earlier and had the nerve to say she would join Cody after the academics departed, doubtless to browbeat her all over again with that ridiculous funeral resort idea.

"Hello?" said the woman on the phone.

"Yes, I'm here," Cody said. "Sorry."

Briar had just thrown up most of her bottle because Cody forgot it was supposed to be warm, and Mel was sound asleep, exhausted by the excitement of the past two days.

"This is Merris Randall. Look, I'm concerned about my neighbor."

Cody propped the phone to her ear and started fixing a new bottle with her free hand. "Uh huh?"

"I think she took the dinghy out, and she hasn't come back."

"When did she go?"

"I don't know. It must be hours ago. We're supposed to be having dinner tonight, and she hasn't come back yet."

Probably a last minute change of heart. Accustomed to blowing smoke for guests having second thoughts about a holiday romance, Cody said, "Well, she could have landed on one of the other beaches. The weather's closing in. Maybe she's walking back."

The voice at the other end grew very cool. "I doubt that. But if you think it's a possibility, we'd better not waste any time. It will be dark in two or three hours."

"Ms. Pearce is a skilled rower," Cody said, trying to sound reassuring. "I'm sure there's no cause for alarm."

If she had taken the dinghy hours ago, it seemed unlikely she would still be out on the water. She was probably wandering home around the bays, collecting shells, as many of their guests did.

Merris wasn't buying. "I'll expect you at the jetty in fifteen minutes. We can take it from there."

"Make it half an hour," Cody said. "I have some other guests turning up shortly, so I'll check whether they've seen her. Okay?"

"Okay." Click.

Cody tested the bottle on her wrist. She had no idea how hot it was supposed to feel, so she opened her mouth and squirted some of the warm milk onto her tongue. It tasted vile, but it was lukewarm — probably just right.

"I can't believe you like this stuff," she told Briar, who grabbed the bottle and started sucking happily as soon as Cody sat down.

This was much easier than dealing with the mushy food,

Cody thought. Melanie had spent about half an hour trying to spoon some pureed banana into Briar before she went to bed. The baby had not seemed remotely interested, drooling it all over her fingers, then wiping them on anything she could reach. On the bright side, after a few weeks of this, Annabel would be thoroughly disenchanted with babies. They weren't so cute when you had to look after them 24/7.

She looked down at Briar, and Melanie's dark serious eyes stared right back at her. Quite suddenly Briar spat the bottle and smiled at Cody like she was the best thing since sliced bread. Grinning despite herself, Cody put the nipple back between her gums. But the baby had lost interest. She reached a chubby hand up to Cody's face and prodded her nose, making odd little sounds.

With her silken black ringlets and her milk-and-roses skin, she was an unusually pretty baby, Cody decided. In a high pitched voice, she said, "You look just like Snow White."

Briar made cooing sounds and pulled at Cody's bottom lip.

"I have to change you now. It's your bed time," Cody informed her. "I hope I can get your pants to stay on this time."

"I could give you a hand with that," suggested a throaty voice, and Dr. Glenn Howick stepped through the French doors from the verandah. "We're early. Sorry if it's a bad time."

"No, it's fine," Cody lied. "Please. Sit down."

"You're not taking me up on that diaper offer? I'm good."

"Well, if you must." Cody tried not to show unseemly relief. "If you don't mind holding her, I'll go get everything."

Glenn Howick seemed genuinely thrilled, lifting Briar from Cody with the assurance of a woman who knew infants well. "She looks just like you," she said, kissing Briar's cheek and making goo goo noises.

"She's not...never mind." Cody glanced at the woman who had followed Glenn in. At the sight of her boss maternalizing all over a baby, Riley Mason looked like she had just trod in dog shit. Cody knew exactly where she was coming from. Pointing toward the kitchen, she said, "Hey, Riley. If you want a beer, help yourself."

When Cody got back, she was relieved to see Riley had made herself useful by pouring a drink for her boss as well. She was gazing at Glenn with a forlorn expression Cody recognized. The poor kid had it bad and it looked like the famous professor was probably a straight woman who had *no* idea.

"Look, something's come up, and dinner's going to be a bit of a problem tonight," Cody said, passing the baby bag to Glenn. "I mean, there's plenty of food, it's just I have to go find one of our guests. I was wondering if you've seen her. Black hair, nice looking. Her name's Olivia. According to her...uh...friend, she took a dinghy out sailing earlier and —"

Glenn stopped the diaper change and looked up abruptly. "A dinghy? What color?"

"Red and green."

The two academics stared at one another. Cody felt the onset of nausea.

"You hadn't seen that wreckage before today, had you?" Glenn directed a question at Riley.

Riley went bright red. "No."

Glenn's hands performed the diaper change, but her eyes were fixed on Cody. "There's some wreckage below the cliffs of Hine te Ana. A small boat."

Cody's legs started to shake. She tried to remember what she had said to Olivia about where to row. There were warnings on each cottage door and inside the island guide. Every new arrival was told to confine their swimming to their own bay and that the south of the island was off-limits for all activities, sailing included. Had Olivia wanted some kind of challenge because she was training for their race?

"Maybe it's some other boat," Riley said. "Stuff washes up on beaches all the time. Or it could be a container that broke up."

Glenn lifted Briar against her shoulder and maintained a swaying motion as she spoke. "Call the friend again, and double-check that she hasn't shown," she instructed Cody. "If she's still missing, we don't have much time before dark."

"I should radio Rarotonga," Cody said. In fact, she and Annabel were the search and rescue team for this zone, but they had choppers and tracking experts on Raro.

"We can't wait for reinforcements. Riley can mind your baby," Glenn said, ignoring her assistant's stifled gasp. "I'll come with you."

MERRIS JUMPED DOWN into the outboard as Cody pulled alongside the jetty. "Any sign of her?" she demanded.

"This is Glenn Howick," Cody said. Her voice sounded like a croak. "She..."

Glenn shook Merris's hand. "I believe I may have seen Olivia's boat earlier today. I'm sorry to have to tell you this. The boat I saw was in pieces."

"What?" Merris sank down on a bench seat. She felt as though someone had just punched her in the gut. "Where is it?"

"There are some cliffs on the southern face of the island."

"The area all the warnings are about?" Merris shot a look at Cody.

"We can't assume it's her," Glenn said in a level voice. "We're going to go get a larger boat and take a look."

"I told her not to go around there," Cody said as they sped along the shoreline. She looked as pale as a ghost.

Merris felt her mouth flood with saliva and her stomach lurch. Gagging, she hung her head over the side of the boat. What in hell kind of place was this forbidden area? And why would Olivia have gone there?

They switched to an inboard cruiser that was anchored off Passion Bay. Around thirty feet long, it was fitted with state-of-the-art equipment, including searchlights.

"There's a Zodiac RIB on board," Cody said, handing out life jackets. "We're registered for search and rescue in this vicinity."

Merris did not know what to feel. She was relieved Cody had a decent boat and likely some experience in search and rescue, but buzzing relentlessly in her mind was an image of Olivia in a tiny boat smashed against a cliff. She cradled her head in her hands, refusing to believe it could be possible.

They circumnavigated the island well outside the reef. There was a five-foot swell, and the wind Merris had noticed while she waited on the jetty was blowing spray high in the air. It had started to rain by the time they approached the cliffs, and Cody increased power, but slowed speed as they chugged along the vertical walls.

"There it is." Glenn pointed toward a rocky mass at the edge of an eyelid-shaped beach.

Cody beamed a spotlight at the area, and they could plainly see a red wooden hull, smashed apart. "That's our dinghy," she said tonelessly.

"Oh, my God." Hot tears spilled down Merris's cheeks.

"Is it swimmable?" Glenn asked.

"There's a chance." Cody trained the light along the beach. "It depends on time of day. There's a rip current off the beach. If she jumped before the dinghy hit, she was probably caught."

"So it depends whether she panicked or not," Glenn said quietly. "I understand there's some kind of path up from the beach."

"Supposedly," Cody said. "But I've never been able to find it."

A small flare of hope burst in Merris's chest. "So she could have made it to the beach and found this path. She could be up there in the jungle?"

"It's possible." Cody handed a loudspeaker to Glenn.

They spent the next half hour calling and searching the surrounding sea and the cliff face until the rain was falling in sheets and waves eight feet high were pounding the cruiser.

"Let's get a search party out at daybreak," Glenn said. "If she's there, we'll find her."

Merris took the loudspeaker and called one last time as they left the cliffs behind. Her voice was lost to the wind and the sea, but she prayed that wherever she was, Olivia would know Merris was coming for her.

Chapter
Seventeen

MOONLIGHT POURED DOWN a narrow limestone throat into a spring of water as silver as a looking glass. Mirrored, a face gazed up—a woman with dark hair and bare breasts. About her neck was a braid of shells, separated by huge, glowing dark pearls. Her mouth was red with promise. In the center of her chest, beneath a wall of bone, her heart beat hard enough to break the skin. Like a rose between her breasts, bloody but perfect, a wound had formed.

Olivia put her finger there. Her blood shone black, like oil. Was she dead? She lifted a huge spiny shell to her ear and listened. There was a pulse. It could be the ocean or her heartbeat. The shell wasn't saying. She had brought it with her from the beach. Up the stony path, through the long tunnel, beyond the golden eyes, and up the high steps to the bedchamber of the princess where she had slept with the taste of ocean in her mouth.

The beach. That had been a surprise. She remembered seeing it far away, grasping air with her fingertips, bubbles teeming from her mouth, a terrible burning in her lungs. She was falling into darkness when something caught her body, and she was dragged up and up into the bright painful light and the hard bounce of a wave. She did not swim to the shore, but was carried there and flung onto the beach as if the ocean had found her unappetizing and spat her out.

Panting, she remained inert on the wet sand until a pain piercing her chest made her move. Beneath her lay a huge pale peach shell. One of its heavy spines had bored into her flesh. Olivia crawled away from the lapping tide, over sand rough with broken shells, then rolled onto her back in the shadow of a giant wall of rock. That was when she heard the song: half lament, half aria, lilting and full of sorrow, in a tongue she did not recognize. The singer stood at the waterline casting her lyrics to the wind and sea. Dark hair hung past her waist where a band of shells held a grassy skirt in place. Full and ripe, her breasts were bare. Around her neck she wore a braid of knotted shells as pale as her teeth. Somehow Olivia knew that this was a princess.

When her song was done, she came to Olivia and held a palm full of water to her mouth. She spoke in a voice that was rich and melodic, but Olivia did not know what she was saying. Her wrists and forearms were tattooed with a geometric pattern of triangles and feathers, dark red-orange against the light brown of her skin. The same design decorated her calves. Something in her face jarred a memory that floated just beyond reach. She seemed familiar. Olivia tried to speak, but her throat was too raw; all she could do was cough.

After a time, the princess took her by the hand and helped her to her feet. She led Olivia up a steep path high above the beach and into a narrow crack in the cliff face. It was cool and pitch dark inside, and it seemed they walked forever. Olivia's fingers followed a trail of shapes carved into the rock walls. Like the princess's tattoo, they were triangles and feathers curved like crescent moons. The path grew wider and, from somewhere high above, a shaft of sunlight lit the way ahead.

The rock was carved into steps so deep and high Olivia had to rest on each and catch her breath. Looking down the way she came, she was nonplussed. Large, dull gold eyes stared up at her, caught by the sun. There were dozens of them, as if the tunnel were home to some strange shy goblins huddled *en masse* where the steps fell away.

Beyond the last step and over a slippery boulder, lay a small cave with crystalline walls that glistened like chandeliers. Strings of shells and beads hung from the rock and crystal formations and water cascaded gently over a lip at one end into a tranquil pool. Olivia caught water from the fresh stream and drank. The princess lifted a necklace from a protrusion of rock and placed it over Olivia's head, then led her to a dry hollow on the far side of the pool. It was lined with mats and heavy *tivaevae* quilts. There, Olivia slept.

MERRIS SAT ON Olivia's bed, fully clothed and smelling of sweat and seawater. Her heartbeat was fast and uneven, like her breathing. She could feel Olivia so tangibly, she knew she must be alive somewhere. Anything else was impossible. She got up and lit the candle that had flickered watery gold across Olivia's flesh the night before. Merris could still feel her, sleek and hot and shaking. She could still hear those small cries of pleasure echoing beyond the silent walls. Impulsively, she tore back the bedclothes, hoping to smell her. But the sheets had been changed.

Merris undressed, leaving her clothes in a damp pile on the floor, and stood beneath the shower picking up Olivia's toiletries one by one. Bath gel, shampoo, and a soap that smelled faintly of spiced roses. It was comforting to be here, surrounded by the simple evidence of Olivia's existence. She washed systematically and wrapped herself in a towel.

As she returned to the bedroom, a gust of wind blew the windows wide open and extinguished the candle. Her skin prickled and the hairs on her neck rose. A person with an overactive imagination would have read something into this, but Merris refused to entertain the idea that Olivia's ghost had just announced its presence. Instead, she fastened the windows and got into bed. She had left the outdoor lights on and a lamp burning in the living room in case Olivia was trying to find her way home in the night. It seemed more likely she would wait until dawn, especially if she were injured.

Merris felt terrible that they could not search the jungle until the next morning. The *makatea* south of Hibiscus Bay was too dangerous. Cody had instructed everyone to get some sleep. She would pick Merris up at first light.

Turning onto her side, Merris conjured up an image of Olivia lying next to her, sound asleep, safe in her arms. Emotion overwhelmed her, raw and untidy. Like a beaten thing, she huddled into herself for comfort. This was unlike any feeling she knew. For the first time in her life, she understood that love was more than sentiment. It was more than fancy wrapping paper around an empty box. Love was a transfusion that found its way into bone and marrow. Nothing could ever be the same again.

Merris was unnerved by the intensity of this feeling. How could she love Olivia so much, so soon? Was it the same for her, too? Merris knew with painful certainty it was not, and maybe it never would be. Could she live with that? Would she even get the chance? She was gripped by an absurd fear that Olivia had been taken from her because she had lied about the "co-incidence" of her presence on the island. She had wanted to come clean, and had only been waiting for the right moment to present itself. But all they'd had were a few days.

Let her come back and I will do anything, she bargained with God. *I'll tell her everything. I'll do right by Allegra and the girls and not begrudge her happiness with someone else. And if this is not right for Olivia, I'll walk away. Anything. Just let her live.*

OLIVIA OPENED HER eyes and inhaled deeply. Her dreams had been invaded by a scent so powerful she had to surface for air. For a moment it seemed to her that she was still dreaming. She was in a small grotto flooded with unearthly light that fractured and beamed off thousands of crystal growths. A thin stream of water spilled into a pool that looked like mercury. Trailing down from the cave opening was a fleshy tangle of creepers and flowering plants. It must be one of these she could smell, Olivia thought. It was unlike any flower she knew, intoxicating as a drug—sensory proof that she was alive and awake, that this was not some unconscious state or death itself.

In her mind's eye she could see the woman who led her here, but she knew she must have been a delusion. No one could have been on that beach with her. She fingered the necklace at her throat. It was real. So was the wound in the center of her chest. Abrasions stung her palms and knees. Her underwear was torn.

She was almost surprised to find the grotto solid to the touch, and the water fresh and good to drink. That she had found this place was miraculous. The woman who had held her hand must have been a figment of her imagination, she decided—a device conjured by a mind under stress. For her it had made the difference between life and death.

Others had found sanctuary here, she thought. The place had the feel of a shrine. Intrigued, she peered down into the quicksilver pool. It was almost hypnotic. At first her face was mirrored back at her, then something hazy rose from beneath the surface to supplant it, and Olivia felt as if she were falling. Her stomach dived and her eyes refused to focus. Dizzy, she clung to the rocks around her and leaned toward the water, trying to make out what was submerged.

Then she was dreaming again. It was one of those dreams that hover at the brink of waking. Olivia knew she was dreaming but could not quite drag herself conscious. She felt like the occupant of a train passing through blurred scenery. She wanted the trip to end, but she was powerless to leave her seat. As if through layers of thick glass, she saw Hunter in a hotel bathroom, sitting on the toilet seat with the lid down, a set of works spread out on the countertop nearby. The door was ajar, and on the bed lay a naked woman. She looked semiconscious.

Olivia tried to shout to Hunter, but her throat made no sound. She watched Hunter shoot up and lean back against the cistern, sagging with relief. There were used hypodermics in the bathtub and clothes strewn all over the floor. Empty Evian bottles littered the room. The discerning addict did not want tap water polluting her body. Hunter staggered into the bedroom and fell across the bed next to her bimbo *du jour* and Olivia could see no more. The scenery accelerated past her window, and suddenly she was at home in Cherry Creek, alone in front of her favorite fire in the library.

A clock ticked so loud it made books fall from the shelves. But Olivia didn't care. She just sat there staring into the fire, tears rolling down her face. Her hair was shorter. She looked older. But everything in the room was the same, and she was playing one of Hunter's albums. Olivia wanted to reach out and shake the Olivia of her dream and yell at her that this was no life. She was wasting her time pining over a lost love that had never had true substance. The fairy tale had ended badly; it was time to close the book.

Olivia stretched her hand out as far as she could, but she was spinning and the room was receding. Her fingers connected with something hard and metallic, and she opened her eyes. The moon had passed beyond the rocky breach, and the grotto was almost in complete darkness. In her hand lay what felt like a heavy round coin. Olivia set it aside and shook the quilt out. It was too dark, and she was too tired to try and climb up to the mouth of the cave now. Merris and probably the others would be looking for her in the morning. Taking comfort in that, she curled up on the mats and surrendered to sleep.

Chapter
Eighteen

ANNABEL STALKED INTO the villa and dumped her gear on the kitchen counter. She was irritated. They had waited at the airstrip for twenty minutes. In the end she had left Violet there with Chris. "Cody?" she called.

"Oh, thank God you're back." Mel appeared in the hallway, face tearstained and eyes welling. Words spilled disjointedly between her sobs. "It's terrible. They're all out looking...and she's probably drowned, and then there was this urgent radio call...the police in Avarua...I'm so frightened."

"Calm down." Annabel put her arms around her cousin and led her to a sofa in the sitting room. She groped in her pockets for some tissues and wiped Mel's face and nose. Trying not to sound as alarmed as she felt, she said, "Slowly now, one thing at a time. First, who's drowned?"

Mel took a shaky breath and recounted a tale about boat wreckage on the Sacred Shore and a guest called Olivia who was missing after taking her dinghy for a row the day before. "Cody organized a search party first thing this morning."

Annabel was stunned. It had always been her worst nightmare that something would happen to a guest. The women who stayed on the island had no idea how closely their hosts kept tabs on them. Between Cody's morning visits, the housekeepers' cleaning schedule, dinner at Villa Luna, and a system of reporting where guests planning hikes and boat trips had to notify Cody of their plans, there was little of which they were unaware. All guests were warned not to explore the south of the island by land or sea, and she and Cody also routinely patrolled the beaches. How could this have happened?

"So far they haven't found anything," Mel said. "Cody came back here a couple of hours ago, and I haven't seen her since."

"They're searching the south of the island?"

"They think if she didn't drown, maybe she climbed the cliffs."

What were the odds of anyone wrecking their boat on the cliffs of Hine te Ana and surviving? Slim to none. Annabel called Olivia Pearce to mind. Was she a fighter? On appearances, Annabel would guess not. But people could surprise you. From her own experience, she knew the instinct to survive was remarkable.

"I feel so useless." Mel blew her nose. Her shoulders were still shaking, but her breathing was becoming even again.

Annabel took her hand and squeezed it. "I understand. But I want you to remember all the things you do, not the things you can't do. You just made a human life, and you traveled halfway across the planet with your baby when you can hardly walk. You're dealing with a huge personal crisis, but you still found the time to help a total stranger who was hurting. You've made a real difference for Chris. She told me. So I don't ever want to hear you say you are useless again. Deal?"

"You're the best." Mel leaned over and kissed Annabel's cheek. With forced humor she said, "Anyway, so here we are in the thick of a real crisis, and the police captain from Avarua radios with an urgent message and, guess what..."

Annabel rolled her eyes. In this neck of the woods, the police thought they were dealing with a serious social problem when someone failed to trim their hedge. "I can't even imagine."

"My brother is in Avarua looking for me."

"You're kidding." Annabel could see why Mel was almost hysterical.

A card-carrying member of Born Again Bigots, Roscoe Worth had already tried to prevent Mel from leaving the USA. He and his scary Tammy Faye-clone wife were hell-bent on getting custody of Briar. Mel had fled to Annabel's mom after receiving a notice that he had commenced legal proceedings, claiming she was unfit to care for the baby. Not one to tolerate bullies, Laura Worth had Mel file charges of harassment against him, then set about getting her and Briar out of the country.

"The Captain called to give you a heads-up. That idiot is accusing me of kidnapping my own child."

"Well, your brother is not in Kansas any more." Annabel carefully controlled her tone. She was livid. It was just like Roscoe to pull a stunt like this. The man was arrogant, hypocritical, and a bully. But thankfully, he was also dumb as dirt. "Don't you worry. I'll handle this. You and Briar are completely safe here." Feeling the tension leave Mel's body, she added, "I need to go now, but when I get back, we're going to have a talk about your brother. It's time we dealt with that moron once and for all."

"SHIT. I BROKE my nail." Trudy thrust a hand in front of Cody.

Cody managed not to yell at her. Politely, she said, "I can take you back any time. Just say the word."

Trudy shrugged. "I've got nothing better to do. At least this way I get a good look around."

"The answer is still no. So why put yourself through this?"

Trudy took an emery board from her *Hello Kitty* backpack and filed the problem acrylic. "I don't get it. There's plenty of room for both concepts. We would gate the resort. Everyone could be confined to the one beach. You'd have the rest of the island to do your women-only thing."

Cody lifted her binoculars and scanned the slopes systematically. "What you don't seem to get is that Moon Island is not women-only just because we like it that way. It's an ancient tradition."

"Yeah, yeah." Trudy heaved a sigh. "How come when white people say something is traditional no one gives a crap, but when it's some tribe no one's ever heard of, well, that's a whole different story? It used to be traditional to crush little girl's feet all over China. Know what I'm saying?"

Cody cast a desperate look toward Glenn, who had so far stayed out of the discussion about the Moon Island Funeral Getaway concept.

"Some customs arise from spiritual belief, and others, such as foot-binding, do not," Glenn cut in helpfully. "In our culture, for example, millions of people believe Jesus was born at Christmastime, so all kinds of customs exist in recognition of this. Do you believe in Jesus, Trudy?"

"Not really. I mean I am a Christian as opposed to like...a Muslim or whatever. But I think all that Jesus stuff is pretty much a nice fairy tale. You know, if it makes people feel good, hey, that's cool. You have to believe in something, right?"

Glenn set down a couple of grid markers. "Do you give presents and have Christmas dinner and decorate a tree?"

"Sure. I love Christmas."

"In other words, you follow the customs even though you really don't believe in their basis."

Trudy seemed interested in this perspective. "You're right. I do. Lots of people do."

"Well, it's traditional," Glenn remarked in her level-headed way. "Imagine if a family of Buddhists from Thailand bought a house in your street and tried to bribe your homeowners' association to ban Christmas lights. How would you feel?"

Trudy was silent, her finely plucked eyebrows drawn

together in a frown of concentration. "I know some Buddhists," she said finally. "They're cool. I mean, they would never do shit like that."

"Why not?"

"Respect," Trudy said with conviction. "They respect other people's rights to believe what they want. Actually, we could all learn something from the Buddhist religion."

"I couldn't agree more. So if you bought a house in their country, you wouldn't expect them to close the local temple, stop all that chanting, and take down their prayer flags?"

"Of course not!" Trudy tugged the Minnie Mouse bows in her hair indignantly.

"Can you give me a reason why the Cook Islanders warrant less respect for their customs than the Thais?" Glenn sounded genuinely puzzled.

Trudy's face was a picture. "No."

"But you've just been telling Cody they should change a custom that's important to them so your dad can lease a block of land here. You think this is reasonable because many of them don't really believe in those goddesses and their curses any more. Kind of like you and Jesus."

Trudy took off her sunglasses and wiped them carefully. "They didn't give you that Ph. D. for eating your lunch, did they? You're really smart."

"I'm no smarter than you. I'm older and I get paid to think about these issues. That's all."

"I wanted to go to college," Trudy confessed. "But everyone said it would be a waste of time. You know. I'd only embarrass myself."

To Cody's surprise, Glenn said, "If you want to apply for college, come and see me in the new semester."

Trudy looked startled. "Really?"

"I think you'd do great. You're open-minded, and you're not afraid to challenge yourself. I wish I could say the same for half my students."

That was nice, Cody thought. Glenn could easily make a lowbrow like Trudy feel inadequate, but instead she was encouraging her to expand her horizons beyond the mall.

Trudy was actually blushing. "You know what? I might take you up on that."

"I hope you do," Glenn said, passing her a new ball of twine and a bunch of markers. "Now, what say you take that zone down there, and we'll climb this rise?"

They watched Trudy until she was in position before starting up a steep incline.

"Did you mean it?" Cody asked Glenn a little later. "About Trudy."

"Trudy is who she is because that's all anyone expects of her. There's no mother in the picture, and I doubt she's ever had any approval from her father that didn't relate to her looks."

"Those breasts," Cody muttered.

"If there's one thing my life has taught me," Glenn said, "that's to look beyond appearances. Things...people...are not always as they seem."

"Tell me about it." Cody grinned. "Once you've run a place like this nothing surprises you."

"Do you think Olivia is alive?" Glenn asked.

Cody met her deep blue eyes. "Something my life taught me is that anything is possible."

RILEY FLOPPED DOWN under a banana palm and took a long drink. It was too soon to give up, but she knew they were wasting their time searching this zone around the cliff tops again. If Olivia had made it up here, which was highly unlikely, she was probably halfway across the island by now. The search party had spent the entire morning combing this area, then Cody had to go back to Villa Luna to check on Annabel's sick cousin. Glenn had suggested they split up to cover more ground and took Trudy with her, a good idea, since everyone was about ready to strangle her.

The only problem with Glenn's plan was that Riley had just spent the last three hours with Merris Randall instead of the one person she came here to be with. "Hey, Merris," she called. "Take a break."

Wiping her face, Merris sat down a few feet away and gulped some water.

"I think we should start working our way up toward the cottage," Riley suggested. "That's where she'll be headed if she's going in the right direction. If she's gotten lost east of here, the others will find her."

"Sounds reasonable," Merris said.

Something in her tone told Riley she was close to breaking. Riley tried to imagine how she would be feeling if it was Glenn who was missing. Insane, she thought. But Merris was not the dramatic type, and maybe she didn't feel for Olivia what Riley felt for Glenn. It sounded like they'd only hooked up on vacation. She felt a pang of envy. Even a short fling with Glenn would be better than nothing.

"How are you doing?" she asked Merris.

"I'm not sure. I keep thinking she's fallen down somewhere and she's hurt and we won't find her 'til it's too late."

"People can survive for days like that, even weeks if there's food and water." Riley did her best to sound confident. "She's got a good chance."

"I can't believe this has happened." Merris gazed out to sea. "I waited my whole life for her. From the moment I saw her, I knew."

Riley blinked. "Love at first sight?" Merris didn't seem the type.

She seemed lost in thought. When she looked up, her eyes were flooded with tears. "The Chinese say an invisible thread connects those destined to meet. It stretches but never breaks. I never understood how that could be until I saw her. It was like a jolt, as if that thread had suddenly pulled tight."

"Do you think that means she's your soul mate?"

"I've never believed in that. People say they've met their soul mate and six months later she's the bitch from hell."

"Not in any big hurry to swap blood vials, huh?"

Merris gave a self-deprecating laugh. "You'll have to ask me that in a year's time."

"Well, look at it this way," Riley said. "If you two are truly meant to be, then she has to be alive."

THE POOL WAS cooler than the ocean. Standing beneath the waterfall, Olivia rinsed her hair of salt and sand, and cleaned the dried blood from her chest. She felt profoundly content. Surviving a near-death situation would tend to do that, she supposed. She shook the water from her limbs and used a quilt to dry herself off. Her bra and panties were as clean as she could get them. She knew she should put them on, but it was hard to give a damn whether she made it out of this naked or semi-naked.

She contemplated the slippery latticework that connected her grotto to the world above. It wasn't that far to climb. About twenty-five feet. If she didn't make it, she could always retreat down the high steps and along the narrow path until she found her way back to the beach. She wondered what time of day it was. A few hours earlier, she had been certain she could hear her name being called and had tried to respond. But her throat was so hoarse that after just a few cries for help, her voice was reduced to an inaudible croak.

Olivia dragged her wet undergarments on, and studied the heavy coin she had found in the pool. How had an old gold guinea found its way to the Cook Islands? Missionaries? She had explored the shallower parts of the pool in case there were more, but this seemed to be the only one. Someone had thrown it in for luck, she surmised, and there it would stay. Making a wish of her own, she cast the coin back into the still waters and fingered the necklace she was wearing. Should she leave it behind?

In her dream, the dark-haired woman had given it to her. It would always remind her of what she had learned here, Olivia thought. There was so much she would take away with her. She had a sharp new sense of her own power, a conviction that she was the author of her own destiny. The Fates had permitted her a glimpse of a present she could not bear to face and a future she was in danger of creating. Like Dickens' Scrooge confronting the ghost of Christmas Yet to Come, she did not like what she saw.

Olivia trailed her hand through the tranquil water. With absolute certainty, she knew there was magic in this place she could never reveal to anyone. She felt as if she had become the keeper of a mystery and that others also knew what she knew but did not speak of it. Feeling a deep sense of gratitude, she removed the plain gold pinky ring that had been her great grandmother's wedding band. She kissed it and placed it behind a small stalagmite, making a pledge to the guardian of the cave.

"I promise to keep your secrets," she whispered. "Now please help me get out of here."

Chapter
Nineteen

MERRIS HOISTED HER backpack onto her shoulders and took a final lingering look out to sea. Riley had gone on ahead of her, marking out the circuitous path they would take back to Frangipani Cottage. Avoiding the tracks they had followed earlier, they would instead skirt a route around the *makatea*, then veer through the center of the island.

Merris picked up her pace to close the distance between them. It was obvious Riley was not happy being stuck with her for the afternoon instead of pairing off with the object of her desire. Merris had a sneaking suspicion Glenn Howick had arranged things that way. She had to be aware her student was besotted. The woman was probably trying to maintain appropriate boundaries. Sharing a cottage couldn't be easy.

She paused to call Olivia's name as she had a thousand times that day. The jungle groaned and creaked in response. A small flock of birds burst from a treetop, raucously decrying her presence. To the east, something stirred just above the undergrowth. Merris trained her binoculars on the spot. It looked like someone or something was making a single palm frond wave above the dense canopy of banana and papaya. It was probably one of the other searchers, she thought, picturing terrible Trudy with a broken ankle. This was roughly the area where Glenn had led her team earlier.

A bolt of hope quickened her weary limbs nonetheless, and she started pushing her way through the heavy leaves. Most likely it was Riley, she reasoned, trying not to set herself up for disappointment. If the younger woman had sidetracked in that direction, maybe she had found something. The thought gave Merris new energy as she struggled over the remains of large trees that had been brought down by the hurricane everyone still talked about. Crossing the steep, jagged *makatea* was frustratingly slow, and as she drew closer it was harder to see the palm waving above the jungle canopy.

Calling Olivia's name again, she jostled through a thicket of creepers almost up to her armpits. Something thrashed against the vegetation a short distance away. Wrenching her way through the tangled plants, Merris broke into a shambling run. There was still no answer to her cries, yet someone was obviously desperate to get her attention. Trampling ferns and orchids, shoving huge leaves out of her face, she yelled, "I'm coming. Stay where you are."

Through a tapestry of light and dark foliage, a pale form moved like a chimera. Merris glimpsed a dark head and familiar shape, then Olivia was in her arms. Sobbing uncontrollably, Merris grabbed a fistful of black hair and buried her face in it, barely able to believe Olivia was real and warm and alive. "I love you," she gasped, and felt Olivia's hand, cool and reassuring against her cheek.

"I know." Olivia indicated her throat, mouthing, "My voice is gone."

Her body was a tapestry of cuts and bruises, her bare feet and hands bloody from the *makatea*. Merris dropped her pack and lowered Olivia to the jungle floor, tearing off her own shirt to wrap it around the woman she loved. "I need to get help," she said.

Olivia grabbed her arm in mute pleading. Her eyes were panicked.

"It's okay, baby." Merris covered her face in kisses. "I'm not going anywhere." She shook out the contents of her pack and found the hand flares Cody had issued that morning.

Trying not to shoot herself by mistake, she turned the arming knob and struck a flare down hard against a rocky ledge. The result was a satisfying orange flame that leapt into the sky and gradually descended in a plume of colored smoke. Just to be sure, Merris set off a second one before hurrying back to Olivia's side.

"That should do it," she said, taking the injured woman's hand. She was terribly cold, Merris observed with alarm. Her skin was clammy, and she seemed to be drifting toward sleep. Certain this was not a good sign, Merris cradled her close and stroked her cheek, urging, "Stay awake, baby. They'll find us soon. Just hang on."

Olivia turned her head into Merris's shoulder, shivering violently. Wracking her brains, Merris tried to remember what she had ever heard about people with shock or hypothermia. She felt for Olivia's pulse and counted. It was very fast, and her breathing was shallow. Foraging urgently in her pack, she retrieved the first aid kit only to stare helplessly at the contents.

Hypodermic, pain killers, vials of who-knew-what, band-aids, antiseptic, candy, bandages. She had no idea what to do with any of it.

A crunching sound cut through her panic-stricken thoughts and she looked up to see Trudy pounce from the undergrowth. Staring open-mouthed at Merris and Olivia, the young woman jumped up and down, waving her arms like a cheerleader, her shrill voice piercing the jungle canopy. "Over here! I found them! Glenn! Help!"

Dazed, Merris could not even manage a hello before a machete lopped the top off a banana palm and Glenn Howick stepped into view looking like a female Indiana Jones. Hands on hips, big white smile, she surveyed the scene with the air of a woman who had seen real danger and judged this child's play by comparison. "Need a hand?" she said.

"TRAUMA AND SHOCK," Violet pronounced many hours later in the living room at Villa Luna. "Twenty-four hours running on adrenalin, and all of a sudden she's safe. Everything caught up with her, the adrenalin took a nosedive, and shock set in."

"I nearly had heart failure," Merris admitted. "She was so excited when I found her, then she just crashed."

"She'll be much better in the morning," Violet assured her. "I've put a few stitches in her feet. And she won't be washing any dishes for a while with those hands. But she's fine. They'll only tell you the same thing at the hospital."

"We'll take her in for a check-up anyway," Cody said. "Annabel will have to pick up the women for the rituals."

Trudy lit up. "Do we get to watch?"

"Only if we're invited," Annabel said, bringing a large platter of shrimp from the kitchen.

Chris came after her with pasta and salad, saying, "Does anyone know where the parmesan is?"

"No idea, but this Chianti is great," Riley said, filling glasses and handing them out.

"I'll take one of those," a voice wheezed from the doorway.

"She insisted," Melanie said, pushing Olivia into the room ahead of her.

"Sweetie." Merris helped her onto a sofa. "You should be asleep."

"And miss my own party? I don't think so."

Glenn stood and raised her glass. "To Olivia, for making it."

Merris closed her hand over Olivia's as they drank. She

knew she was grinning like a fool, but she couldn't help herself. "Last night was the worst night of my life," she said, not caring if she sounded corny. "And tonight is the best."

People were helping themselves to food, but Merris had no appetite for anything except the woman next to her. This was what they meant by *lovesick*, she thought. All she wanted to do was curl up in bed next to Olivia and stare at her all night. Mentally shaking herself, she asked, "Can I get you something to eat?"

Olivia shook her head. Her dark granite eyes held fast to Merris. There was something new and candid in their depths, something meant for Merris alone. Her heart jumped. She was aware of noise and laughter around her, but it was all mere clatter. A silence rich with meaning stretched between her and Olivia. In wordless conversation, they smiled at one another.

Almost solemnly, Olivia kissed Merris's cheek. "I want you with me. I want us to be together."

Merris was sure everyone could probably see her heart pounding. Olivia loved her. She hadn't said the words, but her eyes shone bright with promise. Elated, she said, "You know, I'll never let you go."

Olivia smiled without reserve. "I'm counting on it."

"Get a room, you two," Riley groaned, reminding Merris they had an audience.

Merris slipped her arm around Olivia. "Public announcement. We're an item."

"We kind of had that figured." Annabel's silken drawl was tinted with genuine delight.

"You two met a while ago, didn't you?" Chris asked.

"Actually, we met on Valentine's day," Merris replied. "I was having dinner with a Barbie doll collector, and Olivia was at another table ignoring me. Later, I swept her off her feet by saving her from falling down a flight of stairs." Lifting Olivia's bandaged hand, she planted a kiss on her fingers, adding, "That's my story and I'm sticking to it."

Trudy was enthralled. "Oh, my God. That's so karmic." In case anyone was confused, she explained, "That's Buddhist. It's like when a kind of cosmic coincidence happens. I believe in that."

Violet nodded. "So do I, dear."

"There must be something going on in the stars," Melanie exclaimed. "Chris fell down a cave a couple of days ago, and she found a skeleton!"

"Where was this?" Glenn seemed highly interested.

"The Kopeka cave southwest of here. I fell down a hole and

ended up in a smaller cave. Only someone had beaten me to it. The poor guy never got out."

"A man?" Trudy cast a pointed look at Cody.

"I guess the curse took care of him," Cody said with satisfaction.

"You and Annabel believe this curse is real?" Glenn asked.

"Put it this way," Annabel responded, "I respect the possibility. This is an ancient place. Who knows its karma?" She threw a quick smile of acknowledgment at Trudy.

"Men do come here sometimes," Cody said. "There's our other pilot Bevan, and the chef brings a couple of guys to help her when we're busy. But they're invited."

"Unlike the schmuck in the cave." Chris chuckled.

"What are you going to do about him?" Glenn asked.

"Leave him where he is," Annabel replied. "The goddesses of the island took him."

It seemed so primitive. "But what about his family?" Merris objected. "Surely it's important to try and identify him."

"The bones are centuries old," Annabel said. "I spoke to the *ruahine* about him, and she says the island is his final resting place. I can live with that."

Melanie looked like she wanted to say something, but Chris placed a hand on her arm, distracting her with a comment Merris could not hear.

Glenn glanced at Chris. "I'd love to see the cave if you would show me."

"I'll show you where it is, but I'm not going down there again."

"It can't be Hine te Ana's cave," Annabel said. "It's too far inland."

"I'm starting to think this cave really is entirely mythical." Glenn sounded resigned. "Not all legends are founded in fact."

"Oh, no. I can assure you it does exist," Violet interjected.

Olivia seemed fidgety. Guessing she must be in pain, Merris murmured, "I'll fetch you some Motrin."

"No, I'm fine." She toyed absently with the shell and pearl necklace she had been wearing ever since Merris found her.

"How do you know the cave exists?" Glenn asked Violet.

"Because a woman who lived here told me." Shooting a quick glance at Annabel, she said, "Rebecca found it just before she left the island."

"I knew it!" Glenn got up and paced to the table, pouring herself more wine.

"What's so special about this cave?" Merris asked.

"According to legend, it houses a magical pool of water. If

you drink from it your wish is granted." Glenn recounted the
story of how Hine te Ana swam to the island and sat in the cave
mourning the loss of her daughter who had drowned in the
ocean. "Her tears were so profuse they formed a pool and when
she looked into it, the moon goddess Marama took pity on her
and granted her greatest wish. Between one night and the next,
she could see her daughter once more."

"What a beautiful story," Melanie said. "So they ended up
together again."

"Not exactly. The vision only lasted that single day. Hine te
Ana was so upset she made the moon goddess promise she
would see her daughter again one day. She never gave up
looking. They say she would sit below the cliffs calling for her
daughter and singing a lament, and sometimes she would take
the form of a dolphin and scour the ocean for her."

Merris heard Olivia catch her breath and checked in with her
again. Her cheeks were flushed, and her eyes seemed almost too
bright.

"There are the usual claims about sailors hearing singing or
seeing a beautiful maiden standing on the Scared Shore,"
Annabel commented. "And during the rituals that take place
there, they say the goddess sometimes chooses a woman and
leads her to the cave to have a wish granted."

Glenn turned to Violet. "Is that how Rebecca came to see it?
Was she a participant?"

"I don't think so." Violet's crinkled face was transformed by
memory. It was as if she had to make an effort to return to the
present. Vaguely, she said, "There was a map. Annie mentioned
it to me."

Melanie exchanged a brief, wide-eyed look with Chris, then
lowered her head.

"A map?" Glenn cast an accusing look at Cody and Annabel,
as if they had been holding out on her.

"Rebecca was my aunt's lover," Annabel said. "She was
killed in an accident. If there was a map, my aunt didn't keep it."

"And a good thing, too," Cody said. "Imagine if people
thought they could come here and get a wish granted. It would
make Lourdes look like a picnic."

Olivia tugged at Merris's arm and whispered something in
her ear in an urgent voice. Astonished, Merris said, "You were in
the cave?"

The room fell silent.

Olivia took a sip of wine and a mouthful of the honey Violet
kept pressing on her. In a small voice, she croaked, "I spent the
night there. That's where this necklace came from."

"And I thought you'd blown a years' salary at Harry Winston!" Annabel laughed.

Riley looked stunned. "Where is it? I can't believe you found it. I mean, we searched every square inch of those fucking cliffs."

"Is it true about the magic pool?" Melanie asked hopefully.

"There is a pool." Olivia hesitated. "But...I'm sorry. I don't think..."

Chris took Melanie's hand. "You didn't notice any miracles happening when you drank some?" she asked Olivia. "There was no pot of gold or anything?"

Olivia studied her hands. Guardedly, she said, "It's very lovely, but it's just water."

Merris had the distinct impression there was something she wasn't saying. She looked more closely at the necklace. It was finely woven from leather and some kind of thread. Delicate shells were dotted between huge silver-gray pearls she recognized from past experience. They were the South Sea kind Allegra had blown serious money on. If such a valuable trinket had come from this legendary cave, what else was there?

Glenn looked like she had just won the lottery. "Annabel, I can guarantee not to publish the location. All I need is a few photographs of the interior for verification." She turned to Olivia. "If you could take us there..."

"I'm not sure if I can locate it. I can't remember much about finding my way out." Olivia seemed uneasy. "Anyway, it's not for me to decide. I can't tell you any more without breaking the *tapu*."

Obviously the subject was upsetting for her. It was part of the trauma she had just been through, Merris surmised. If Glenn and Riley wanted to revisit the area, she would take them herself. She would not allow Olivia to be stressed.

Annabel looked torn. "I don't think I can make that decision either. We'll need to speak to the *ruahine*."

"I DON'T SEE the problem," Riley said, pushing the cottage door open. "It's not like you'd be printing a map."

Glenn followed her into their modest sitting room. They'd spent the walk from Villa Luna to Annie's Cottage discussing the photographs and statements they would need to support her thesis. Glenn wanted to feel optimistic that the *ruahine* would grant the access they needed, but she knew it was unlikely.

"The cave is sacred to women," she said. "If we publish photographs, men will see them. I imagine the *ruahine* would consider that a breach of the *tapu*."

"That's ridiculous," Riley retorted. "I mean, it makes sense not to let men into the place, but a photograph is just ink on paper. Who cares if a guy looks at it?"

"It's not that simple. Even in our own culture we don't have the right to publish a picture of another person or a private event of theirs without a release." Glenn sat down in an armchair and shook out her ponytail. "I think we're on thin ice dismissing the constraints imposed by a different culture, then conveniently failing to observe those of our own. Either we respect the *tapu*, or we are guided by privacy law and copyright. We can't disclaim both."

"That's all very principled, but if we don't do this, sooner or later someone else will." Earnest in her outrage on Glenn's professional behalf, she added, "Then they'll get the credit for proving your theory."

"Which would be hard to swallow," Glenn conceded.

The ethics of this project had troubled her since the outset. She had committed enormous energy to documenting spiritual traditions that existed outside of the dominant patriarchal paradigms. When women knew the truth of their own spiritual past, they could reclaim a part of their heritage the major religions sought to deny. Surely the importance to the many outweighed the concerns of the few.

Yet Moon Island was home to a living spirituality, perhaps one of the last vestiges of woman-centered belief on the planet. If laying bare its secrets contributed to its final disappearance, was she any better than the arrogant missionaries who had attempted to wipe the old traditions out?

Riley was watching her with the usual combination of hero-worship and lust. But there was also disbelief. No doubt she was entertaining the appalling possibility that Glenn was about to tumble from her pedestal. *If she only knew the half of it.* Glenn twisted the golden butterfly at her throat and contemplated her options. She liked Riley, and she had hoped that working with her more closely might help her move beyond her obvious crush. Failing that, Glenn would have to shut her out and keep her at a distance as she did most people.

There was a third option, but Glenn had no plans to reveal a truth that could destroy her credibility as a feminist scholar. Like someone in a witness protection program, she was constantly haunted by a past she feared would catch up to her one day. Ten years had passed since she had completed gender reassignment, and she had built a new life where no one knew the man she had once struggled to be. She had kept only her name as a symbol of her parents' confusion over a child whose gender doctors could not determine at birth.

"Can I ask you something?" Riley said, her voice edgy.

Bracing herself for a declaration of undying love, Glenn said, "Sure."

"I was wondering why you chose me for this."

Because you're an outsider too. It was not the only reason, but it factored. "Why do *you* think you're here?"

Riley started to speak, then stopped. "Well, it's not because I'm academically gifted, is it?"

"That's subjective. When something interests you, your work is very lucid and—"

"You have to know I'm in love with you," Riley cut her off, eyes blazing. "And please don't label it a crush."

Glenn mentally voiced the neatly worded rebuffs she had prepared for this moment. The rational discussion about the ethics of teacher-student dating, the power imbalance, their age difference and the fact that Riley had already dated another faculty member with unfortunate consequences. But that was intellectual.

Weighing her words, she said, "I'm honored that you care for me, Riley, and I truly wish I felt the same way. But I don't."

"You're not gay. Is that it?" Riley looked crestfallen.

Wanting to let her down as gently as possible, Glenn avoided answering.

Taking her silence as affirmation, Riley said, "Now I feel really stupid."

"Don't. We should have had this conversation a long time ago."

"I'm sorry if I've embarrassed you."

"I'm not embarrassed. I'm flattered."

Riley regained a little of her usual self-assurance. "Does that mean you'd date me if you were gay?"

"Who knows," Glenn said. "I hear a lot of women find you irresistible."

Riley gazed at her with a mixture of hope and dejection. "Way too many," she commented darkly.

She would get over it, Glenn thought. She was only twenty-three. Feelings took on mammoth proportions at that age, but they also changed as one grew. Glenn had moments of attraction to Riley. In another time and place, she might have acted on them. Right now, however, Riley Mason needed a mentor more than she needed a lover, whether she knew it or not.

Glenn extended her hand. "So...friends?"

Riley took it. "Just don't tell anyone about this. Okay?"

GAZING ACROSS THE fruit-covered mango trees toward Passion Bay, Annabel said, "The initials on the map...R.J.G. Those were Rebecca's initials."

"Your aunt's lover?" Chris felt a small pang of disappointment. It was all falling into place. This Rebecca must have found the map and explored the marked spot. What she had discovered was not treasure but this legendary sacred cave.

"She must have resealed the map and written the warning in Maori," Annabel said. "I suppose we could just put it back with the skeleton. Let sleeping dogs lie."

The idea offended the lawyer in Chris. "Why risk someone else finding it and deciding to keep it?"

"You're right," Annabel said. "I'll put it in a bank deposit box."

"You're not curious about the cave?"

"I think if ever I'm meant to see it, I will. Anything else seems like a violation." Pensively, Annabel continued, "I live in the most beautiful place on earth. I'd like to keep its guardians on my side."

Chris watched the sky flood with wild dark peach. The jungle seemed to be holding its breath in anticipation of the first shock of sunlight. For the first time in months, she felt excited about life. "Your idea about hanging out my shingle in Avarua — I'm going to think about it."

Annabel smiled. "Well, you already have friends here."

It was a good feeling, Chris thought, as they went indoors a little later. Maybe she would go back and pick up her life where she had left off, or maybe she would embark on a whole new future. The choice was hers.

WITH A CONTENTED sigh, Olivia smiled up at Merris. "I'm glad we came back here instead of staying up at the Villa."

Her body felt raw all over, and she was sluggish from the painkillers she took before bed, yet she felt intensely alive. Snuggling closer, she recalled the first time they'd made love. It was just two nights ago, here in this plain bed in her cottage, yet it seemed to belong to another life.

Merris's arm tightened around Olivia. "If you want to go home I can change our flights."

"I have a better idea. Why don't you change your reservation? We could both stay here in my cottage "

"If I must," Merris said.

Olivia gave her a playful prod. "Well, we could stay at your place. But you know, since mine is bigger..."

Laughing, Merris pushed Olivia flat on her back, trapping her in a firm embrace. "We'll see about that." With sensual deliberation she kissed her, claiming her mouth with such intensity Olivia's stomach plunged.

As their kiss deepened, Olivia opened her eyes. Dilated with moonlight and passion, Merris's pupils shone liquid black. The two women gazed at one another, mouths fused, hearts keeping time. They had said they would not make love tonight, yet Olivia could not imagine falling asleep without feeling Merris inside her once more. The very thought made her moan softly with anticipation.

Merris instantly drew back. "God, I'm sorry." She tenderly kissed Olivia's cheek.

"You didn't hurt me." Olivia kept an insistent hold on her. "Please. I want you."

"Baby... " Merris cupped her face. "We have all the time in the world."

Olivia rested her bandaged hands above her head and kicked the bedclothes off. "Indulge me," she said playfully. "I'm not sore *everywhere.*"

Merris rested her forehead against Olivia's. "I love you."

Olivia knew she should simply echo the words but her mouth refused to form them. Wrapping her legs around Merris, she pulled her down hard. "Show me," she said.

Chapter Twenty

THE *RUAHINE* WAS a big woman in every sense of the word, but what struck Olivia most forcefully were the tattoos on her arms. Bands of reddish-orange triangles encircled each wrist, and a sharply cut featherlike pattern extended up her forearms. Almost six feet tall, the priestess wore a plain orange cotton *pareu* skirt and a short-sleeved white top printed with orange flowers. Her black hair was streaked with gray, and a garland of waxy frangipani encircled her head.

Olivia was not sure what she had had expected; a more exotic tribal costume, she supposed, feeling like a silly tourist. The *ruahine* also seemed interested in her, glancing past the women clustered around to make eye contact. Olivia felt her stomach flutter when she said something to the group and came toward her carrying an *ei* of cream and pink flowers. She wondered how she was supposed to address this important woman. Annabel called her Aunty Akaiti, but they knew one another.

"*Kia orana* Olivia." She placed the flower garland around Olivia's neck.

"*Kia orana.*" Olivia returned the Cook Island greeting everyone in this part of the world used.

The *ruahine* shook her hand. "I'm Akaiti Rataro. I heard about your swim."

How was she going to explain her appalling breach of *tapu*? Bad enough she boated around the forbidden cliffs, let alone set foot on the Sacred Shore. "I'm terribly sorry..." Olivia began.

With a big rich laugh, the *ruahine* enfolded her in a powerful hug. "Child, what are you sorry for? We've been expecting you." She held Olivia at arm's length and looked her up and down. Her light brown eyes seemed drawn to Olivia's necklace. Moving the fragrant *ei* aside, she lifted it reverently. "I know this *tàhei.*"

Awkwardly, Olivia smiled. How was it going to sound when she admitted she had helped herself to it from the cave? In defense of this *faux pas*, she recounted her hallucination. "I had a dream that a princess took me to a cave. She gave me the necklace. When I woke up I was really there." Olivia started to remove the necklace to return it, but the *ruahine* stopped her.

"No, this belongs to you."

Olivia's eyes fell to her tattoos. "She had these, too. The woman in my dream." She met Akaiti's eyes. "Who was she?"

Akaiti raised her eyebrows as if it were blindingly obvious. "Hine te Ana."

The goddess of the legend? Olivia was amazed, yet not entirely surprised. Somehow she had known it from the start.

The *ruahine* smiled and called the other women over, speaking to them in rapid Maori. Pausing, she placed a hand on Olivia's shoulder and adopted a more formal tone. "*E mihi ki te tamāhine o Hine te Ana.*"

Apparently this was some kind of introduction. In response, the island women formed a line and each in her turn shook hands with Olivia and kissed her cheek. A few yards away, Merris was smiling, but Annabel had an odd look on her face. Olivia felt embarrassed. She supposed they were making a fuss of her because she was living evidence that Hine te Ana's legendary swim was indeed possible. Glenn had certainly found this inspiring.

An old, stooped woman leaning on an elaborately carved stick took her hand, and Olivia bent low to receive her greeting. "Our mothers waited for you," she said in halting English.

Olivia smiled at this sweet welcome. The elderly woman had probably translated literally some popular phrase in her own language. Hoping her response was appropriate, she said, "Thank you. I'm honored to be here."

When the formalities were through, the *ruahine* walked Olivia over to Annabel, whom she took aside, saying, "The return of the daughter is a great day for us."

Glenn seemed acutely interested in their conversation. To Olivia, she said, "They say the gods finally promised Hine te Ana that one day her drowned daughter would return to these islands. Until then, the goddess was destined to roam the oceans forever in the form of a dolphin, searching for her."

"Oh my God. They think it's me?" Olivia exchanged a dumbfounded look with Merris.

"My team just finished interviewing all the women here. They believe the daughter's return signals a period of good fortune for their people."

"Oh, no," Olivia said. "I feel like such a fraud."

"The *ruahine* doesn't think so."

"You're saying they think Olivia is a reincarnation of their goddess's daughter?" Merris sounded dubious, but also proud.

"Belief in reincarnation is common to most of the world's non-Christian religions," Glenn said. "The Cook Islanders were converted less than two hundred years ago, so the concept still endures for many of them."

Knowing Merris's question was not completely academic, Olivia said lightly, "For all that I believe in reincarnation, this does seem a little far-fetched. I'm a white woman born in London."

Riley had joined them and seemed shocked by this statement. "You think reincarnation occurs along intra-racial lines?"

"Do I strike you as a fascist?" Olivia coolly responded.

Before Riley could answer, Cody joined their group, plainly brimming with news. "You'll never guess what they're talking about," she said, cocking her head toward Annabel and Akaiti, who were still deep in conversation. "The *ruahine* has invited us to join them on the Sacred Shore tonight for part of the rituals. All of us, I mean. Me and Annabel, all the guests on the island, and even you guys from Anthropologists Anonymous."

"That's incredible," Glenn gasped. "I don't know what to say. Thank you."

"Don't thank me, thank her," Cody glanced at Olivia. "As far as Aunty's concerned, you're flavor of the month. It's pretty incredible. They've never invited outsiders before, not even me and Annabel."

"They think she's some kind of goddess," Trudy chipped in, arriving to offer a fruit platter around.

"They do not," Olivia said, disconcerted by the attention. "They mistakenly believe I'm the reincarnation of Hine te Ana's daughter. And I'm going to go over there right now and tell the *ruahine* it's not the case."

"Spoilsport!" Trudy protested. "I want to see the ceremony, and so does everyone else. Anyway, how do you know you're not this *tamàhine* person they're talking about?"

"You have to admit it was astounding that you survived," Merris said gently. "What's the harm in letting them believe it was more than plain dumb luck?"

Olivia took a slice of watermelon from Trudy's platter and bit into the crisp pink flesh. *Plain dumb luck*, she repeated the phrase mentally. The truth was something quite different. But who would believe what had actually happened to her? By putting an end to this speculation, she could at least avoid awkward questions.

"I suppose I'm not comfortable because this feels like

cultural voyeurism to me," she said finally.

"I understand where you're coming from," Glenn said. "But they've invited us, and it would be an insult if we declined. Whether you believe you're the *tamàhine* or not, their *ruahine* has identified you. Do you really want to humiliate her by telling everyone she doesn't know what she's talking about?"

"In case you hadn't guessed, Glenn *really* wants to see these rituals," Cody remarked, lightening the tension.

Glenn had the grace to look embarrassed. "I'm sorry if that came across as emotional blackmail."

"It doesn't mean you're wrong," Olivia said. "This is their land and their beliefs." Aware of relief breaking over the faces around her, she added, "I guess if we're going to this ceremony tonight, I should get some rest."

ANNABEL WATCHED MERRIS help Olivia onto the jetty, then signaled the all-clear to Cody at the helm.

Watching the two women walk away holding hands, Akaiti raised her eyebrows and playfully prodded Annabel, saying, "*Kua kòwhiria e ia he whakapiringa wahine takàpui.*"

Smiling, Annabel said, "We're everywhere, Aunty."

Merris and Olivia turned to wave, and the entire boat waved back, some of the women giggling as they added two and two. In the Cook Islands, homosexuality was illegal for men, but lesbians received no mention in the law. Annabel had met a few gay Cook Island women, but most could not bear the pressure, within their community, to marry and have children. Eventually they left Rarotonga to live in New Zealand.

Since living in the islands, she had encountered none of the overt homophobia she had known back home. But she was never quite sure whether the officials and organizations she dealt with knew that she and most of Moon Island's guests were lesbian, or whether they simply chose to ignore it. Aunty Akaiti often joked that she wished her own four daughters had chosen women instead of their lazy husbands. But Annabel knew the *ruahine* pitied her childlessness. She had once clipped an article on artificial insemination from a magazine and slipped it into Annabel's hand.

A couple of the women were pointing and chattering, and Annabel crossed the cruiser to see what the excitement was about. To her astonishment, a lavishly appointed yacht was approaching. Grabbing some binoculars, she caught the name *Avarua Maiden*, one of charter vessels that frequented the Cook Islands.

"They must be doing at least six knots," Cody said when Annabel joined her. "They're headed straight for us."

"Maybe they're in trouble," Annabel said. It was rare to see a charter boat this close to Moon Island.

Cody radioed the coast guard for their call sign. "Let's talk to them," she said, slowing to headway speed and bringing the cruiser port side. She spoke briefly into the radio, rolled her eyes, and handed it over to Annabel. "It's George Toki. He wants permission to land a passenger."

Annabel muttered a mild expletive. Every now and then a journalist tried to cover the Moon Island rituals. The last one had hired a chopper and almost crashed it into the cliffs. But that was nothing compared with the saga unfolding in her ear. George's passenger was none other than her cousin, Roscoe Worth, who claimed to be here at the express behest of his personal savior the Lord Jesus Christ. In other words, his wife had ordered it.

"I don't believe this," Annabel said, her fury building by the second. "Melanie's brother thinks he's going to pay us a call."

Cody's jaw dropped. "The guy with the assault rifle under his mattress and the family values website? Want me to board them and give him a knuckle sandwich?"

"Don't tempt me." In her most formal tone, Annabel responded, "Landing is denied. Yes, I know he's my cousin."

Muffled voices argued at the other end, then George poured a tale of woe into her ear about how the big American wasn't going to pay the rest of his charter fee if he couldn't land. Worse still, Roscoe claimed to know the minister at George's church and he would be shamed next Sunday.

"Tell my cousin I will see him in Avarua tomorrow. Okay?"

"He says he's coming back with the police."

"George, do you know who I have here with me? Akaiti Rataro." She caught a faint whimper. "Do you really want me to tell her about this?"

"I already told him he's going to get cursed," George whined.

"It won't just be him who gets cursed. What's your wife going to say when everything starts shrinking?"

"Please. No, I'll..."

An American voice took over. "Don't you go filling his fool head with native superstition. This is a Christian country."

"Go back to Avarua, Roscoe. You have no business here."

"I'm here on the Lord's business," her cousin snapped predictably. "You may choose the path to damnation, but I will not stand back and see my own flesh and blood contaminated by a fetid plague of godlessness and perversion!"

Annabel had heard it all before. "If you attempt to land, I'll charge you with trespassing, and you can spend a couple of nights in jail."

"I will not leave these islands until I have plucked that innocent babe from the halls of abomination."

"Have you no shame? Your sister is a sick woman, and here you are, trying to steal her child."

"My wife and I offered to open our home and our hearts to my sister," Roscoe declared with impassioned pomposity. "There is still time for her to repent and be saved. Would you deny her the chance to spend her final days safe in the bosom of our Lord?"

Annabel sighed. There was no reasoning with a brainwashed bigot like her cousin and her anger would only excite him. "I hear you, Roscoe, but this is not the time or place. You need to go back to Rarotonga, and I promise I will come and talk with you soon. Now, put George back on."

She was mildly surprised when he complied, but figured he probably needed to go on deck and smoke.

"Your cousin. He's a crazy man," George rasped into the radio.

"Yes, he is." Once more Annabel reminded the unhappy Cook Islander that his days of virility were numbered if his passenger was brought ashore. For good measure, she added, "And if I see your vessel in my lagoon, I'll sink it."

"Aw, shit," George moaned, adding a few additional comments in his mother tongue. "No worries. Okay? We're going back. No worries."

"Happy to hear it," Annabel said. "Have a great day. Over and out." She replaced the radio and drew a calming breath. With a quick glance at Cody, she said, "I trust that asswipe about as far as I could throw him. Let's drop the women off and get back ASAP."

Chapter
Twenty-one

"THERE'S A FAT guy in a sailor hat stealing bananas down there." Trudy pointed vaguely toward the trees below Villa Luna.

"A man?" Chris asked. "Are you sure?"

Trudy gave her a look. "Duh."

The color fled Melanie's face. "Oh, God. It's my brother." She scrambled off the chaise lounge, urging Chris, "Don't let him see me."

Chris swung her into her arms, instructing Trudy, "Delay him, would you, sweetie?"

"You got it," Trudy said with the confidence of a woman who snacked on men with comb-overs.

"What are we going to do?" Melanie burst into tears. "Do you think he knows?"

"He couldn't possibly," Chris said, carrying her indoors to her room. "I haven't filed anything yet."

"What if he stops us? He knows people. He has influence."

"Not in this part of the world." Chris stroked Melanie's hair off her face. "Take a deep breath. He can't do a thing. Trust me. Cody is a New Zealander, and Annabel automatically has residency as her domestic partner. They are about to legalize gay union there. Remember?"

"Yes. And the adoption papers are filed there, not back home." Melanie wiped her tears. "I'm being silly."

"She's your child. It's not silly at all. Listen to me. That lunatic will not set foot in this house while I'm here. You and Briar are completely safe."

Wide-eyed with panic, Melanie nodded. "Okay."

"Everything's going to be fine. Now if you'll excuse me, I have some ass to kick."

Melanie's hand caught hers. "Chris? If I was gay, I'd ask you to marry me."

Chris grinned. "Got a thing for lawyers, huh?"

The comment elicited a small giggle. "Maybe."

Relieved to see the tension clearing from Melanie's face, Chris closed her bedroom door and sidled a few paces along the hallway, listening carefully. Trudy was working it, from what she could hear. Chris briefly pondered her options, and decided killing the guy with her bare hands was probably a bad idea. Instead, she hurried to the sitting room where she'd left her backpack.

ANCHORED, THE *AVARUA Maiden* bobbed against the silver horizon north of Passion Bay, an outboard tied alongside. Cody put down her binoculars and said, "We've got company."

"That moron!" Annabel stored their life-jackets. "I knew he'd try his luck."

"Is there anything he can do? I mean, we're not going to jail over this, are we?"

"Chris says it's unlikely Roscoe could obtain a deportation order, and even if he did, the New Zealand government wouldn't honor it because their human rights legislation outlaws discrimination against gays."

Cody cut the motors and prepared to drop anchor. "Yeah. Back home, we're allowed to adopt same as anyone else."

"Whether we can risk taking Briar to visit Mom is another matter. She'll still be an American citizen."

"They could take her from us?"

Annabel sighed. "Conceivably."

"That's outrageous!"

Cody was surprised by her own reaction. Originally, she had felt bushwhacked when Chris and Annabel came back from Solarim full of their bright idea. Melanie was thrilled, and Annabel spent half the night talking in bed about converting Cody's seldom-used office to a playroom and eventually schooling Briar at home. Chris had lectured her on what a great thing it was she could do for her partner and how lucky they were that they would soon be able to tie the knot legally. Their union would provide Briar with the protections straight people took for granted.

Chris planned to visit New Zealand before heading back to the States and would engage a law firm there to complete the adoption. If Melanie couldn't make the trip for the court appearance, she could give a deposition in Avarua. The Cook Islands were a New Zealand territory, after all.

In the end, Cody had agreed to sign the papers with as much good grace as she could manage. Briar was a nice little baby, and she could see Annabel would be doing most of the mothering. It didn't seem like such a big price to pay for keeping everyone happy.

She lowered the outboard into the water, and they climbed down the ladder and dropped into the hull.

Annabel was as irate as Cody had ever seen her. "How dare he set foot here!" she fumed. "If he upsets Mel, I'll kill him."

"Maybe he could, er...disappear. We could tell his wife the local cannibals ate him."

Annabel managed a half-smile. "It's funny. I know he can't do anything to us, legally speaking, but the thing is, the guy is a nut. They don't play by the rules. I wouldn't put it past him to do something totally crazy."

"He already is," Cody said. "Now is not the time for any bloke to set foot on the island."

"You forget, Roscoe is wearing the armor of the righteous. You know, the kind that deflects heathen curses." Annabel's drawl was laced with irony.

Cody snorted. She wasn't sure if she really believed in the curse herself. On the other hand, in Australia everyone knew that if an Aboriginal pointed the bone at you, you were stuffed. In Haiti they stuck pins in dolls. Why should a Cook Islands curse be any different?

"How could you have a cousin like him?" she exclaimed. "What went wrong in the gene pool?"

"Well, my father's older brother married a woman whose fertility, shall we say...was not in question."

"Do you think it's occurred to Roscoe his dad might be some other guy?" Cody asked, as they waded to shore and started up the slope toward Villa Luna.

"Not in a thousand light years," Annabel said. "The saint who gave birth to him couldn't possibly be a fallen woman. He tells everyone he was premature."

"What I don't get is why he and Tammy Faye don't breed their own damn kids."

"God has not seen fit to bless them at this time."

"He's shooting blanks?"

"I didn't ask."

They both fell silent at the sound of loud giggling squeals coming from the verandah.

"What in hell—" Cody began.

Annabel caught her arm and they hid behind a mango tree. "Wait. I want to see this," she whispered.

Cody craned for a better look. Trudy and Annabel's cousin were all over one another. It was disgusting. She glanced sideways. Annabel had one hand clamped firmly over her mouth, trying to contain herself.

"I'm putting a stop to this," Cody said, but Annabel grabbed her and pointed to the opposite end of the verandah.

Hanging from a ladder, Chris Thompson had her camera trained on Roscoe's hypocritical butt.

Cody gave a low whistle. "Man, is he in trouble."

They waited a few more minutes until Trudy cried with well-staged disgust, "Get off me, you pig! Help!"

Apparently Roscoe mistook this for appreciation. He started wrestling his way out of his pants.

"Roscoe!" Annabel marched up the verandah and stood a few feet from the action, hands on her hips. "I'm placing you under arrest for attempted rape." As Cody dragged him off Trudy, she continued, "You have the right to remain silent, and I advise you to do so since no court of law in this part of the world is going to believe a word you say."

Chris had joined them. Smugly, she waved her camera. "A picture is worth a thousand words."

"Shall I cuff him?" Cody asked.

"Absolutely," Annabel said.

Telling Chris to keep the prisoner restrained, Cody ran indoors to fetch the handcuffs. In the absence of any formal policing from Rarotonga, Annabel, as the official Justice of the Peace for Moon Island, had the delegated responsibility for maintaining law and order. She could even preside over minor court cases herself. Cody had expected that box of police equipment issued with the job might come in handy one day.

"You can't do this to me!" Roscoe yelped as she tightened the cuffs around his chubby wrists. His comb-over had flopped to the wrong side and his nose was red with fury. "I'll sue you. By the time I'm done, I'll own this degenerate hellhole."

Very calmly, Annabel said, "Roscoe, you need to know that I am empowered to convene a court right here, and I could sentence you to up to two years jail for assault on a female."

"She wanted it." Roscoe glared at Trudy who was rearranging her pigtails and buttoning her shirt. "She's a whore and a temptress."

"Hey, asshole." Trudy landed a sharp kick in his shins as she walked past him on her way into the villa. Pausing, she kicked him a second time, adding, "And that's for Melanie!"

"Let me get this, er...straight. A lesbian staying on a lesbian island wanted to get into your pants real bad; this is what you'll be telling the court?" Chris enquired.

Flicking through the digital images on Chris's camera,

Annabel commented, "Just wait 'til Jolene shows these to her divorce attorney."

"The way I see it, Mr. Worth, you have two choices," Chris said. "You can slither quietly into the night, and so long as we don't hear from you, you won't hear from us. Or you can cause a problem, in which case your wife will see these pictures, and if you are anywhere in these islands your ass will be in jail."

"This is entrapment," Roscoe spluttered.

Annabel smiled. "God works in mysterious ways."

Chapter
Twenty-two

BLOOD, BLACK IN the moonlight, seeped down the hands of a young woman sitting naked on the beach, her back supported by two companions. Centered in the flickering glow of three fires, positioned to form points in a triangle, the oldest woman in the group was tattooing a braid of feathers around each of her wrists.

Merris was intrigued. The old woman seemed almost blind, yet her work was precise and unstumbling. When she was done, she led the girl to the sea and washed the blood away. Her companions then applied some kind of salve to the tattoos, and everyone came up to admire them.

This was far from the somber, worshipful gathering Merris had anticipated. The atmosphere had been warm and celebratory from the moment they'd set foot on the Sacred Shore, tumbling out of the Zodiac like children as the waves bounced them to shore.

Several women had been tattooed so far, and it now seemed that part of the proceedings was over. The *ruahine*, in a cloak of leaves and flowers, called the women together. Standing between the fires they listened as she made a speech. Merris wished she could understand the honeyed language. Every now and then, the entire group responded to their leader with a word or a brief chant. After a time, she stepped away from them and walked to the rocky outcrop at the western end of the bay. The women promptly broke into rhythmic clapping.

Next to her, Olivia joined in, keeping perfect time with the odd staccato beats. She looked completely mesmerized, her dark eyes bottomless in the night, her hair spilling over her bare breasts. The women had carried her across the sands as soon as the Zodiac landed, casting her shirt and *pareu* aside and dressing her in a long skirt of soft grass adorned with a wide belt of frangipani. Olivia said she had wanted an *ei* around her neck to cover her breasts, but the *ruahine* had refused, instead placing a garland on her head. It was something to do with the necklace and what it symbolized, Olivia informed Merris.

The clapping continued, and the three women who had just been tattooed circulated, carrying coconut cups they offered to everyone in turn. These contained a pale fluid with a bitter tang and an edge of anise. Merris sipped politely, but the young woman tilted the cup, insisting she swallow more. A few feet away Cody caught her eye, and the two exchanged the commiserating glances of stricken beer drinkers at an herbal tea-tasting event.

The evil brew was circulated a few more times, leaving Merris's mouth unpleasantly dry and her head fuzzy. Angling her head to Olivia's, she murmured, "Are you stoned?"

"I think so." Olivia smiled at her, still clapping in time.

She seemed to be enjoying herself, Merris thought, pleased. In fact it looked like everyone was. Violet, Trudy and Chris were sitting on the sand next to Melanie who was in a portable deck chair covered with a light quilt. Standing nearby, Cody had her arm around Annabel's waist, and baby Briar was sound asleep in a pack on her back. Glenn and Riley had been joined by the rest of their research team that morning and they all seemed transfixed.

The clapping grew faster until it was abruptly silenced by a single profound note. The *ruahine* stood, her arms swaying above her head as if she were drawing the ocean to her. The note flowed into a song that was hauntingly beautiful. Akaiti had the voice of an opera singer.

Olivia was entranced. "I know that song," she said, and started walking toward the singer.

The women stepped aside for her, murmuring some greeting in their own language. Merris felt awkward following her and soon dropped back to stand with Cody and Annabel. Olivia stepped up onto the rocks and took the hand Akaiti extended to her. Directly in front of them the sea exploded, and a dark, sleek shape arced high in the air.

"Wow," Cody said. "We don't get many dolphins around here."

Moving to the water's edge, the women began their clapping once more, this time singing a new song, led by their priestess. The atmosphere was electric.

Joining Merris and Cody, Glenn said, "They believe this dolphin is Hine te Ana herself and that she has come to see her daughter."

Merris could just make out the shape of a dorsal fin piercing the breakers a few yards out. Lifting its head above the water, the dolphin clicked at the singers, and Merris was startled to realize it was in synch with their clapping. Stepping out into the sea, the women started stomping the sand, making the water splash and boil. The *ruahine* led Olivia out in front of them, and they began walking east. Automatically Merris and the others followed, Chris carrying Melanie.

Almost in the dead center of the half-moon shaped bay, they halted, and Merris watched uneasily as Akaiti and Olivia handed their skirts to the women and walked naked out into the sea to waist depth. In the waves breaking around them, the dolphin hovered close, then it was between them, and Olivia began caressing it and speaking to it.

The *ruahine* pointed at Melanie, commanding, "Bring the woman with the weak shadow."

Chris looked shocked, but carried Melanie out into the breakers, and together with Akaiti, held her in the water so she, too, could touch the dolphin.

"Close your eyes," Akaiti told her. "And Hine te Ana will speak to you."

Her hand lightly on the dolphins flank, Melanie did as she was bade, and after a few seconds broke into a huge smile and lay her head against the creature, plainly overwhelmed.

When Chris moved to lift her away, Akaiti placed a staying hand on her shoulder. "Hine te Ana knows your grief. She says your woman misses you, too. Your sorrow is her sorrow. If you speak to her now, in your heart, she will hear you."

She signaled two strong young women, who lifted Melanie from Chris's arms and carried her up the beach, removing her wet clothes and wrapping her in her quilt. Annabel went over and sat with her, holding her hand. Merris could not hear what they were saying. They both started to cry, holding one another close. Not wanting to intrude on this private moment, she looked away.

Chris stood in the water for some time, her head lowered, the dolphin clicking softly at her. Finally, looking dazed, she hugged Akaiti and walked past the women. With a brief nod at Merris and Cody, she headed along the beach, obviously needing time to herself.

The *ruahine's* next choice was quite a surprise. Summoning Trudy, she said, "Hine te Ana has a task for you."

"For me?" Trudy could not get into the water fast enough.

Akaiti removed the beaded bands from Trudy's pigtails and said something to one of her women, who hurried along the beach and returned with an *ei*. Placing this on Trudy's head, the *ruahine* steered her alongside the dolphin, instructing, "Listen carefully."

It was Olivia who spoke, leaning over the creature and murmuring into Trudy's ear.

"She's probably telling her to remove the implants," Cody said irreverently.

"Is it just me or is this getting weird?" Merris asked.

"Put it this way. I'm glad it's not my girlfriend out there in the nude, talking to a fish." She gave Merris a nudge. "I'm being facetious. Still, this is bizarre, but since we're all on drugs—"

"Tell me about it. I don't know what they put in that drink, but my consciousness is altered, that's for sure."

Trudy had returned to the beach. Brimming with zeal, she rushed straight up to Cody and declared, "I'm going to tell Daddy this place stinks, and it'll never work for a deluxe transition retreat." She paused to emit a small squeal of excitement. "This is way better than *Survivor!*" With that, she bounced off to join the startled academics standing a few yards away.

"What was that about?" Merris asked.

"I'm sure it's a long story. But wait, there's more." Cody pulled Merris closer to the water. "This we have to hear."

It was Glenn's turn to stand before the *ruahine*, who stared at her intently. Merris wasn't sure if it was her imagination, but Glenn seemed uneasy, casting apprehensive glances past the Islanders toward Riley and the rest of her team.

"You have no reason to fear," the *ruahine* said. "A woman's spirit may take more than one form—our goddess lives this life as a dolphin. Yours is a path unlit by the flames of others. Cast off the weight of their fears, daughter. Do not doubt your truth."

These mysterious pronouncements seemed to make complete sense to Glenn, who walked from the water as if she'd just shrugged off an enormous burden.

"Weirder and weirder," Cody whispered.

The *ruahine* took Olivia by the hand and said a few words in Maori. They embraced warmly and the women surged around them, piling one garland after the next around their necks. Triumphantly, they swept Olivia up and proceeded along the beach to the western end of the cliffs.

"Now the *tamàhine* will sing her own song for us," Akaiti announced.

This was greeted with an expectant silence.

Olivia looked bemused. "But I only know songs in English."

"We don't mind," someone called out.

With an embarrassed laugh, Olivia said something in Maori and everyone giggled and clapped. To the east, a faint smear of pink washed across the horizon signaling the imminent dawn.

Even the clouds seemed lighter, shifting from charcoal to ghostly gray. Merris could not believe they had been on the beach for almost eight hours. She knew it would be impossible to describe the experience to anyone who had not shared it.

Olivia was staring out to sea. Smiling as if at some private joke, she sang a line Merris recognized from one of Hunter Carsen's hit songs. Olivia must have written the lyrics. Their eyes met, and Olivia sang directly to her, "Baby, this sweet day belongs to you and me. Make it what we will. When midnight comes, let's have no regrets, for what has slipped away. This sweet day..."

Merris felt Cody give her a nudge, and blushed as women turned, all smiles, to look her up and down. Olivia's voice was not the off-key disaster she had claimed it was when Merris asked her one day if she ever sang her own songs. Still slightly husky from the throat infection she'd had, it was warmer and smoother than her speaking voice, and perfectly pitched.

Cody and Annabel joined in and even Merris found herself singing the chorus.

As she hit the final note, Olivia cut a path directly through the milling women to wrap her arms around Merris. "I'm ready to go home," she said.

IT WAS DAWN when Olivia and Merris fell exhausted into bed.

"Will you tell me something?" Merris asked, caressing her back. "How did you get to the shore?"

Olivia knew Merris had been avoiding pressing her for the details. Closing her eyes, she saw the bubbles rising above her head and heard the click of a dolphin pierce the eerie calm beneath the waves. A lithe gray shape swam up and under her, buoying her gently. Recognizing the dark feathered stripe on that dorsal fin, Olivia clasped hold of it with both hands. Like a magnet, the Scared Shore drew them closer and closer until suddenly she was released, lifted by a wave and cast down hard against the rough white sands.

"That dolphin we saw tonight...it came to me when I was rowing in Hibiscus Bay," Olivia said, explaining that she had followed it around the coast where they were joined by the entire pod. "I couldn't resist swimming with them. To cut a long story short, the boat was wrecked, and I was swept out to sea. I was drowning, and the dolphin rescued me and swam me to shore. I know that seems incredible, but it's true."

"I believe you." Merris drew her so close their bodies seemed fused, as if fashioned from clay. "After everything that's happened here, I'm starting to believe in magic."

"I was very lucky," Olivia said. She thought about her vision of Hine te Ana singing at the water's edge. There was an odd similarity between the rhythm of that haunting melody and the way the dolphin clicked. She called that face to mind, a face strangely familiar to her. She thought about the goddess who took the form of a dolphin to seek out her lost daughter across the expanses of time and ocean.

Love did not die, she realized. It lived within. It harnessed hope and refused to surrender to the bitterness of defeat or death. Love endured. It took new form.

Smiling, Olivia fingered the necklace about her throat. It was time she came home to herself. Rolling onto her side, she faced Merris, eyes open for her to read. "I love you," she said.

Merris looked profoundly moved. "And I love you."

In silence they studied one another, co-conspirators in the story they would write together, that of their love. Beyond their simple room, an evanescent moon shared the sky with a freshly gilt sun. In a few hours the lovers would step out into the brightness of the day, and so would begin the first page in the book of their life together.

Epilogue

AN EARLY EVENING breeze rifled through fragile pink hibiscus petals and carried the scent of ocean and wood to a small grove below Villa Luna. Annabel planted the last clump of violet and stood up, wiping her face. She hoped they would grow here in the protective shade of the mangos. Mel had always loved them.

A small hand tugged her shorts. "Bel?"

With both hands Briar held out a glass of juice. Framed with glossy black ringlets, her toddler face was grave with concentration.

"Sweetheart. Thank you!" Annabel took the drink and crouched to give the little girl a hug.

Dark doe eyes examined her face and Annabel felt a crushing sadness. Sometimes it seemed Melanie looked out through her daughter's gaze. It had been six months since her passing. Briar would be two soon. She had recently started calling Annabel *Mama* at bedtime. Annabel had corrected her at first, then she stopped, knowing it was what Mel had wanted.

"Guess what," Cody joined them, camera in hand. "Hine is in the bay."

Annabel smiled. "What are we waiting for!"

Cody swung Briar up onto her shoulders, and they cut through the trees down to the warm white sands. Just a few yards from the shore, a supple silver form shot through the glistening sea and hurled itself high in the air, scattering diamonds of water across the lagoon.

Cody set Briar down, and they watched her toddle along the water's edge, squealing and waving her arms in excitement. After a moment, Annabel slipped her hand into Cody's, and they ran after her, as parents do.

"I love you," Annabel shouted to Cody through the splashes.

Cody grinned. "Lucky me." Tucking Briar under one arm and slinging the other over Annabel's shoulders, she steered them out a little deeper.

The dolphin was aware of them, clicking and calling, flaunting its lissom power in surges and leaps. Hine had first arrived in Passion Bay one day when Annabel and Melanie were swimming. Mel could no longer speak by then. Neither could she write. Her fingers had lost all power to grasp. Cradling her in the soothing warmth, Annabel had been startled when the water broke just yards away and a dolphin looked her in the eye.

The animal had seemed to sense Melanie was sick. Approaching them, it lay on its side gazing at her and making tiny clicks. Annabel had wanted to leave the water, worried it would knock Mel accidentally. But Melanie's eyes urged her to stay.

To Annabel's astonishment, the dolphin slid beneath Melanie, helping buoy her. Between them, they swam her the length of the bay and back before the dolphin steered them resolutely toward the shore. She lingered for a moment as if to say farewell, then vanished.

In the months that followed, the dolphin visited regularly, sometimes screeching a summons so loud Annabel heard it from the villa. Cody had named their visitor Hine, suggesting it could be the dolphin they had encountered on the Sacred Shore months earlier. They had no way of knowing, but it was nice to believe it could be so.

At the times when Annabel felt saddest, both before and after Melanie's final days, it seemed Hine would show up by some irrational coincidence.

Was there such a thing? Was the universe so randomly ordered? Annabel listened for the muted click and cry she had come to recognize as Hine's goodbye. There was no such thing as coincidence, she decided. It was a word invented to disguise a truth neither religion nor science wanted to recognize — that there was some larger scheme at work in all of our lives and in the life of our planet.

Annabel drew closer to Briar and Cody. Neither of these people had entered her life by accident. They were meant to be. She waved farewell to Hine and watched, transfixed, as she arced joyously in the air.

Lifting Briar onto Cody's shoulders, she said, "Let's go home."

Behind them, a feathered dorsal fin slid beneath the water, and the sinking sun painted Passion Bay as red as a lovers heart.

The End

Also available from
Yellow Rose Books

Passion Bay

Book I in the Moon Island Series
(2nd edition)

Two women from different ends of the earth meet in paradise. Mourning the death of her favorite Aunt, Annabel Worth is stunned to find she has inherited two things—an island in the South Pacific and a mystery that can only be solved by traveling there. Disillusioned with life as a securities trader in Boston, she rashly decides to exchange one world for another. New Zealander Cody Stanton has made the same choice. Dumped by her lover, laid off from her job, she rents a beach villa on remote Moon Island, expecting to take comfort in sea, solitude and simplicity. Then she meets Annabel.

Haunted by a secret that threatens to derail her relationship with her mother, Annabel resists their powerful attraction. Cody, too, is burdened with a secret that could destroy the passion growing between them. When Hurricane Mary strikes the island, each woman must make a choice that will change her life forever.

A runaway bestseller with seven reprints in its first edition, *Passion Bay* has been re-released in a second 'author's cut' edition, extensively revised, updated and expanded.

Here's what the critics say: "Send your customers looking for the perfect beach book to *Passion Bay*...this novel absolutely has it all." ~ Feminist Bookstore News

ISBN 1-932300-25-2

Saving Grace

Book II in the Moon Island Series
(2nd edition)

Champion swimmer and Olympic hopeful, Dawn Beaumont has been injured in a car crash she caused. Haunted by guilt over the death of a passenger, her career in ruins, her body damaged and scarred, she flees to Moon Island. Scientist Grace Ramsay welcomes her cute new neighbor, imaging Dawn could be a pleasant diversion from her secret mission to evaluate Moon Island for corporate purchase by a chemicals giant looking for a waste dump far from civilization. But Dawn won't play ball, in fact she denies she is even a lesbian. Beset by troubling nightmares rooted in the past, and increasing ambivalence over her job, Grace sets out to prove otherwise. Meanwhile Annabel Worth, the owner of the island, is determined not to sell her home to a chemicals conglomerate. But then her plane goes down in the Pacific in suspicious circumstances.

Here's what the critics say: "*Saving Grace* has all the elements a reader looks for in a good novel: romance, adventure, danger and intrigue. Jennifer Fulton has taken these ingredients and created a novel the reader will have a hard time putting down." ~R. Lynne Watson, Mega-Scene

ISBN 1-932300-26-0

Another Jennifer Fulton book to look for in the
coming months from
Yellow Rose Books

A Guarded Heart

Book IV in the Moon Island Series

In her life Lauren Douglas never imagined she would
wake up one day and find herself the star of the hottest soap
on daytime television. But as wholesome, smart and lovely Dr.
Kate, she is plastered over the media as a role model and
inspiration for young women. As she is about to sign a bloated
new contract, Lauren is publicly outed. Scrambling for damage control, her father, a Congressman, wants her banished
abroad and her network writes her temporarily out of the
show in a plane crash, while they consider her future. As if the
slavering press doesn't have enough to report, a creepy fan
enraged by the revelation, shoots her. All of which means zip
to FBI Special Agent Pat Roussel whose hunt for the Kiddy
Pageant Killer has consumed every waking moment for three
years. Suffering from burnout, and hoping fresh new eyes
might come up with a break in the case, Pat reluctantly elects
to take a few months leave without pay. The last thing she
expects to find herself doing in her time off is an illicit private
security gig babysitting a celebrity. But she owes a friend a big
favor. Her first assignment sounds like hell-a month on a tropical island as bodyguard for a TV star with a bullet wound.
Only Lauren is not the spoiled narcissist Pat is expecting.

Jennifer Fulton lives in the shadow of the Rocky Mountains with her partner and animal companions. Her vice of choice is writing, however she is also devoted to her wonderful daughter and her hobbies: fly fishing, cinema, and fine cooking. Jennifer started writing stories almost as soon as she could read them, and never stopped. Under pen names Jennifer Fulton and Rose Beecham, she has published eight lesbian novels and a handful of short stories.

Printed in the United States
108946LV00003B/303/A

9 781932 300352